The GAME

VI KEELAND

The GAME

The Game
Edited by: Jessica Royer Ocken
Proofreading by: Elaine York/Allusion Publishing,
www.allusionpublishing.com, Julia Griffins
Cover Model: Nicky John White
Photographer: Marq Mendez
Cover designer: Sommer Stein, Perfect Pear Creative
Formatting: Elaine York, Allusion Publishing,
www.allusionpublishing.com

"IN THE END...
We only regret the chances we didn't take,
the relationships we were afraid to have,
and the decisions we waited too long to make."
— Lewis Carroll

Chapter 1

Bella

"I STILL CANNOT believe this is all yours..." Miller ducked his head to look out the passenger-side window from the driver's seat.

"It's not *all* mine—twenty-five percent is owned by an investment group."

"Whatever. You're still the queen of that castle. Are you sure you don't want me to come in with you?"

I glanced over at the imposing building. "I love you for offering, but I think this is something I need to do by myself."

"Okay. But I don't have to be at the office until this afternoon, so if you change your mind, just give me a call." He winked. "You may need an assistant to go ahead of you into the locker room and make sure all of those sweaty football players are decent before you walk in."

I leaned over and kissed Miller's cheek with a chuckle. "You're such a giver. Thank you again for driving me."

I opened the car door and paused, taking a deep breath as I stared at the tremendous arena. Up ahead was a guy wearing a hoodie and carrying what looked like at least a dozen pizza boxes.

Miller pointed. "Shouldn't you go in a different entrance than the delivery people?"

"I have no damn idea. But if my lovely siblings have anything to do with it, I'm sure my entrance will lead straight to a dungeon."

"Don't let those spoiled, rich pricks intimidate you. And straighten your damn glasses. They're crooked again."

I sighed and pushed my glasses up my nose. "I'll do my best."

The walk from the parking lot to the entrance of Bruins Stadium felt a lot like walking a gang plank, especially since I knew there were sharks waiting for me inside. When I got close to the door, I noticed a few people milling around with cameras. I wasn't sure if they were here for me, since I'd had people camped out in front of my apartment again lately, or if maybe they'd come because the players were practicing today. But I lowered my head to avoid eye contact and kept walking until I was safely inside. A security officer stopped me two steps into the building.

"Can I help you?"

"Ummm, yes. I work here."

"Never saw you before. New?"

I nodded. "Today is technically my first day."

He picked up a clipboard. "Name?"

"Bella Keating."

He scanned his list and pointed to the X-ray machine a few feet away. "Just like the airport. Cell phones, laptops, and any other electronic devices have to be removed from your bag and run through the machine. When you're done, wait on the yellow line to be called before walking through the metal detector."

I followed the instructions and set my cell phone in a small round dish before placing my laptop in a larger gray tray. Two more security officers stood talking on the other side of the metal detector while I waited on the yellow line. Up ahead, I watched as the pizza guy with the hoodie stopped to talk to a woman. She twirled her hair and giggled at something he said before he got into the elevator car and disappeared. A few seconds later, the doors to the adjoining car slid open and a young guy wearing a suit walked out. His nose was buried in his phone as he strolled toward security. When he finally looked up, his eyes widened and his casual amble turned to a sprint. I glanced behind me, wondering who he was running for.

"Ms. Keating! I'm so sorry I'm late." He frowned at the two security guards who, until now, had been ignoring me in favor of quoting stats about last weekend's game, while I waited patiently on the yellow line as instructed. "*Excuse me.* Do you know who this is that you have waiting?"

The guard who had checked my ID shrugged. "Last name's Keating, right? She's new here."

Suit Guy put his hands on his hips and shook his head. "And what's the name of the new owner of the team? The person whose name will be on your next paycheck?"

The guard's eyes grew wide. "Holy crap. You're Ms. Keating?"

I hesitated before nodding. "Yes, I'm Bella Keating."

"I'm very sorry." He took my elbow and guided me to walk through the metal detector. It buzzed as I passed through, and I stopped, but the guard waved it off. "It's fine. You don't need to go through security at all."

The young guy in the suit shook his head. "I'm sorry, Ms. Keating. I wasn't expecting you until later. I was com-

3

ing down to make sure security knew you would be here today, and to tell them to call me as soon as you arrived." He extended his hand. "I'm Josh Sullivan, your assistant. Well, I mean, I was Mr. Barrett's assistant. We've spoken on the phone a few times."

"Oh, sure...Josh." I smiled. "It's nice to finally meet you."

"Would you like me to give you a tour of the arena, or would you prefer to go straight to your office?"

Considering I wasn't even sure I *had* an office, I figured that would be as good a place to start as any. "My office would be great."

Josh held his hand out for me to walk first. I took a few steps, but then remembered my stuff had gone through the X-ray machine, and I'd never collected it. I pointed. "Almost forgot my electronics."

In the elevator, Josh inserted a keycard into a slot on the button panel. "You can't access the executive suites without a security card. I have a set of cards and a bunch of keys you'll be needing waiting for you in your office."

"Thank you."

The top floor of executive suites was nothing like my old, dingy office. The bright halls were decorated with framed action shots of players and an array of awards and accolades. When we came to the end of the hall, Josh took keys out of his pocket and unlocked the door.

"This is your office." He pushed the door open, but stepped aside for me to enter.

"This is an *office*?"

He chuckled. "It is, and it's all yours."

I walked over to the long wall of glass that looked down into the stadium. A few athletes were out on the field below, stretching. "You do know I've asked Tom Lauren to stay on as acting team president, the position he's held since John Barrett passed, right? I'm co-president, but it's just in name. I have a lot to learn. So maybe Tom should have this office."

Josh smiled. "His isn't too shabby. It's down the hall. I booked you a sit-down with him at eleven today, and there's a luncheon staff meeting at twelve thirty. Then at four, you have a quick meet and greet with the team when practice ends. Otherwise, your calendar is wide open so you can get settled in."

"Okay, great."

"By the way, do you prefer an electronic calendar, a physical planner, or both?"

"I would prefer a physical planner, if you don't mind."

He smiled again. "Your father did, too. Sometimes old school just works better."

I nodded. Keeping a paper-and-pen calendar wasn't that unique, yet I clung to that tiny bit of information about John Barrett. I knew so little about him, but I had a feeling that would change quickly now that I was here.

Josh motioned to the window. "Practice starts at ten, so it'll fill up soon." He pointed to the biggest desk I'd ever seen. "I ordered you a new laptop and set you up on the team's management portal. It gives you access to everything you'll want to know about the team and the individual athletes—stats by player, injuries, medical reports, salary, discipline reports—you name it, there's a report for it in there." He motioned to a door on the wall behind the desk. "That leads to a private bathroom. It's equipped with a shower and a massage room."

"Massage room?"

"Mr. Barrett often utilized the team's massage thera-pists. I can set you up with whatever appointments you'd like." He walked over to a floor-to-ceiling bookcase. "All of the team's playbooks are printed out and shelved, as are dossiers on each team member. There are also books on potential recruits the recruiting staff is following and a book on all players within the league whose contracts are up in the next twelve months. Through that door—"

Josh suddenly stopped. My eyes had still been stuck on the dozens of thick books on the *many* shelves. When they shifted back to his, he smiled. "I'm sorry. This must be a lot to take in, and I'm rambling, aren't I?"

"It's fine."

"Why don't I go grab us both some coffee and give you a few minutes to settle in?"

I exhaled loudly. "That would be great. Thank you, Josh."

He closed the door behind him, and I stood in the center of the giant space. It was surreal that I was here, not to mention that this was my office. I'd barely gotten to look back over it all when the door burst open and my nightmare of a half-sister walked in.

"Ready to call it quits yet?" Drizella snarked.

Of course, Drizella wasn't her real name, but that's how Miller and I referred to my new half-siblings, Drizella and Anastasia—the evil stepsisters from *Cinderella*.

I plastered on a fake smile. "Good morning, Tiffany."

She sneered. "This is such a joke. I can't believe you're going to attempt to run the team. Have you ever even watched a game?"

6

I ignored her. "I'm glad you agreed to stay on. Your experience is obviously invaluable."

"Of course I'm invaluable. Because *I know football.* Unlike you."

"Well, I'm hoping I can learn a lot from you." I smiled sweetly. Over the last two years, since my life had been turned upside down, I'd figured out that the best way to combat Tiffany's evil was to bludgeon her with kindness and compliments. She only knew how to fight with me. So after a while, if I didn't take the bait, she'd lose the wind in her sail and float away. And that's exactly what happened now. She turned and strutted her too-skinny ass back to the door. As she did, the pizza delivery guy passed by. It was the third time I'd noticed him, and it dawned on me that it was a little strange.

"Who gets pizza delivered before eight AM? What place is even open that early?"

Tiffany glanced down the hallway after the guy and turned back with an evil smile. "You want to make yourself useful?"

I assumed it was a rhetorical question, but she waited for an actual response. I sighed. "Of course, Tiffany."

She pointed down the hall. "That pizza delivery guy has been harassing women. Only last week he made a comment about my ass. As the new leader of this organization, perhaps you can let him know behavior like that will not be tolerated."

I blinked. "Oh. Wow. That's terrible."

"That's why I'm suggesting you do something about it. Unless you're too busy...or maybe you don't care how the women here are treated."

"Of course I care."

"Then I look forward to hearing how your discussion goes. I'll see you at the staff meeting later."

Tiffany huffed and disappeared. I figured I'd speak to Josh about the delivery guy when he returned, but a minute later, hoodie guy passed by my door yet again. This time the pizza boxes were gone. I normally dreaded confrontation, but I was going to have to get used to it if I was going to do this job. So I walked out into the hall.

"Excuse me..."

The guy turned around.

Damn. This close he was *really* good looking.

He pointed to himself. "Are you talking to me?"

"Yes. Do you think we can speak for a moment?"

He flashed a megawatt smile that was pretty damn dazzling. His teeth might've actually gleamed a bit. No wonder this guy thought he could say and do whatever he wanted. Though being handsome certainly didn't give him the right to harass women.

Hoodie guy followed me to my office. I stepped aside and extended my hand. "Please, come in."

I closed the door behind me before offering my hand. "I'm Bella Keating."

"I know who you are. I've seen your picture in the paper." He clasped my hand. "Christian. It's good to meet you."

"Obviously this isn't the ideal topic of conversation when you first meet someone, but I'm afraid I need to discuss a complaint I've received about you."

Christian's forehead wrinkled. "Complaint? What kind of complaint?"

"One of the employees has informed me that you've been harassing women here at the Bruins. She mentioned one particular instance where you made a comment about her backside."

Christian's eyebrows jumped. "Harassing? I don't think so. Some of the women like to flirt, but they're just fooling around."

"That's actually a common problem. One person thinks they're flirting, but the other person feels like they're being harassed. The line between the two can often be very blurry. Here at the Bruins, we have a zero-tolerance policy for harassment, so I'm afraid I'm going to have to ask you to refrain from delivering your pies here in the future. What pizza place do you work for?"

"Pizza place?"

"Yes, I'd like to know who your employer is."

The guy's full lips curved to a grin as he planted his hands on his hips. "You don't know who my employer is?"

"If I did, I wouldn't be asking."

He chuckled and walked toward the door. "I gotta go. But it was fun meeting you, Bella."

I couldn't believe the audacity of this guy. He was laughing? "You know I don't find sexual harassment funny, nor do I take approaching someone to discuss a complaint lodged against them lightly. I wasn't going to call your boss, but I think perhaps I should, considering how flippant you're being."

"By all means, call her. That oughta make for an interesting conversation." He opened my door and looked back over his shoulder. "And hey, as long as I'm harassing people, I might as well tell you that you're much cuter than your pictures in the paper. Would you like to have dinner sometime?"

My mouth dropped open. Before I could close it, Josh returned. He lifted his chin to the delivery guy. "What's up, Christian. I guess you met the boss?"

"Sure did. Bella here wants to know what pizza place I work for. Maybe you can fill her in. She'd also like my boss's number. Gotta run." Christian blew me a kiss. "Later, beautiful. By the way, your glasses are a little crooked."

Josh held out a coffee, shaking his head. "That was weird."

"Tell me about it." I adjusted my glasses on my face. "I hope you know who he works for."

Josh thumbed toward the door. "Christian?"

"Yes?"

"Well, since you own the team now, I guess he works for you."

My nose wrinkled. "The pizza delivery guy works for the team?"

Josh studied my face. "Oh crap. You have no idea who that was, do you?"

"Uhhh...the pizza delivery guy?"

"That was Christian Knox. The starting quarterback for the Bruins and your team's captain."

I shut my eyes. *I'm going to kill Drizella.*

———

"How was your first day?"

My head lolled back against the headrest the moment I pulled Miller's car door shut. "Do you remember what happened on my first day when we worked together in college?"

"You mean Mr. Big Balls?"

"The one and only."

"What about him?"

"My mistake with him was less embarrassing than today."

In our sophomore year, Miller had gotten me a job at the place he worked—he did tech support for a payroll-software company. I should've known before I started that it was a bad idea. Clients would call in when they had a problem, and we'd share our screens, showing them the steps to get through the issue with our software. There was also a chat box on the bottom of the screen where you could see the client's profile picture and they could see yours. Third client into my shift, this guy pops in for some help, and his profile pic shows him standing. I could see down to his mid-thigh. I swear, to this day, I still have no idea what was going on in that photo, but on my screen it looked like he had *giant balls*. I don't mean a pronounced bulge. I mean two round softballs trying to escape from his pants. I managed to get through the support chat, but before we disconnected, I took a screenshot of the profile pic with my phone so I could show it to Miller. Then I *thought* I disconnected the guy. You can see where this is going already...

Long story short, I proceeded to send the screenshot to Miller through our employee DM chat, where we had a lengthy discussion about whether balls could grow that big. I even did things like google conditions that could cause testicular swelling and then searched the guy on social media to see if his profile picture had been distorted somehow or if he really looked like that. Needless to say, I hadn't actually disconnected, so Mr. Big Balls had watched everything I'd done on his screen before he called my boss. Miller and I were both fired, and my very first day became my very last.

"What could you have done that's worse than Mr. Big Balls?"

"Oh, I don't know. Maybe mistake the best quarterback in the league for the pizza delivery guy and then give him a lecture on sexual harassment in the workplace."

Miller's eyes flashed to me and back to the road. "What the hell happened?"

"*Drizella* happened."

"But how can you not recognize him? You memorized the statistics of every player on the team."

"You know me and faces don't mix well. I memorized his numbers, not his appearance—which, by the way, is breathtaking. The man's jawline could make a sculptor weep."

Miller shook his head. "I hate to tell you, but you're not building algorithms anymore. You're going to have to start paying attention to people. Use the tricks you've always used when you had to put faces together with names."

I pouted. "I'm not a people person. I'm a mathematician."

"Not anymore, princess. You're a billionairess who owns an NFL team."

"I think I want to go back to my old job. I'm done peopling."

Miller chuckled. "You'll get better at it. I promise."

Chapter 2

Christian

"**WELL. WELL. WELL.** Look what the cat dragged in. Took ya long enough."

I walked over to Coach and automatically went to extend my right hand, but caught myself at the last second and offered my left. Coach's right side had been impaired since his stroke a few years back. It was also the reason he used a wheelchair.

We shook. "How's riding the bench treating you?" he asked.

I patted him on the shoulder with my free hand. "I like it about as much as you like riding this chair, old man."

Coach chuckled. Marvin "Coach" Barrett and I had been busting balls as far back as my pee-wee football days. He'd been my first football coach, but he was also the father of John Barrett, one of the greatest football players of all time and the owner of the New York Bruins. Well, John had been the owner until he passed away from pancreatic cancer two years ago. Now the organization was apparently being run by a woman who thought I was the pizza delivery guy and lectured me on sexual harassment.

"So what's going on? How's the recovery?" Coach asked.

I'd had surgery to reattach a torn ligament to my knee a month ago, after being injured in a game. "I feel good. I'm killing it at physical therapy, and my knee hasn't been this limber since my college days. But Doc won't sign off for me to come back for at least three more weeks."

"I'm sure they know best. Remember that time you cracked two teeth in the third quarter of a game in middle school? You didn't tell anyone until the game was over because you were afraid they would make you sit out the last eight minutes. And if I remember correctly, your team was up by more than twenty points, too. You had to get nine stitches because you cut up the inside of your mouth so badly. It looked like you ate a razor blade. Doctor's right for not trusting you to make the decision yourself."

I waved him off. "You want to go outside and get some fresh air?"

"Yeah, why not? Walking around with you is better than walking around with a puppy. All the ladies want to stop and coo, and I get a good visual from where I'm sitting—right at chest level, if you know what I mean."

I chuckled. "Still a dirty old man."

Outside, Coach and I walked around his little neighborhood. After his stroke, he'd moved into a continuous care retirement community. He had his own townhouse and lived pretty independently, but there were healthcare workers and others on staff to provide extra support from time to time. We walked around the lake and into the park, where we often played checkers when I visited.

"Should I kick your ass again today?" He snickered.

"You got lucky last time. I was still on painkillers, so don't let it go to your head. Besides, even a blind squirrel finds a nut sometimes."

Coach cackled. "Still a sore loser, I see."

"You want to put your money where your mouth is?"

"Okay, but I don't need your money. If I win, you're bringing me a pastrami on rye from Katz's deli."

"Fine." I scratched my chin, thinking about my wager. "When I win, you're going to wear a T-shirt with my face on it and sit in the visiting team's bleacher seats at the next home game."

"That's just cruel." He grinned. "I like it."

I positioned Coach on one side of the concrete checkers table and set up the board. "Age before beauty. You go first."

Coach slid one of his black checkers forward into a square. "So have you met my granddaughter yet? She was supposed to take the helm this week."

"I did. Yesterday. She's...interesting."

"She's the whole package, that one. Smart and pretty. Graduated first in her class at Yale. Too bad I couldn't be proud when it happened, considering I didn't know she existed at the time."

When I visited Coach, our talks almost always centered on the game, not our personal lives. So I only knew what most people knew from reading the papers—that his son John Barrett had left the team to a daughter he'd never acknowledged while he was alive, and not to his two daughters who already worked for the organization. The newspapers had followed the story for more than two years while his family contested the will, and the final appeal decision had only come down a few weeks ago. So I was definitely curious about Bella Keating.

"Have you met her?" I asked.

Coach nodded. "She comes to visit almost every Saturday morning. First time she came was a few weeks after the will was read. She was looking for answers I didn't have. Like why my dumbass son didn't acknowledge her existence while he was alive."

I'd had no idea. "How do you think she's going to handle running the team?"

"I think Bella's going to surprise everyone." He wagged his crooked finger. "You know, she used to develop algorithms to determine the buying patterns of millions of people. She's not going to have a problem learning a sport that two blockheads like us could master. Bella just needs to get out of her head and work on her people skills. She'll get there."

People skills like recognizing the players on her team might be a good place to start. I kept that thought to myself. No good ever came of criticizing another man's family, even if the person was a new addition.

Coach pushed a checker forward. "She doesn't look much like her sisters, does she?"

Definitely not. Tiffany and Rebecca were tall and rail thin, with olive skin and dark hair and eyes like their father. They were attractive, but there was something harsh about them—maybe it was their angular jaws or their eyes; I wasn't sure. But Bella had porcelain skin with bright green eyes and auburn hair. Her full lips curved into a cute little V at the top center, almost forming a bow. She was probably only five foot three at best, but she had curves in all the right places. Thinking about her thick-rimmed glasses, slightly crooked on her face, made me smile. "No, I didn't notice any resemblance," I told him. "What's the story about why John left the team to her and not Tiffany and Rebecca, if you don't mind me asking?"

Coach shrugged. "Only thing I know for sure is what he wrote in the letter he left with his will—that those two are spoiled enough. I couldn't agree more. And he apologized for leaving Bella to struggle after her mom died. Bella's mother was Rose, a real sweet lady. She worked for Bruins Stadium as a hospitality manager in the luxury boxes. That's a fancy title for putting up with a bunch of rich people's shit and serving drinks and whatnot to guests who probably didn't even say thank you. I met Rose plenty of times over the years, but never had any clue that something was going on with my son. I suspect the reason he left the team to Bella was because he had a lot of guilt he wanted to get off his chest in his final months. Rose and Bella didn't have an easy life, especially after Rose died when Bella was only a teenager. But don't worry, unlike my son, Bella is as stand-up as they come. Do you know she offered to sign the team over to me? I had to talk her out of not handing it over to her bratty damn siblings, too. She didn't feel like it should have gone to her because she hadn't done anything to earn it." He shook his head. "Can you imagine the other two thinking they needed to *earn* anything? I love 'em, but my other granddaughters think it's their birthright to inherit the Earth."

I didn't know Rebecca that well, but Tiffany was definitely entitled. A few months back she'd decided she was entitled to some of my dick and called me into her office to take it. She'd started to strip out of her clothes like she was the only one who decided if we fucked. But I wasn't going there. Don't get me wrong, she was attractive. It wouldn't have been a hardship to give her what she wanted, but a woman like that is never satisfied with just a lay. She's *waaayy* more work than I was up for.

Over the next hour, I beat Coach at checkers three times. He now had to wear a T-shirt with my face on it, hold up one of those big foam fingers with my number on it, and hang my jersey from a pole attached to his wheelchair, flying it like a flag. I'd still bring him his damn sandwich from Katz's deli next time I stopped by, though, because the guy was more like a father to me than my own ever was.

At the end of my visit, I made sure he was settled back in his living room in his electric recliner before I said goodbye. "Anything you need before I go?"

He shook his head. "I'm all good. But can you do me one favor?"

"Name it."

"Check in on Bella for me from time to time. I can't imagine too many people in that ivory tower are happy with her steering the boat. She could probably use a friend."

I patted his shoulder. "Sure. I'll see if she likes pizza and bring some by..."

—

Two days later, I was upstairs at the arena for a meeting with Carl Robbins, VP of Community Relations. I was scheduled to toss the ball around tomorrow afternoon with some of the kids from the youth league the team sponsored, but my coach was being a stickler about my restrictions and had pulled the plug on me even doing that. Instead, they wanted me to give a talk about the hard work it took to get to the NFL. Carl had written some bullet points, as if I couldn't figure out what to tell kids even though I was the one who'd managed to get here. *Whatever.* I knew he meant well, and some of the guys on the team would've made him write every word they were going to say for an appearance.

Carl liked to talk, so he was still rattling on as he walked me to the door of his office at the end of our session. I stepped out into the hall and tried to cut him off politely, but did a double take upon finding a certain green-eyed beauty heading right toward me. Bella's steps faltered, giving Carl someone new to yammer at.

"Bella," he bellowed. "Have you had a chance to meet Christian Knox yet?"

Her eyes jumped to me and back to Carl. I figured she was trying to figure out how much to say, so I decided to have a little fun and answer first.

"We actually met the other day." I grinned. "Bella asked me for some recommendations on local places to order lunch. I suggested Three Brothers' Pizza, though I told her she might want to pick it up because their delivery guy has been having some issues lately."

Bella's lip twitched. "Hi, Christian. It's good to see you again."

"Christian here is going to give a speech over at the youth league we sponsor," Carl said. "I'm still putting together the list you asked me for of charitable events you might get involved with, but this is one you'd probably like.

It's an all-girls' football team here in the City. They're really good, too."

"Oh really? An all-girls' team? That does sound interesting." Bella nodded toward her office. "I have to run to a meeting in a few minutes, but Christian, maybe you could tell me a little bit more about it."

"Of course." I shook Carl's hand and told him I'd see him tomorrow afternoon. Then I followed Bella down the hall. I couldn't help noticing her great ass, but I forced my eyes back up as fast as they fell, not wanting *another* sexual-harassment lecture.

Inside her office, she closed the door behind us.

"Maybe you shouldn't shut that." I folded my arms across my chest. "I wouldn't want you to think I was trying to get you alone so I could *harass* you."

Bella sighed. "I deserve that. And it seems you figured out that I had mistaken you for someone else."

"The womanizing pizza delivery guy..."

"I owe you a big apology. My half-sister apparently had a little fun at my expense. Though I need to take responsibility for my mistake. I should have recognized you."

I wasn't really mad. Once I'd realized she wasn't actually accusing me of harassing someone, I found it kind of amusing. So I let her off the hook with a shrug. "Apology accepted."

"Really?"

"Would it make you feel better if you had to grovel first?"

She sighed again. "Actually, it probably would. People being nice around here makes me suspicious."

"Not a friendly reception, I take it?"

"My sisters hate my guts, and the mostly male staff all use a patronizing tone."

"You want to know how I would handle those people?"

"How?"

"*Fuck 'em.* Ignore them all and do your own thing." I tapped two fingers to my temple. "Don't let them get in your head."

"Thanks. I appreciate that." She smiled. "Why were you carrying all those pizza boxes at eight o'clock in the morning anyway?"

"It's a tradition. When we win a home game, everyone gets pizza for breakfast the next morning, courtesy of Three Brothers' Pizza. The owner's a huge fan and has been doing it for longer than I've been around. Whatever sucker is out on injured reserve has to go get them."

"What if you lose?"

I frowned. "No pizza."

Bella laughed. "Do you think we can put the pizza-delivery incident behind us and start over? Pretend this is the first time we met?"

"I thought we already did, but alright." I extended my hand. "Christian Knox. It's nice to meet you."

She put her hand in mine. "Bella Keating. I'm excited to meet you, Christian. I'm a big fan."

I raised a brow. "Think that might be pushing it, since you didn't even know what I looked like."

"I don't usually tell people this, but my being unable to place a face isn't from lack of interest. I have prosopagnosia."

"Prosopo—what?"

"Prosopagnosia. It's the inability to recognize people by their faces."

"That's an actual thing?"

She smiled. "It is. It's a cognitive disorder often caused by a head injury, but it can be congenital, too. I fell off the monkey bars at the park when I was five, and it affected the fusiform gyrus, which is the part of the brain that controls recognition."

"No shit?"

"Brad Pitt has it too. Though I think his is congenital." Bella laughed. "I don't even know why I just told you any of that. I've only ever told three people about my condition. I can hide it pretty well by memorizing non-facial cues about a person, such as their walk, or voice, or the way they dress. Even a necklace a person wears or their build can help me identify them better than a face."

"You told me because you didn't want my ego to be bruised."

"I didn't want you to think I wasn't a fan. Because I am. I've studied your career."

I rubbed my lip with my thumb. "You've studied me, huh?"

She straightened. "Sixty-seven-point-four completion rate last year. Five-thousand-two-hundred-and-seventy-four yards. Forty-four touchdowns and eight interceptions. The season before that, sixty-one-point-eight completion rate, four-thousand-six-hundred-and-eleven yards, forty touchdowns, and twelve interceptions. The year before that, sixty-four-point-two completion rate, four-thousand-nine-hundred-and-six yards, forty-three touchdowns, and twelve interceptions. You went to Notre Dame for college, where you led the Fighting Irish to two league championships. You have a twin brother—identical not fraternal—

who is also a quarterback. He was on injured reserve this week, the same as you, though he's due to come back Sunday, and you will most likely be out for another few weeks. And you have a second brother, who played for Michigan State but didn't make it to the NFL. I believe that brother is a cop in New Jersey."

"Who was my pee-wee team's football coach?"

Her face fell. "I don't know. But I'm hoping that's not relevant to prove my point, that I know who you are as a player, even if I didn't recognize your face."

I shook my pointer at her. "I wouldn't be so sure of that. You can't figure out everything through facts and figures. You're not building algorithms anymore."

She tilted her head. "Sounds like you've done your homework, too. You know what I previously did for a living..."

My phone alarm buzzed. I slipped it from my pocket and turned it off. "I gotta run. Practice starts in ten minutes. I'm not allowed on the field while I'm injured, but I can sure as hell coach the guy keeping my spot warm from the sidelines. Maybe we can talk about the all-girls' youth team another time?"

Bella smiled. "Sure. And thank you again for being so understanding about the other day."

I nodded and walked toward the door. "By the way, just to be clear, is it sexual harassment when two people work together and one of them asks the other out?"

"I think if it's done in a manner so that the other party feels comfortable saying no, if they're not interested, it wouldn't be considered harassment."

I let my eyes do a quick sweep over Bella as she watched. "Good to know. I hope I see you around, Bella."

Chapter 3

Bella

"WHY ARE YOU sitting over here?"

The following week, I attended my first official home game as the team's owner. Right before halftime, I'd been sitting in the owner's box with friends when the jumbotron zoomed in on a man in the visiting team's bleacher seats. *My grandfather.* I knew he had season tickets right behind the home team bench, so I went down to check on him.

My brows furrowed when I saw his shirt. "And what in heaven's name are you wearing?" I bent for a closer look.

"Lost a damn bet with Knox."

Oh my God, is that Christian's face? "What bet did you lose?"

"He beat me at checkers, so I have to sit here with all this dumb shit on."

"Why were you playing checkers with Christian?"

"Because he's a sore loser. I won last time, so he had to have a rematch."

I shook my head. "But why were you playing with him at all?"

My grandfather shrugged. "You've seen the outdoor park in my complex..."

"Yes? What about it?"

"They have those concrete tables with checkerboards painted on the top."

"Okay…"

"We sometimes stop there when we go out for a walk."

I was still confused. "Christian comes to see you?"

"Once or twice a month. He used to come to my team's practices, but since I retired, he comes to the house instead."

"I didn't realize you two were friendly."

"Ever since I coached his pee-wee football team—too many years ago for me to count. I followed his career through the years after that, made your father come down and watch a few of his high school games. That's how he became interested in Knox for the Bruins."

Pee-wee football. And here I'd thought Christian was poking fun at me for being a stats geek and not knowing people so well. I had no idea my grandfather had been his coach.

"Well, the jumbotron found you sitting on the visitor side, and the announcers are having a field day with it. Why don't you come up to the owner's box for the rest of the game?"

He shook his head. "No can do. I'm no deadbeat. A bet's a bet."

I sighed. "Okay…well, my friend Miller is here with some friends, so I'm going to go back up. But I'll come back down in a little bit to keep you company."

"You enjoy your friends. I'm fine right here by myself watching the game."

I smiled. "I'll be back anyway."

The second half had already started by the time I made my way back to the fancy skybox. "Is everything alright with your grandfather?" Miller asked.

"Yeah, he's fine. Apparently he lost a bet, so that's why he's sitting on the opposing side, wearing a T-shirt with Christian Knox's face on it."

"Sounds like something we would do." Miller sipped his wine and motioned to the private seating area outside where his new boyfriend, Trent, and Trent's brother, Travis, were sitting. "So what do you think of Trav?"

I squinted. "I thought you said this wasn't a fix up."

"It's not. But he has a great smile, doesn't he?"

Sadly, I hadn't even noticed. Though I had noticed, from all the way up here, that Christian Knox had a fantastic one as he stood on the sidelines. It was less of a smile and more of a smirk. On his official player photo, you could see one dimple. But in some of the interviews I'd watched this week, a second one made an appearance too. And no, I hadn't stalked. I'd done research. I was the team owner now and needed to know who my players were. At least that was what I'd told myself on more than one occasion as I clicked on his photo in the team portal.

I shrugged. "I guess so. But you know I just started dating Julian."

"Not dating. *Date.* You had one. Speaking of which, has he called yet?"

"No, but it's only been a week."

"I called Trent five minutes after our date ended to see if he wanted to go out again. He was literally still on my block, walking to the train he takes home."

"Not everyone likes to go at warp speed in relationships like you do. Besides, I've known Julian a long time.

He's not the type of guy to rush into things, even with projects when we worked together. It was one of the things that gave us a lot of compatibility when I was doing the math on us."

"The math on us." Miller scoffed. "I know you're a math genius, but not everything can be solved using a formula. If you're going to pick men to date with some sort of dumb algorithm you developed—"

I interrupted. "I didn't develop the algorithm. I used the Gale-Shapley model. It's been proven to work for dating apps like Hinge, college admissions, and matching residents to hospitals. It's a solid solution to stable matching problems. The developers won the Nobel Prize for it. Besides, you're the one who pushed me to find someone I could have a long-term relationship with so..." I made air quotes. "I don't wind up an old maid."

"I *meant* to go out and meet people or go out with a guy more than five times, not feed all the men you know into a database."

"You have your ways of doing things, and I have mine."

"Fine. But if you're going to score men, you should at least know the deets on Travis. He's single, a contractor, has an *eight twelve credit score*, drives a Tesla, and owns his own home. He also doesn't purchase single-use plastic bottles because he's concerned about the environment."

"And you're telling me this because today was *not* a setup."

Miller grinned. "That's right."

"I'm going to grab a drink and go back outside to watch the game."

He guzzled the remnants of his wine and held the glass out to me. "As long as you're at it... I need to tinkle."

Travis smiled when we joined them outside. Miller was right; his smile was nice. But I found myself comparing it to Christian's. Which was absolutely ridiculous.

"So, what's it like running a football team?" he asked.

"Well, it's only been two weeks, but it's pretty much meeting after meeting. I'm not used to that. I think a lot of people really like to hear themselves talk."

Travis chuckled. "I'm not a meeting person either. I actually changed my career because of that."

"Miller said you're a contractor. What did you do before?"

"I went to school to be an architect. Once I graduated, it took me less than a year to realize that while I loved building things, I wasn't cut out for the job. I spent more than half my time in meetings with owners, inspectors, the building department, or my bosses. So I quit and bought a house that was falling down near me. Moved into one room while I fixed it up, and then I sold it. A friend of my dad's loved the renovations I'd done and asked me to work on his summer home. Things snowballed from there, and I transitioned to being a contractor."

"Do you like owning your own business?"

He turned in his seat to face me. "I do. The good thing about being the boss is that if you don't like parts of your job, you can assign those to someone else. My assistant handles all the building-department issues, and my site manager handles all the homeowner issues. So I pretty much get to focus on the building part, which is what I like."

"Well, that's something to look forward to. I'm pretty sure I don't even know all the different parts of my job yet."

"You will soon enough. When I started at the architecture firm, I found myself asking tons of questions of the contractors I'd work with. Looking back, I realize I was more interested in that job than the one I was hired to do, from the very beginning."

I smiled. "I asked a million questions of the Director of Analytics the other day."

"What does he do, exactly?"

"He keeps all the statistics the coaches use to manage the players and prepare for games against each opponent."

"I guess that's up your alley?"

I tapped the three-ring binder sitting on my lap. I'd been jotting things down in it all day. "I've started working on an algorithm that predicts game stats, just for fun, in my spare time. I'm better with numbers than people."

"I don't know about that. You're doing pretty well right now."

He seemed like a sweet-enough guy, but I needed to stay focused on the team, and talking to him kept me from tracking the stats I wanted to record. So a little while later, I excused myself and went to go sit with my grandfather. I learned more spending a quarter and a half next to him than I had reading a hundred books on football over the last two years.

When the game was over, I'd started to wheel him from the row when Christian Knox appeared on the sideline directly beneath us.

He banged on the backstop wall. "Nice shirt, old man!"

"I'm going to use it as a rag when I get home," my grandfather yelled. "By the way, you looked great out there today... Oh wait, that wasn't you who led the team to victory. It was the guy gunning for your job."

Christian clutched his chest. "Low blow, Coach. Low blow."

The two men smiled. Christian lifted his chin to me. "What's going on, boss lady?"

"Not much. Just got more of an education on the sport of football in an hour than I did over the last two years trying to learn it on my own."

"It's annoying as hell, isn't it? I think I know it all until I sit with him. You guys sticking around for a while?" He thumbed over his shoulder. "I gotta run to the post-game meeting. But I can grab the PT van from Doc and give you a ride home, if you want, Coach." He looked at me. "It's wheelchair accessible, and they don't care when I take it to drive him."

My grandfather put a finger up. "I'll take the ride. Lenny Riddler dropped me off, but I know his daughter is in town, so I'd rather not make him go out of his way again." He pointed to Christian. "You, on the other hand, I don't mind wasting your time."

Christian laughed. "You guys going to be around here?"

"Actually," I said, "I have some friends up in the owner's box. Why don't you meet us there?"

He nodded. "Will do."

———

Forty-five minutes later, Christian strolled into the owner's box carrying three pizzas. He winked at me. "Thought you might be hungry."

I shook my head with a smile. "I'm never going to live that down, am I?"

He grinned. "Probably not."

Miller and his boyfriend walked over, with Travis in tow. I could see the stars in their eyes, so I made the introductions. "Christian, this is my friend Miller, his boyfriend, Trent, and Trent's brother, Travis."

Christian shook everyone's hand.

"I'm a huge fan," Miller said.

"Yes, huge fan." I rolled my eyes. "He asked me what inning we were in earlier."

Christian chuckled. "Well, at least they stock these things with alcohol and food."

Miller leaned down and picked up a serving dish full of hors d'oeuvres. "Not just food. Caviar and champagne. If I had known this is how games were, I might have tried out for the football team instead of the badminton team."

"Um...you didn't actually try out for the badminton team," I reminded him. "You were the water boy because you had the hots for the twenty-five-year-old coach."

Miller waved me off. "We don't need to be all technical now..."

I took the pizza boxes from Christian with a laugh. "What can I get you to drink?"

"Whatever you're having is fine."

"She drinks Mike's Hard Lemonade," Miller said. "I had to smuggle them into the stadium. I figured they didn't stock them in their fancy wine fridges up here."

Christian looked amused. "I don't think I've had one of those things since high school. But I'll take one."

Travis turned his head and sneezed. He was five feet away from me and covered his mouth, yet I held my breath and started to count anyway. Miller caught what I was doing and smirked, while Christian glanced back and forth between us.

"What am I missing here?" he said.

I pointed to Miller since I hadn't reached fifteen yet.

He rocked back and forth on his heels. "She holds her breath for fifteen seconds after people sneeze."

Christian's smile was crooked. "Why?"

"Germs."

Christian chuckled, but didn't pursue it further.

For the next half hour, my guests pretty much formed a circle around Christian. If he minded, no one would ever have known it. He was gracious as could be. At one point, he excused himself to go to the bathroom, and when he came out, I was packing up my things.

"Did you drive here?" he asked, rolling up the sleeves on his white dress shirt.

My eyes snagged on his muscular forearms, and by the time I tore them away, I'd completely forgotten what we were talking about. "Umm... I'm sorry. What did you ask?"

The corner of his lip twitched. "I asked if you drove here."

"No, I actually don't drive. I came with Miller."

He looked over at the three men now talking with Coach. "Double date?"

"No... Well, at least not that I was aware of. Though I think Miller might've had other ideas."

"Can I drop you home then? We can take Coach first."

"I actually live in the City."

"So do I."

"Oh. Then I guess yeah, sure." I smiled, but felt a bit nervous. "I need to let Miller know."

Miller was still standing with Trent and Travis when I walked over. "Hey," I said. "I'm going to go with Christian to drop off my grandfather. He'll give me a ride home after."

Miller's eyes sparkled with excitement, and I noticed Travis's smile wilt a bit. When I went out to the seating area to double-check that I hadn't left anything behind, Travis joined me.

"Hey." He shoved his hands into his pockets. "Do you think maybe I could get your phone number? Take you out to dinner sometime?"

I always felt terrible saying no when a guy asked me out, especially when he was nice. In fact, I'd gone on a few dates solely because I'd felt bad declining. At least this time I had a reason to give him, not that I needed one.

"I'm sorry. I recently started seeing someone I used to work with, and I have so much going on at work these days, I just don't think it's the right time."

Travis forced a smile. "Oh, yeah. Of course."

"But it was really nice meeting you."

"Sure. You, too. Thanks for having me today. I had a great time."

When Travis turned away, I noticed Christian watching me through the glass. Unlike when most people get caught staring, he didn't look away. Instead, he smirked and kept his eyes trained on me as I approached the door and opened it.

"Broke his heart, huh?" His grin widened as I walked through.

"How do you know what Travis and I talked about out there?"

"I know the look of defeat."

"Oh really? So a lot of women turn you down?"

"Nah." He grinned. "I'm usually the reason they're turning down some other guy."

I rolled my eyes. "Full of yourself much?"

Christian shrugged. "Just being honest."

"Come on, honest Abe. Let's get out of here. The cleaning crew has looked in a few times to see if we're still here. I'm sure they'd like to go home in the near future."

———

An hour later, we'd dropped off my grandfather, and Christian and I were alone in the van.

"So today was your first time sitting in the owner's box, right?" he asked.

I nodded. "I went to all the team's games over the last two years, but I sat in regular seats. My sisters weren't going to welcome me unless they had to."

Christian was quiet for a moment. "It must've been crazy to find out who your father was and that he'd left you a football team, both on the same day."

I nodded. "It was. Most people probably think I won the lotto by inheriting the majority of shares of a professional football team, but it didn't feel like that at all. It made me sad to realize my father had known I'd existed and didn't bother to get to know me."

"You really had no idea he was your dad, huh?"

I shook my head. "My mom was only nineteen when she had me. She always said my father was a guy she met at a concert out of state, and she didn't even know his last name. After she died, I went to live with my aunt for a short time. I asked her if she knew more about who my father was, and she admitted that my mother had confided that he was a married man. But she didn't know his name, and she suspected my mom might not have told whoever it was about her pregnancy."

Christian's eyes slanted to mine. "But John obviously knew, if he wrote you into his will."

I nodded. "Though I have no idea if he knew from day one or found out years later. My mom was a hostess in the luxury boxes at the stadium for sixteen years, from the time she was eighteen. She sometimes worked in the owner's suite. They could've had a long-term affair or only a night together. When I first found out, I tried to talk to my half-sisters and find out what they knew. But they weren't exactly amenable to speaking to me, much less sharing anything personal they knew about their dad."

"Not surprising, knowing Tiffany and Rebecca."

"Yeah."

"They must've freaked out when the will was read."

"I would imagine. I wasn't there for the actual reading. One day a lawyer knocked on my door and said a bequest had been made to me from John Barrett. I didn't even know who that was until the attorney explained he owned the Bruins. I figured maybe he had been friendly with my mom." I shook my head. "Anyway, I had to work, so I didn't go to the reading. I found out what I'd been left that night on the news."

"Holy shit."

"Yeah. It was a crazy time. One day I was living my quiet life, and the next I couldn't go anywhere without a reporter sticking a microphone in my face. And my lovely new half-sisters held a press conference saying I was a gold digger who'd manipulated a sick man, even though I'd never met John Barrett."

"Jesus, and I thought I had a lot of pressure."

"My grandfather likes to say pressure makes diamonds. He forgets it can also cause a nervous breakdown."

Christian looked over once again and smiled. "Nah... you got this."

A little while later, we pulled up to the address I'd given him. Christian's brows dipped as he looked over at the crappy old building. "Do you need to stop at the store or something?"

I laughed. "No, this is where I live." I pointed up to the third-floor window, two stories above the fruit stand downstairs. "It's a walk up, but it's rent controlled, and I have a skylight."

"How long have you lived here?"

"Since I was sixteen. I worked for Mr. Zhang, the owner, in exchange for a place to stay until I finished college and got a full-time job."

"You said your aunt took care of you after your mother died, right?"

I nodded. "She did, but she died during a routine hernia surgery six months after my mom. She had a reaction to the anesthesia. So the state placed me with a cousin of my mom's. That didn't work, so I moved out on my own."

"At sixteen? The state didn't care?"

"They didn't know. Social services is so overwhelmed with people who don't have places to stay that they don't check on people too often who are taken in by family."

Christian was quiet as he glanced toward the grocery store again. "I guess it's convenient to get fresh fruit."

I smiled. "That it is. And I'm guessing you live somewhere a little more swanky?"

Christian squinted at the building. "How do you get in?"

"Through the store. There's a door in the back that leads upstairs to the two apartments."

"What about when the market is closed?"

"It's open twenty-four hours. So it's never been a problem."

Christian grinned. "You really jumped into the billionaire lifestyle, huh?"

"Totally." I chuckled. "Well, thank you for the ride home—and for dropping off my grandfather."

"Hang on. Let me find a parking spot, and I'll walk you."

"That's not necessary."

"Maybe not. But it's dark out, and I'm going to do it anyway." He looked around. The street was lined with bumper-to-bumper cars, so he hit the button for the flashers. "On second thought, right here looks good."

Christian got out of the van and jogged around to my side to open the passenger door. He held out a hand to help me. Being the klutz I am, I somehow dropped my binder as I stepped to the curb. It fell to the sidewalk and bounced, spilling the contents all over the street.

"Shit." I bent to scoop up the papers, but the breeze caught a few pages and sent them sailing down the street.

Christian chased those down, while I corralled the others. When they were all cleaned up, he went to hand me the ones he'd gathered, then pulled them in for a closer inspection. "You're keeping your own stats? You know there's a team analyst who does that—more than one, actually."

"I know. I used their stats to build an algorithm to try to predict the success rate of certain plays in the future."

"Really? You can do that?"

"I thought so. It worked pretty well for some players, but not so much for others."

"Which ones?"

"Which ones what?"

"Did it not work for?"

I shuffled the loose papers around until I found the ones with the most red ink. "Yates, for one. His was completely off. And so was Owens."

Christian smiled. "Ah, you're missing the human factor."

"What do you mean?"

"Yates's girlfriend dumped him this week. He's a great player, but he's also emotional as shit. He was off his game at practice all week, too. And Owens is worried about his contract renewal. His wife recently found out she's pregnant with their fifth kid, and he's in his early thirties. He's got a lot riding on his shoulders with an uncertain future."

"Oh wow," I said. "I didn't know any of that."

Christian extended the papers in his hands to me. "Numbers are only half the equation. You need to get to know the people, too."

I scrunched up my nose. "I'm not so great at that."

He smiled. "I can help, if you want. I'm benched for a while still and mostly sitting around twiddling my thumbs."

"That's kind of you to offer. Normally when I tell people the things I'm doing for fun, they just look at me like I'm nuts."

Christian walked me to the entrance of the fruit stand, which was only twenty feet away. "By the way, what was the reason you shot down the guy who asked you out earlier?"

"Umm... I recently went out on a first date with someone I used to work with, and my life is kind of busy right now."

His eyes dropped to my lips for a half second. If I'd blinked, I would have missed it. "You and the guy you worked with exclusive?"

"No." I shook my head. "Not yet anyway. But I also think I need to get settled in my new role and let that be the focus for a while—at least get to know all the different people in the organization and learn who I can trust and who I need to look out for."

Christian rubbed his bottom lip with his thumb. "Alright. I get that. I'll see you tomorrow then."

"Tomorrow?"

"Yeah. I know everyone in the corporate organization pretty well, and all of the players. I'll come by after practice and help you figure it all out." He shrugged. "Sooner you're settled, the sooner you can have dinner with me."

"I never said I'd have dinner with you."

Christian leaned in and kissed my cheek. "We'll work on that, too. 'Night, boss lady."

Chapter 4

Bella

"THE LAST THING we need to talk about is *Sports Illustrated*."

"What about it?" I asked.

Beau Fallon, VP of Publicity, tapped his pen to his notepad. "They still want you for the cover. The president of the conglomerate that owns the magazine called me himself to ask what it would take to get it done."

"Like I told you, I don't think it's a good idea for me to have a high profile right now. I need to make friends with the people who work here, not alienate them further by flashing my face all over and acting like I think I'm a rock star."

"I know, and I agreed when you made that decision. But I wanted to raise the issue again because they brought up a good point—you're the youngest person to ever own a team, and a woman. It could be inspiring to other young women to know someone who looks like them is on top at an unlikely place."

I shook my head. "Maybe down the road, but now isn't the right time."

He pulled something out of his leather bag on the floor and plopped it on the table. It looked like a stack of magazines wrapped in plastic.

"I'll let them know. But they sent me these and asked that I give them to you."

"What are they?"

"Some of their issues with trailblazing women in sports on them." He pointed. "Billie Jean King, Serena and Venus Williams, Katherine Switzer..."

"Who's Katherine Switzer?"

"She was the first woman to complete the Boston Marathon, back in '67. Women weren't allowed to compete, so she entered as KV Switzer. During the marathon, one of the refs realized a woman was running and tried to chase her off the course. But she was the first official female entrant to complete the race." He pushed the stack of magazines forward. "You just made the point they were trying to make by giving you these. People don't know about women's accomplishments unless their stories are told."

"I can definitely appreciate that it's important to tell women's stories. But I'd like to actually accomplish something before being hailed."

Beau smiled. "You sound like your father."

"I do?"

He nodded. "The man had made it to the NFL, broken a dozen records during his career, and then amassed a fortune through wise investing in oil and gas—enough to buy a team by the time he was forty. Yet he never felt like he deserved accolades."

I had so much trouble reconciling the positive things I heard about John Barrett with the father who didn't step up to take responsibility when I was born. But so many of the people who worked here revered him, so I kept that thought to myself.

"Anything else we need to discuss?"

Beau shook his head. "I don't think so."

The rest of the afternoon flew by. I had meetings with the legal department and operations team, and then sat in on the sales-team meeting. It was after five by the time I walked back down the long hall that led to my office. On my way, a photo I'd passed a dozen times finally stopped me. It was of my father and Tiffany and Rebecca. They were holding the Super Bowl trophy in the air, while ticker tape rained down all over them. I studied my father's smiling face, again trying to figure out who the man was. A minute or so passed...or maybe it was longer. I was so lost in my head that I really had no idea until a man's voice snapped me out of it.

"That was one hell of a crazy day."

I hadn't even heard Christian approach. "Oh, hey."

He lifted his chin to the framed photo. "Did you watch that game?"

I shook my head. "I doubt I even knew the game was being played or what teams were in it."

"I like how honest you are."

"You might be the only one in this building."

Christian smiled. "Apologies for being late getting up here. My knee was swollen today, so PT made me go for a scan."

"Are you okay?"

"Yeah. Probably pushed it a little harder than I should've in therapy. You ready for Bruins people training 101?"

I shook my head. "You really don't have to do this."

"I know, but I want to."

I wasn't quite sure what to do with that answer, so I tilted my head toward my office. "Come on."

Inside, Christian pointed to the couch. "Mind if I sit there and prop my foot on the table? I need to elevate it to reduce the swelling so Doc doesn't have a heart attack on me." He stopped and put his hands up. "Wait, will that freak you out because you're a germaphobe?"

"I'm not a germaphobe. Why would you say that?"

"You held your breath when someone sneezed yesterday."

"Oh, that. I just don't like sneezing. Did you know pathogens can fly from the human body at almost a hundred miles an hour and travel up to twenty-seven feet?"

"That's a great little factoid. Do you spring those on people at parties? No wonder you need people training."

I narrowed my eyes. "Put your foot up, wiseass."

Christian chuckled. "You're cute when you're tough. Especially with those crooked spectacles."

"Oh my God. Again?" I took my glasses off, bent one side a bit, and put them back on. "Better?"

Christian smiled and lifted his foot up on the table. "Nah. I was only screwing with you before. But now you really made them crooked."

"You are such a child." I fixed my glasses a second time, then grabbed a notebook and pen, along with my trusty algorithm binder, and sat down across from him.

"So what do you want to start with?" he asked. "The players or the corporate crew?"

I was about to say whatever he preferred when I noticed the stack of magazines on the coffee table from earlier today. It reminded me of what Beau had said—how I was so much like my father. "You knew John pretty well, didn't you?"

"Barrett? Your father?"

I nodded.

"I think so."

"What was he...like?"

Christian looked back and forth between my eyes. "He was a great guy. I'm not sure if that's what you want to hear, considering how he handled things with you. But it's the truth." He shrugged. "At least from what I knew of him."

I said nothing for a long time. "If you had to pick one word to describe him, what would it be?"

"The first thing that comes to my mind is honorable. Which doesn't seem right to say to you. But the man I knew was a man of his word. There's a lot of posturing and gambling in sports. Owners and coaches want to put together the best team possible, and that often means stepping on someone to get where you want to be. Everyone is always searching for the next best player. You can be the king one year and traded for a new royal the next. You're only as good as your last game. There's not too much loyalty. But when my first contract was up for renewal, and John put his hand on my shoulder and told me not to worry about it, I didn't."

I shook my head. "I guess I'm having trouble reconciling the man people around here talk about and the man who would let a child be passed around to different homes after the death of the only parent she ever knew."

Christian frowned. "I don't blame you. I am also."

"Miller thinks I need to stop holding a dead man accountable, or I'll never move on. But for me, it's less about forgiveness and more about understanding why he did what he did. I'm the type of person who can't leave a puzzle three quarters of the way done."

Christian nodded. "I get it. I think sometimes we feel unsettled because we're meant to know more."

"Exactly. Why can't Miller understand my logic like that?"

"I take it you two have been friends a long time?"

"Since he walked up to me the second day of class in ninth grade and told me never to wear orange again."

"Why didn't he want you to wear orange?"

I pointed to my head. "It looks terrible with my auburn hair."

"He just walked up unsolicited and told you that?"

"Yep."

"And you didn't mind?"

"I did at the moment. I told him to go screw himself. But then when I went home and looked in the mirror, I realized he was right. I wore green to school the next day. Miller told me the color was *intoxicating* on me and handed me half of the brownie he was eating. We've been inseparable since. He has boundary issues, but he's the best friend a girl could ask for."

My cell phone started to ring from my desk on the other side of the room, so I excused myself to check whether it was anything important. Finding Wyatt's name flashing, I smiled. "I need to answer this. I'll only be a minute."

"Take your time."

I swiped and brought the phone to my ear. "What's going on, Trouble?"

45

"I'm calling to remind you about Wednesday night."

"Do I ever forget your games?"

"You missed half of the last one."

"Yes, but that's not because I forgot. I got on the wrong second bus. There's a difference."

"Is Miller driving you?"

"No. Miller wants to come, but he has a big project at work, and they can't start on it until the rest of the office is gone for the day."

"So you're going to take the buses again? That's gonna take like an hour and a half with all the stops and transfer-ring."

"It's okay. I'll have my laptop to keep me busy."

"You know they have this thing called Uber now..."

I smiled. "I'll be there when it starts this time, I prom-ise."

"My friend Andre can drive you home after. He's a pretty good driver."

"Does Andre have a license?"

"He's got his learner's permit."

"That's not a license to drive. I hope you're not getting into the car with him."

"You know, you used to be cool. Now you sound like my mom."

"I'm going to take that as a compliment."

"You do that..."

I laughed. "I'm at work still, so I need to run. I'll see you Wednesday, okay?"

"A'ight. Later."

"Later, Trouble." I brought my cell over to the couch with me after I hung up.

"You going to the Philly game?" Christian asked.

"Philly game?"

"You mentioned a game on Wednesday. The league is trying out weekday nights a few times this season. Philly game is this Wednesday."

"Oh." I shook my head. "No, I'm going to a high school game, not a league one. Wyatt and his mom are old friends. He actually grew up playing soccer, but when he got to high school, the football coach drafted him as the kicker. He's really good. Hoping to get a scholarship, but he goes to a catholic high school in Queens that doesn't get a lot of attention from colleges."

"What school?"

"St. Francis."

Christian nodded. He was sitting on the couch, with one arm slung across the top and one foot propped up on the coffee table. It certainly didn't look like he was in any rush to get up, and he seemed perfectly content just talking about, well...nothing.

I tilted my head. "Can I ask you something?"

He shrugged. "Sure."

"Why are you here?"

"You mean at the Bruins?"

I shook my head. "No, here with me at this moment. You must have plenty of other things you could be doing right now that are more fun than listening to my drivel."

"Maybe I like drivel."

I snort-laughed. "No one likes drivel."

He smiled, and his eyes dropped to my lips for a fraction of a second. "Maybe I like *you*."

I shifted in my seat to face him. "Why?"

47

Christian shrugged again. "I don't know. I think you're interesting."

My eyes narrowed. "What about me is interesting?"

"You're a billionaire who lives in a rent-controlled apartment over a fruit stand and tried to give the team you inherited to your grandfather. What's *not* interesting about you? Given your situation, most people I know would live in a penthouse by now and take car services, not walk twenty minutes to the stadium every day after getting off the train or humping it on two buses to Queens to see a high school game."

I raised an eyebrow, and a grin spread across Christian's face.

"Plus, you're hot."

That last part made me smile. "And technically, I'm your boss."

His grin widened. "That makes you even hotter."

I chuckled. "Tell me about yourself, Christian. I feel like you know so much about me, but I don't know anything about you, other than your stats, of course."

"What do you want to know?"

"Do you have a girlfriend?"

"You think I'm hot too, don't you?"

I laughed. "Just answer the question, Knox. Something tells me your ego gets stroked enough."

"Yes, ma'am." He shook his head. "No girlfriend."

I tapped my lip with my pointer. "What do you do in the offseason?"

"Recover. Let my body heal. Sleep. Fish. I have a cabin on a lake up in Maine. Spend time with friends. Travel. Keep up with my training."

"That sounds so...normal."

"The season is anything but normal when you play in the NFL. It's tough on the body and mind. You're on the road all the time, the media follows your ass around, women hand you underwear with their numbers written on them and sneak into your hotel room. So normal is good."

My face wrinkled. "Women give you their underwear?"

Christian smiled. "Any other questions?"

"Am I demented if I'm curious to know whether the underwear are clean or not?"

He laughed. "Maybe. But I like the way you think."

A little while later, Christian's cell chimed. He slipped it from his pocket and swiped. "I promised PT I'd stop back down before they close at seven thirty for a quick recheck of my knee, so I have to run."

I tapped the screen on my phone to check the time. "Oh, wow. I can't believe it's seven fifteen already. We never even talked about the players or the staff."

"Which means I have to come back." Christian winked and stood. "Unless you want me to come back after and we can talk over dinner?"

I smiled. "I should probably get going."

He nodded. "Another time, then?"

"Sure."

He walked to the door. "I'm going to hold you to that *sure*."

Chapter 5

Bella

"HEY, KIDDO." I waved to Wyatt from the bottom of the bleachers as he ran over. He'd just kicked a forty-yard field goal to end the second quarter and was all smiles as he thumbed back toward the uprights.

"Did you see that? Where's my contract? The Bruins gotta get them some of this."

I laughed. "I think you should try finishing high school and college first."

He waved me off. "Man...school's for dummies."

"I went to four years of college, did my master's, and three quarters of a PhD. What does that make me?"

Wyatt grinned. "Wasteful. You own a football team. You didn't need to do all that."

He was teasing, so I spared him the lecture about the value of a good education. "Is your mom here? I didn't see her in the stands."

"She's gotta work late again. She said she'd try to make the end of the game. But I told her not to. I don't want her taking two trains to get here only to see the last sixty seconds. There's a game next Saturday she can come to."

"I'll cheer you on for both of us."

He waved. "I gotta get to the locker room before Coach kicks my ass. See you after the game?"

"*Butt*—before the coach kicks your *butt*. And yes, I'll find you after the game is over."

Wyatt ran back to join his team.

I took a seat on the bleachers and spent halftime catching up on emails from my phone. It was hard to imagine how most people in the Bruins organization got anything done with the amount of emails and meetings they had to manage. Five minutes into the third quarter, I noticed a news truck pull up in the parking lot not too far away. Then another one, and another. I really hoped they were here for the team and not me. I slouched down into my seat, just in case. By the end of the third quarter, there had to be a dozen trucks crammed into the already-full lot of cars. But none of the media had come in. They'd gotten out of their vans and were standing around waiting for something. I tried to focus on the game and pretend they weren't there.

At one point, Wyatt's team was behind by three, and it was third and twelve. Their offense hadn't been too reliable making the long first downs this game, so the coach signaled for Wyatt to get ready. I watched with a smile on my face as he shot practice kicks into the net on the sideline behind his team's bench. It seemed like only yesterday I was babysitting, and he was taking practice shots on me in front of the soccer goal.

As had been the case for most of the game today, his team didn't convert for a first down. So Wyatt jogged onto the field to set up for a field-goal attempt. I nibbled my lip, feeling tightness in my chest as I waited for him to take his shot. I had no idea how professional players managed the stress. My heart felt like it was going to jump out of my chest, and I was only a spectator at a high school game. I might've held my breath as he ran toward the ball and reared his leg back for the kick.

But I jumped up and down and screamed when the ball sailed through the uprights. "*Great job, Wyatt!* Woo-hoo!"

"Damn, I didn't see you jumping around like that when McKenzie knocked the ball in for three last Sunday right before halftime." A man's voice startled me.

"Christian?" I turned and blinked a few times.

He smiled. "Bella?"

I peered around him, though I had no idea what I was looking for. "What are you doing here?"

He shrugged. "Bringing the media."

"What do you mean?"

"You said your friend's son is a good player, but his school doesn't get much attention. I figured I'd help out."

My mind was still boggled that Christian Knox was standing next to me, here at the field of St. Francis Prep High School in Queens. Not to mention, he looked ridiculously sexy in a backward baseball cap, so it took my brain some time to catch up. "But how did you know there was a game?"

"You told me the other day in your office, after you hung up from your call with the kid. I believe you referred to him as Trouble."

I shook my head. "Oh, yeah...right."

I wasn't used to most men listening when I said something important, much less paying attention when I mentioned something in passing. "I can't believe you're here. Do all those news trucks follow you wherever you go?"

He shook his head. "I had one of the team's publicists leak where I was heading." Christian lifted his chin toward the scoreboard. "Your boy just tied it up, huh? I saw him knock it in while I was walking from the parking lot."

"Yeah, he's doing great. That's his third field goal of the game."

The reporters huddled in the parking lot were now spread out along the sideline, setting up their tripods. Christian noticed me looking around.

"I told them I'd talk to them after the game, but to keep their eye on the home team kicker until it's over."

"That was so kind of you. Thank you. Wyatt is going to freak out when he realizes all of these reporters are here to see him." I paused. "Well, they're here to see you, but you know what I mean."

"No problem."

We stood side by side, watching the game for a few minutes in silence. "Is your friend here?" Christian asked. "You said it was your friend's son."

I shook my head. "She couldn't make it. She had to work. I try to come to all of Wyatt's games anyway, but I like to make sure I'm here for the evening ones because I know she often can't be." From the corner of my eye, I noticed Wyatt and half of his teammates standing on the sideline, pointing our direction. I motioned across the field. "I think you've been spotted."

Christian waved to them. "I remember the feeling they probably have right now. Coach came to all of my games. I was about their age when he brought his famous son the first time." He smiled. "I remember running across the field after the game was over. I couldn't wait to meet him. Halfway, I tripped over my own two feet and fell right on my face."

I covered my mouth. "Oh my God."

"I thought for sure John would never come back to another game, but he did." He paused. "You know, Coach would probably love to come see a high school game like this. Have you brought him yet?"

I shook my head. "I haven't. It's kind of hard for me to bring him anywhere since I don't drive, and he doesn't get around so easily."

"You know they have these things called *car services* now. I'm pretty sure it's the billionairess's preferred mode of transportation."

"Cute," I said.

Christian lifted his backward baseball cap off his head and spun it around forward. "That's what the girls call me."

I chuckled. "I'm sure they do."

We watched the game for a while. Toward the end of the fourth quarter, the coach put Wyatt in for another field goal try, which he nailed. I clapped. "Four for four!"

"Kid's got some leg. The soccer coach must not have been happy when the football coach nabbed him."

"He wasn't actually. And Wyatt's mom was against him playing football. But Wyatt has a way of talking people into anything, especially me and his mother."

"It sounds like you two have been friends a long time."

I nodded. "We have. I also used to babysit Wyatt when his mom had to work. So we're pretty close."

"Is that before or after you started to work for Mr. Zhang and live above the fruit stand?"

"God, you even remember my landlord's name. You have a very good memory."

"Only when I'm interested in what I'm hearing."

My stomach felt all mushy, which I tried to ignore. "To answer your question, it was both before and after I started working at the fruit stand. Talia, Wyatt's mom, and I lived in the same shelter for a while when I was fifteen. That's how we met."

Christian's face fell. "I'm sorry."

"There's nothing to be sorry about. I wouldn't change that year because without it, I wouldn't have Talia and Wyatt in my life. Talia was only sixteen when she had Wyatt. She and I are five years apart, so Wyatt was just four when we met. Back then, she watched my stuff while I went to school, so it would be there when I got back, and I watched her son while she worked an evening shift at McDonald's." I looked out to the field and over at Wyatt. "When I got my apartment above Mr. Zhang's, they stayed with me for a while until she made assistant manager and could afford a place of their own. We've been close ever since. She and Miller are my family, the ones I chose."

Christian shook his head. "I don't get how John could have let his daughter live in a shelter with all that he had."

"I wish I understood a lot of things about him better..."

After the game was over, Wyatt came charging across the field. I leaned over to Christian as he neared. "Glad he didn't trip."

"Holy crap! I can't believe Christian Knox is here!"

Christian stretched a hand over the fence. "Nice game, Wyatt."

Wyatt's eyes bulged. "You know my name?"

"Sure. I came to watch you play." He lifted his chin to the reporters still positioned along the edge of the field. "So did they."

"Really?"

"Yep. But if your coach is anything like my high school coach, he's not gonna be happy that you're over here. So why don't you go back and join your team for the end-of-game talk. I'll come over and say hello in a few minutes."

"Okay!"

Wyatt bolted back toward his team without even glancing in my direction.

"I don't think he noticed I was standing here."

Christian's eyes swept up and over me. "Trust me, he's the only one."

I felt my cheeks heat. "You know, I am your boss."

"Not right now you're not, and there are about six layers of coaches and management between us, so I'm not worried about it anyway." He gestured toward the media. "I gotta go give them some time for coming. You want to join me, or do an end run and go the other way?"

I normally avoided the media at all costs, but I appreciated them being here today, and one hand washed the other in the world of business, so I decided to walk over with Christian.

The first reporter we stopped at was Reggie Carter. He was older and more polite than a lot of the young guys. "Ms. Keating? I thought that looked like you. Damn, this must be an important kid for both of you to be here."

Christian looked to me to answer. I smiled. "He is. And I appreciate you coming to see for yourself."

He dug a small notebook from the leather satchel at his feet and flipped to an open page. "Tell me a little bit about him..."

———

"So what do you want to major in at college?" Christian glanced in the rearview mirror, speaking to Wyatt. After more than an hour of throwing the ball around with the team, he'd insisted on driving us both home.

Wyatt was so busy tapping away on his phone, he didn't respond.

"Wyatt?" I said. "Christian asked you a question."

"Oh...sorry. My Snapchat is blowing up because of the pictures I posted of Christian and me having a catch." Wyatt lowered his cell. "What did you ask?"

Christian smiled. "What are you thinking about studying in college?"

Wyatt shrugged. "I don't know. I just want to play football. Whatever is easiest, I guess."

"You know, a lot of excellent players never make it to the NFL. But even if you do, every time you step out on that field, you risk having your career end because of an injury. You should take some time to think about what you're interested in and pick something that offers you a solid future. Every smart player has a backup plan."

"What was your major?"

"Archeology."

Wyatt's face wrinkled. "You mean like the bones of dead people that you dig out of the ground?"

"That would be the one."

"I don't know what I'm interested in, but it's definitely not that."

Christian chuckled. "You don't have to like what I like, but you should try to figure out what you have a passion for."

A giant grin spread across Wyatt's face. "I already know. Pizza, girls, and football."

Even I had to laugh at that response. When we got to Wyatt's home, Talia was still at work. She must've had to stay even later than she'd expected. I walked Wyatt in but didn't stay long since Christian had double-parked out front.

"What are you doing for your birthday?" I asked at the door. "It's only a few weeks away."

He shrugged. "Nothing."

"How about if we have a little party in the owner's box at Bruins Stadium? You can invite your team for a game."

"The *whole* team?"

I mussed Wyatt's hair. "Sure. There's enough room."

"Will Christian be there?"

"Christian will be down on the field with the team."

"Oh."

"But maybe I can get us a field pass, and we can go down and say hi before the game starts, or after."

"*Really*?"

I pointed a finger. "*If* you give some thought to what Christian said in the car. Come to the game with five subjects or jobs you think you might be interested in, and I'll get you down to the field for at least a few minutes. Deal?"

"Deal." He nodded.

Even though I was pretty quick, a traffic cop was at

Christian's car when I came back out. I got in on the passenger side, expecting the officer to be harassing him, but the cop—a woman—was all smiles.

Christian signed his name across the face of a parking ticket. "You're not going to forget to void this, right?" He handed it back to her.

"I got you." She took the ticket back. "This baby is getting framed, not going into the system."

"Thank you. Have a good night, Officer."

After she walked away, Christian looked over at me. "You ready?"

"I am. But did you just smile your way out of a ticket?"

"She recognized me and offered. I didn't ask."

"What else do you get for free?"

Christian looked over his shoulder before shifting into drive and pulling away. "It actually makes me uncomfortable when people won't take my money at restaurants and stuff."

It was nice that he didn't feel entitled. "I can see that. I've never been very good at taking a handout."

Christian glanced over at me and back to the road. "You might be genetically similar to Tiffany and Rebecca, but the resemblance stops at DNA."

"I still can't get over Tiffany making me give you a lecture on sexual harassment. I think she's going to hate me forever."

"I think that little stunt was aimed at both of us, not just you."

"What do you mean?"

"I haven't been on Tiff's good side lately."

"Oh? How come?"

He was quiet for a few seconds, as he seemed to consider his answer. "Let's just say, I don't always take the free stuff offered like I did getting out of that ticket with the cop."

My brows furrowed. "Tiffany offered you something for free? What?"

His eyes caught mine for a brief second. "Her."

It took a couple seconds for me to sort that out. Then my eyes widened. "You mean she *solicited* you? Like for sex?"

Christian shrugged. "Subtlety isn't her strong suit."

I shook my head. "So she harassed you and then accused *you* of harassing *her*."

"It wasn't a big deal."

"It is a big deal. If a male executive did that to a woman, would you think it was okay? Someone in a position of power should not be making unwelcome sexual advances."

Christian pursed his lips. "You're right. I wouldn't. But I never felt threatened by it. It's just the way she is."

I shook my head. "It's still very wrong."

He drummed his fingers on the steering wheel in the silence. "Wyatt seems like a good kid."

"He is. He's very different around kids his own age than he is around me or his mom. Believe it or not, he's pretty shy. Football has really helped him come out of his shell. And I'm pretty sure he's going to be king of his school for a while after this evening. Thank you again for doing that."

"No problem."

"He is definitely starstruck. I told him I'd bring him and his friends to the owner's box for his birthday, which is coming up in a few weeks. And the first thing he said was 'Will Christian be there?'"

Christian shook his head. "Damn. Your sister wants to hang out with me, and your little buddy does... What do I have to do to get that kind of attention from you?"

I smiled. "You have my attention. But I don't think anything more than friendship is a good idea since I own the team you work for. I mean, your contract is up for renewal this year."

"You just said yourself, someone in a position of power shouldn't be making sexual advances. But I don't have the power here. You do. Though I'm just going to put it out there—if you get the urge to make sexual advances, they wouldn't be unwelcome."

I laughed. "I'm flattered. Really, I am. And to be honest, it's very tempting. But—"

Christian held up his pointer. "I wasn't done. I need to address your other point. My contract *is* up this year. But rumor around the organization is that you're letting Tom Lauren run the show while you learn the ropes. Is that true?"

"Well, yes...but—"

He shrugged. "I don't see any problem then."

"It's not only the circumstances; it's also how it would look."

"I stopped giving a shit about how things look a long time ago. You learn that real quick when your face is splashed all over the newspapers every week and half the time the headline is made up."

"Even if we remove all of the work issues, I've just started dating someone. Julian and I have known each other for a few years."

"You've known him for years and he only recently asked you out? He sounds like an idiot to me."

I smiled.

Christian sighed. "Okay. I'll back off. *For now*. But if you want me to, I'll still help you with the team stuff that might affect your algorithm and fill you in on what makes people within the organization tick."

"I'd like that. Thank you."

He pointed up ahead. "Are you hungry?"

I hesitated, though I was actually starving.

Christian noticed. "It's not a date. I'm asking you to have a completely platonic meal with me at my favorite burger joint." He pulled up at a red light and looked over with puppy-dog eyes. "Not that you owe me anything, but the reason I haven't eaten yet is because I went out of my way to drive to Queens during rush-hour traffic to see Wyatt play."

I chuckled. "That wasn't manipulative at all."

He flashed a crooked smile. "Is that a yes?"

I nodded. "Sure. I'd love to share a platonic burger with you."

About a half mile down the road, Christian parked, and we walked down the block to an unassuming little eatery. There was a handwritten sign taped to the door: CASH ONLY. I stopped as Christian opened the door.

"Shoot. I don't think I have any cash on me."

"You don't need it. I'd never let my date pay."

I squinted at him. "I thought this was the platonic sharing of a burger, not a date."

He put his hand on my back, guiding me inside. "My ego is bruised enough. Just let me pretend."

Chapter 6

Christian

BELLA'S PHONE JUMPED around, vibrating on the table with *Julian* flashing on the screen.

I wasn't being nosy. Her phone was sitting almost in the center of the table, between our plates of burgers. But I was definitely curious about what she was going to do now...

She stared a few heartbeats, and her eyes lifted to meet mine.

I grinned. "Phone call..."

Her cell continued to shimmy around on the table while our eyes stayed locked. Eventually, after three more rings, it stopped.

I tilted my head ever so slightly. "Why didn't you answer?"

"Because we're in the middle of eating."

"Ah." I nodded. "And Julian wouldn't be happy to hear you're sharing a meal with a handsome athlete?"

"First of all, full of yourself much? But I meant it would be rude of me to talk on the phone while we're in the middle of having dinner."

"So it's about manners, then? Julian wouldn't be upset you were on a date?"

"This isn't a date."

"Whatever. It wouldn't bother him?"

"He and I have only been on one date."

"How long ago was that?"

"Two weeks, maybe?"

"Why no second yet?"

"I don't know. Jeez, you're nosy."

I smiled. "Interested. Not nosy. Job that has him traveling the last few weeks?"

"He's the head of artificial intelligence at my old company." Bella shook her head. "There's no travel involved in his job."

I debated how far to push the conversation and decided *just a little bit further* as I stretched my arms across the top of the booth. "What does he have that I don't?"

"Julian?"

I nodded.

"Humility, for one."

I chuckled. "How tall is he?"

"I don't know. Not quite six foot, I guess."

"I'm six-three."

"Does that give you a point on your imaginary scorecard?"

"Definitely."

"Julian is probably not the tallest or best-looking guy, but he has a lot of great qualities."

"Like what? Big dick? Because if he gets a point for that, I think it's only fair that I get to show you mine. I have a size fourteen foot, you know."

Her lips moved, but she managed to contain her smile. "I'll keep that in mind in case I ever need to buy you *socks*. Julian and I have a lot in common, if you must know."

"Like what?"

"I don't know. Off the top of my head, we both work in artificial intelligence, love math and technology, and neither of us likes sneezes."

My forehead wrinkled. "He holds his breath too?"

"No, but they make him irrationally angry."

"Sneezes? Who the hell gets angry over sneezes? It's a bodily function that can't be helped. If that's the best you got for what you have in common, I hate to tell you, but the relationship is doomed."

"It is not."

"Sweetheart, you don't even have artificial intelligence in common anymore. You work in football now. That's a point for me, not Bozo." I reached over and swiped a French fry from her plate. "Have you ever dated an athlete?"

Bella leaned toward my plate and took one of my fries. She wagged it at me before shoving it into her mouth. "Can't say that I have."

"Hear me out. You can't know what you like until you try it, right? So how do you know dating an athlete isn't way better than dating some average-looking dude who... what, plays with robots all day?"

"You know what, you have a point." She tapped her finger to her lip. "I wonder if Patrick Mannon has plans next Friday night?"

I smirked. Patrick is the Bruins' center. "He's married with kiddo number two on the way."

Bella gave in and laughed. "Our conversation has taken a strange turn."

A little while later, we'd both finished our burgers and fries. I was full, but ordered dessert anyway, not ready to drop her off yet. The waitress brought my chocolate lava cake and French vanilla ice cream and set it down in front of me with a spoon.

"Can we get another spoon, please?"

"Sure thing."

Once it came, I slid the cake to the middle and motioned for Bella to dig in as I scooped a piece from my side. "So how did you get into developing algorithms? Were you a computer nerd in high school?"

"More of a math geek than computer nerd. I was actually working toward my PhD in mathematics, hoping to become a math professor, while I worked part time as a data analyst. My job was to track how buying trends came in compared to what the algorithm developers had forecasted. But I'm not very good at letting go of things that irk me, so when the variances were big, I liked to figure out what had gone wrong in the algorithm. Eventually they asked me to join the algorithm-engineering department to help them find out what's off before the buying happens. I had to learn a lot of coding and different software, but I loved the job."

"Did you ever finish your PhD?"

Bella shook her head. "I took a leave from the program to try working full time as a developer and never looked back."

"So you're saying you almost wound up working in a career that would have probably left you unfulfilled, had you not given something new a try?"

Bella laughed. "You have an uncanny ability to work any conversation back to being about you, huh?"

"It's a gift."

"Anyway, I was planning on leaving my job to head up my own algorithm group at a bigger company, where I would be able to work from home. I was due to give my notice the day after a random lawyer knocked on my door to say a man I didn't know had left me something. Needless to say, that threw a wrench in my plans. Had that not happened, I probably would've been living up in Vermont right now."

"Vermont?"

She nodded. "I love it up there. Since I could work from home, I was going to try living outside the City. I've only ever lived in Manhattan."

"See? We have more in common than you think. I love New England, too. My cabin in Maine isn't too far from the Vermont border. I'll have to take you some time."

"Maybe." Bella scooped a hunk of the lava cake onto her spoon, then sheared off a layer of the ice cream on top. She pointed the full spoon at me before shoveling it into her mouth. "Tell me more about you. I was surprised when you told Wyatt your major was archeology. Were you into digging in the dirt and playing with bones?"

"Growing up, my brothers and I stayed with my grand-parents in Colorado for two weeks every year. Summer of ninth grade, a new family moved in next door to them. The daughter volunteered at a nearby camp—Crow Canyon. It's an archeological research center. Her name was Shelby Minton, and I was in love. So I asked my grandmother to sign me up for some week-long summer program that introduced you to archeology. I had zero interest in it at the time—really zero interest in anything but football and girls—but I wanted to be near Shelby."

"So a girl got you interested in archeology?"

"More like a woman. Shelby was twenty-three, I think."

Bella covered her smile with her hand. "You were in ninth grade? What is that, fifteen? And had the hots for a twenty-three-year-old?"

I nodded. "She drove a Jeep Wrangler with no doors or top, even when it rained, and she had big boobs. I'd wait outside for hours until she came home on a rainy afternoon, just so I could check her out in a wet T-shirt."

Bella's eyes glittered with amusement behind her slightly crooked glasses. I loved the way her whole face smiled, even when she was laughing at me.

"Did you follow Shelby around during the summer camp?"

"I did the first day. Then I saw her making out with another woman. I figured I had no shot after that."

"It took finding out she liked women for you to realize you had no shot? The fact that you were fifteen and she was twenty-three didn't give you a hint that it wasn't going to happen?"

"Nah. I was six inches taller than all the boys in my grade already, the co-captain of the varsity football team in my first year playing high school football, and popular with the girls. I thought I was the shit. I had no clue she was out of my league."

Bella laughed. "You must've been a handful."

"Anyway, once I realized Shelby was a lost cause, I started to pay more attention at the camp. By the end of the five days, I knew I wanted to go to college for archeology."

"What do you like about it?"

"I guess the mystery of it. It's like putting together a puzzle without knowing what picture you're making." Bella's eyes roamed my face. I thought maybe I had some chocolate on it, so I rubbed at my cheek. "What? Am I wearing dessert?"

She smiled. "No. You're just different than I thought you'd be."

"What did you think I'd be like?"

"I'm not sure. Just different."

"Is it a bad or good different?"

"It's a good different."

I wiggled my brows. "So does that mean you'll go out with me?"

Bella laughed. "No. But nice try."

———

A little while later, we pulled up at Bella's building. Like last time, I double-parked, hopped out, and jogged around to open her door, offering her a hand down from the truck. Except this time, I didn't let go once her feet were on the ground. Instead, I tightened my grip around her petite fingers and brought the top of her hand to my lips for a kiss.

"Thank you for having dinner with me. Even though you're going to pretend it wasn't a date, I had a good time."

"I did, too. And thank you again for coming to Wyatt's game. It was incredibly thoughtful."

"Anytime." We walked side by side to the entrance of the fruit stand. "Are you going to the game in Colorado this weekend?"

"I am. I think I'm going to hop a ride on the team's plane, for the way there at least. I'm sitting in on a meeting with an advertiser a little outside of Denver the day after the game, so I'll probably take a different flight home. But I'd like to let the players and staff know I'm accessible and trying my best to learn the ropes."

"That's a good idea. Practice ends early the day before. Maybe I can finally get around to telling you a little about the players and team's management?"

"I feel like I've monopolized a lot of your time lately."

I shook my head. "I don't mind. Do you?"

She smiled. "I think most of my days are filled with meetings until five. What time does your practice end?"

"Doesn't matter. I'll come up about six, if that works."

"Okay, thanks."

I winked. "It's a date. Another one."

She rolled her eyes, but the smile on her face told a different story. "Goodnight, Christian."

"'Night, boss lady."

Halfway back to my car, I yelled. "Hey, Bella?"

"Yes?"

"Are you going to call Julian back tonight?"

She shook her head. "Probably not. Maybe tomorrow."

I grinned. "Yeah, it's a date."

Chapter 7

Bella

"WYATT COULDN'T SLEEP last night, he was so wired from the afternoon." Talia laughed. "He must've come into my room a half dozen times while I was trying to fall asleep to tell me something about Christian that he forgot to tell me during his two-hour ramble that started the moment I walked in the door."

Talia had called early this morning while I was in the first of a string of meetings, and it had been after five by the time I called her back. I shouldered my cell so I could use both hands to tug at the bottom drawer of my desk, which was stuck, but it wouldn't budge. A week ago, I would never have imagined needing to use all of the storage in this ginormous desk, but suddenly I had reports and documents piled up everywhere.

"I haven't had a chance to see if any of the reporters who were at the game ran the story about why Christian was visiting the team," I told her.

"They sure did. Wyatt has been sending me videos and screenshots of articles that mention his name. He's not home from practice yet, but he asked me to pick up a scrapbook for him." She laughed. "Pretty sure his inflated head isn't going to fit into a helmet for a while."

"He deserves it. He's a great kid."

"Oh, and the coach told him he got *two* calls today from colleges interested in him! They asked the coach to send a highlight reel and stats and said they'd be in touch. I can't believe it. I don't know how to thank you, Bella."

"I didn't do anything. I had no idea Christian was going to show up with all the media in tow. It was all his doing."

"Well, please thank him for me," Talia said. "What's the deal with him, though? Is he trying to earn brownie points with the new owner or something?"

I'd been trying to figure that out myself. Why *was* Christian Knox being so generous with his time? Sure, he'd made it pretty clear that he wanted to take me out. But men who looked like him and played professional football did *not* have to work so hard for a date. "I'm not really sure what his motive is. But...he did ask me out."

"*Are you serious*?!"

I had to pull the phone away from my ear to avoid the shriek she let out.

"Why didn't you call immediately and tell me you were going out with the hottest man on the planet?"

"Because I'm not."

"What do you mean you're not?"

"He asked, but I declined."

"Is that third stair at your shitty apartment still coming loose, and you fell and hit your head?"

I chuckled. "I'm his boss, Talia. Besides, things between Julian and me just got going, and I don't want to mess that up. We're really compatible."

"I didn't realize you two were getting cozy after the lame first date that ended in a handshake. So things are progressing?"

I frowned. "We haven't actually gone out again. I think he's taking things slow. Which is actually fine with me. I'm overwhelmed with all the changes in my life anyway."

"But you're talking on a regular basis?"

"He called me yesterday." Which reminded me, I hadn't called him back yet...

"Don't tell me that's the first time he made contact since you went out weeks ago."

I sighed. "He's...shy."

"There's shy and then there's plain stupid. Who goes out with a woman and doesn't call her for weeks? And you're not going out with an Adonis because of this? You want to know what I think?"

"No."

"Too bad. I think you actually like Christian and that's why you won't go out with him."

"Oh yeah, that makes a lot of sense. Because I prefer my relationships to be with people I don't like..."

"No, you don't *have relationships*, Bella. You sleep with men who are nice looking, and then you dump them before they can dump you. You've been doing it since you were seventeen—ever since you gave that twenty-five-year-old dirtbag you were crazy about your virginity. Yes, he ditched you the next week after chasing you for months, but that's not going to happen every time. You never go out with a man who has real potential."

"I went on a date with Julian, didn't I?"

"Yes, because some insane dating formula you created picked him for a good match. That's not normal, Bella.

Besides, I'm guessing you're fine continuing things with him because you see him as safe."

Beau from Publicity knocked on my open door. It was the second time he'd stopped by today, so I figured it was the perfect excuse to nix this conversation. I held up a finger to him. "Tal, I have to run. I'll call you soon, okay?"

"Uh, you definitely will. Because my son told me you're hosting a party in the owner's box for his birthday?"

"Yeah, I'm sorry about that. I realized after I said it that I should have run it by you first. I hope you don't have other plans."

"I do. But I can scrub the floor and do laundry another day."

I laughed. "Alright, great. I'll call you over the weekend so we can talk about the party."

After I hung up, I waved Beau into my office. "Sorry. It's been one of those days."

He smiled. "Been here seven years. I'm waiting for it *not* to be one of those days."

I motioned to the round table in the middle of my office. "Thanks, Beau. That's encouraging."

"I won't take up much of your time. I just wanted to speak to you about your visit to St. Francis yesterday."

"Oh, sorry. I didn't even think about people calling you today."

"It's fine. But I am getting some calls. So do you mind sharing how your visit came about? I could use a few speaking points. Unlike most people here, I can't ignore the media when I feel like it, because they're often my partners in crime. If I want them to show up at the things I want spotlighted, I have to give them at least a snippet when they're the ones doing the calling."

"Of course." I nodded. "I understand."

"I left a message for Christian, but haven't heard back from him yet. Can you tell me who Wyatt Kane is?"

"Sure. He's the son of a good friend of mine. He used to play soccer, but the football coach recruited him as kicker, and he's broken every school record since he started."

Beau scribbled on his notepad. "And he's a junior?"

"That's right."

"Committed to a college yet?"

"No. That's actually the reason Christian decided to come to the game. Wyatt and his teammates haven't received many visits from college coaches."

Beau smiled. "I'm guessing that's about to change..."

I smiled back. "It has already."

"And you and Christian?"

My forehead wrinkled. "Went to the game?"

Beau chuckled. "Sorry. I was trying not to be too nosy. But a reporter asked how long you and Christian have been a couple."

I blinked. "We're not. Why would they ask that?"

Beau pulled out his cell phone. He punched in his code and swiped for a minute before setting the phone on the table and turning it to face me. "Sean Haggerty from Sports Network sent me these and asked for a comment."

In the first shot, Christian and I were standing together on the sidelines at Wyatt's school. We were looking at each other. I was laughing while he sported a dimpled smile. There must've been a breeze, because my hair was blowing back, giving the moment an oddly romantic feel. I swiped through to look at the rest. There were a few more of us looking cozy at the game, and then the last few were me getting into Christian's truck. One showed him opening the door for me, while the next few showed his hand on my back while he made sure I climbed in okay. I felt a sinking feeling in my stomach.

"This isn't what it looks like. Christian and I were just talking. We stayed to ourselves so he wouldn't get bombarded by fans, and then he was only being a gentleman by opening the car door and helping me in. His SUV is really high."

"So the official statement is nothing is going on."

"Well, not just the official statement. It's also the truth. Everyone around here already has such low opinions of me. I don't need more gossip."

"I'm sorry. I didn't mean to upset you. Sean Haggerty is the only one who asked that question, and he's a decent guy. I'm sure I can get him to bury the photos."

I sighed. "I'd appreciate that. Thank you."

Beau and I spoke for a little while longer, and when he had everything he needed, he closed his notebook and stood...just as Christian appeared at my door. He flashed his signature boyish smile and held up a bag. "I brought tacos for dinner."

Beau looked between Christian and me. He didn't say a word, but his face questioned everything I'd told him over the last ten minutes.

"Hey, Christian." He lifted his chin, then nodded to me. "I'll get out of your way. No one likes cold tacos."

I felt a little deflated, yet forced a smile. "Thanks again, Beau."

Once Beau walked out of my office, Christian stepped inside. He thumbed behind him. "Should I shut the door?

Probably don't want people hearing us talk about the team."

I sighed. "Please. They're already talking about us..."

Christian set the bag on the table. "Who's talking about us?"

"At least one reporter. He snapped some pictures of you and me on the sidelines laughing and looking oddly cozy. He wanted a statement from Beau about our relationship."

A devilish grin spread across Christian's face. "Everyone seems to see it except you..."

"Just shut up and give me a taco."

He reached into the bag and offered me something covered in silver foil. "You're one of those who gets hangry, huh? I'll have to keep that in mind for when you stay over so I have breakfast ready." He winked, and I pointed to his eyes.

"Next time you see the team doc, you might want to get those checked. That one keeps shutting on its own."

Christian smiled and dug into his food. "So how was your chat with Julian?"

I opened my taco and motioned to two small plastic containers. "Are these both hot sauce?"

He gestured to a red dot on one of the lids. "That one is extra hot. I like spicy, but this place crushes up the seeds in the habaneros in that. It's like eating fire."

I took the other one. "Thanks for the warning. I love spicy, but lately I've been getting the worst heartburn."

"Stress." He nodded.

"Really? Stress gives you heartburn? I assumed it was because I've been eating more takeout than usual."

"It could be. But stress can cause it too. When my mom got sick a few years ago, I kept getting the worst burning in my chest. Team doc made me get a battery of tests to make sure it wasn't my heart. Turned out to be heartburn. I'd never had it before. Doc prescribed something, and it went away."

"I'm sorry about your mom. Is she okay?"

Christian nodded. "She was diagnosed with pancreatic cancer the day before the first game of the season. The survival rate is low, and it was tough to not always be with her during her treatments. But she's been cancer free for three years now with no recurrences. Anyway, your heartburn could be stress, too. What do you do for that?"

"To treat the heartburn?"

He shook his head. "No, to treat the stress."

"Umm...eat too much chocolate and drink wine?"

His left dimple deepened. "You're going to need something better than that, being in the NFL."

"What do you do for stress?"

A dirty smile spread across his face. "I could show you, if you'd like."

My belly fluttered a bit. *God, I bet he's really good at destressing.*

"In all seriousness," Christian said, "you should find something that helps you clear your mind. Do you exercise?"

"Does walking up the stairs to my apartment count?"

"Afraid not. If you don't like exercise, maybe give meditation a try. My brother swears by it. He's even into oils and stuff. I tried it, but it wasn't for me. I need something more physical. So I usually work out until my muscles ache, and then I go to my happy place."

"Your happy place?"

"Grass. Barefoot in the grass, specifically. It makes me feel content. Started when Coach coached my pee-wee football team. We'd practice hard all week and usually had games on Saturday mornings. But the last practice on Friday afternoons ended a half hour early, and Coach would have the ice cream truck come. We could all get whatever we wanted, and then we'd take off our cleats and run around the field barefoot, trying to tackle each other and stealing the ice cream from anyone we could get to the ground. I always got a Chipwich, vanilla ice cream between two chocolate chip cookies. It was my favorite time of every week, and ever since then, when I'm stressed, I have an ice cream and stand barefoot in the grass."

"It's not easy to find a patch of grass you'd want to stick your feet in anywhere in Manhattan."

He grinned. "I know. That's why I planted a ten-foot-by-ten-foot patch of it on my balcony. The guys make fun of me, saying it's like my child because I'm always watering it and telling people not to be too rough on it."

I laughed. "I'll have to try that sometime. Though I think the closest thing I have to grass in my neighborhood is some fuzz on the fruit that's been hanging around too long at Mr. Zhang's."

"Your toes are welcome in my grass any time."

We were both smiling when my office door suddenly whooshed open. Tiffany did *not* look happy. "What's going on here?" she barked.

I took a deep breath. "Hello, Tiffany. It's nice to see you. As you can see, Christian and I are in the middle of eating, but what can I help you with?"

"Why are you eating together?"

"Christian is helping me with a project."

Her hands gripped her hips. "What project?"

I put down my taco and cleared my throat. "Did you need something, Tiffany?"

She looked between Christian and me. No, actually, she glared at us. "Have you seen the board of directors meeting minutes binder from 2020?"

I shook my head. "I don't think so."

Tiffany waved her hand at the wall full of binders. "It's probably one of those."

"Actually, it's not. I've gone through those, and I didn't come across one with board-meeting minutes."

"You went through *all* those binders?"

I nodded. "Last week."

"I doubt it. But whatever. Can you just look for it? The players' union wants a copy of a policy we adopted at a meeting, and I'm missing 2019 and 2020. My father always kept them in here."

"I'll double-check. But I don't think I have them."

Her lips pursed as she turned her attention to Christian. "I didn't think you were the kind of man who preferred chuck to filet mignon."

"Don't let the door hit you in the ass on your way out, Tiff," Christian said.

She smirked. "The ass you've seen."

The door slammed shut, and I struggled to digest the last ten seconds. "You've seen Tiffany's ass? You two—"

Christian shook his head. "Definitely not. Remember when I told you she sort of solicited me?"

"Yeah?"

"I wanted to spare you the visual, but a few months ago she called me into her office and locked the door, then started to strip out of her clothes."

"Are you joking?"

Christian shrugged. "Nope. By the time I got her to stop, she was bent over her desk, aiming her ass at me, wearing nothing but a thong."

I rubbed my temples. "And I guess her chopped-meat comment means she thinks we're...a couple of some sort. My God, does the entire world think we're together?"

Christian smirked. "Maybe the entire world knows something you don't, and you should reconsider..."

I couldn't help but laugh. "God, that woman hated me already."

"I hate to break it to you, but you were never going to be doing each other's hair and having sleepovers where you stay up late talkin' about boys."

I sighed. "I was never one of those anyway. I spent my Friday nights in high school trying to disprove Noether's theorem."

"Another theorem?"

"Noether's theorem, as in Emmy Noether. The German mathematician who proved differentiable symmetry."

Christian's brows drew inward. "Why would you want to do that?"

"Because I'm a geek, Christian, or haven't you noticed?"

His gaze dropped to my lips, and he took his time making his way back up to meet my eyes. "Hadn't noticed."

Oh my. Another flutter moved through my belly, this one lower than the last.

I had no retort. In fact, I was pretty sure all of my words were stuck somewhere behind the swarm of butterflies blocking passage from my belly. Sitting up straight, I cleared my throat. "Why don't we get started talking about the team?"

———

"I can't believe it's almost eleven o'clock." I leaned back in my chair and stretched my arms over my head. Christian and I had been working on tweaks to my algorithm, based on human factors related to the players, for close to five hours.

"I think I'm going to have to put in for overtime with the boss."

I smiled. "It would be well worth it. You're a wealth of knowledge, Christian Knox. I'm excited to make the changes and see how my performance predictions come out for this week's game."

"There are still a lot of variables. You have the stats of the opposing team, but you don't know what's going on with their people."

"True. Think you could buddy up to the Colorado captain and get their team's dirt?"

Christian laughed. "I'm sure he'd be open to sharing who's having an off week with me."

I closed my notebook. "I really appreciate you taking the time to help me."

"My pleasure. By the way, how was your call with Bozo today? Did he ask you out on another date?"

"If you mean Julian, I didn't call him back yet. The day flew by with back-to-back meetings."

Christian flashed a gloating smile. "Uh-huh."

I squinted. "Don't read into it. I was very busy."

"Not reading into it. Just looking at the facts."

"What facts?"

He shrugged. "No time to call Bozo. Spent the last five hours with me."

"This is work-related."

His smile grew more smug, if that were even possible. "Sure."

I had a page of notes on the table. I wrinkled them into a ball and chucked it at his face.

Of course, he caught it. "Maybe I'll keep these, so I have to come back again."

I tapped my finger to my temple. "Not necessary. They're all up here already."

Christian chuckled. "I have an MRI early tomorrow before the team meeting, so I'm going to head home. I want to put my leg up to bring down any swelling—I need my knee to be perfect so they'll finally clear me to play. You want a ride?"

"I think I'm going to stick around for a while and go through the binders—see if I might've missed the one Tiffany is looking for. If I find it, it might work as a peace offering."

Christian shook his head. "Don't count on it. She's a grudge holder."

He was right, of course, but I still wanted to do my best to be helpful. Whether it was appreciated or not. "It's okay. I'll still look."

"I can wait or even help you try to find it?"

"Thanks, but I'm good."

Christian looked disappointed, but he nodded. "How will you get home?"

"It's late, so I think I'll take one of those fancy car services you told me was the preferred mode of transportation for billionairesses."

He smiled. "Good. I'll see you on the plane tomorrow evening?"

I nodded. "You will. And thanks again, Christian."

I walked over to my desk and opened the top drawer to stick my laptop in. I'd made a habit of keeping it there. But when I closed it, the stuck drawer underneath caught my attention.

"Hey, Christian?"

"Yeah?"

"Would you mind seeing if you can pull open the bottom drawer of my desk? I've tried a few times, and it's stuck."

"You sure it doesn't have a key?"

I shook my head. "I don't think so. There's no lock."

Christian came behind the desk and gave the drawer a yank. It didn't budge. He knelt down and felt the bottom and around the sides, then peered into the gap at the top. "I don't see a lock. You sure you want me to get it open? The door might come off."

"Either way, I'll have to get it fixed. But if you're able to open it, I'd like to see whether the binder Tiffany is looking for might be in there."

He shrugged. "Alright. But step away in case it snaps off."

"Okay." I walked around to the other side of the desk and watched Christian give it a firmer tug. When it didn't open, he lifted one foot onto the frame of the desk and leveraged his weight with a third pull that was so strong, I was surprised the desk didn't fly into the air.

But it worked. The drawer opened, though the pull was now in Christian's hand and no longer attached to the desk. He looked down at it and frowned. "Sorry."

"It's fine. Thank you for opening it." I walked back around the desk. "Is anything inside?"

"Yeah, it looks pretty full."

The drawer was crammed to the very top. "Oh wow. Yeah, that is pretty packed."

Christian leaned down and lifted the top item from the pile. It was a black, leather-bound daily planner with an orange rubber band wrapped around it. The bottom center had three faded, gold-foiled initials: JWB. My father's. Underneath, it looked like the year was printed, but all I could make out was the two and the zero, not the last two numbers.

I leaned over and lifted the next book from the pile. It was exactly the same as the first, though I could read the year on this one. Looking through the drawer, there had to be at least twenty of them. "They're all the exact same planner. One for each year, I guess. It looks like the date and initials got rubbed off of most of them."

"My CPA tells me to keep my planner for tax purposes. I'm supposed to write down travel and business meetings and stuff—in case we ever get audited for things we deduct, like mileage and entertainment. But I'm not that good at it. Mostly I have a bunch of empty planners in a file," Christian said.

I fanned the pages of a few of the books from the pile. They were definitely not empty. "These are well used.

There are notes at all the time slots, with appointments and meetings and stuff, I guess."

"Did you get a lot of John's personal belongings?"

I shook my head. "Nothing. I wouldn't know his handwriting if I saw it. The office had been cleaned out before I arrived. So I should probably give these to Tiffany and Rebecca."

He held the book in his hands out to me. "You sure you don't want a ride home?"

"I'm sure. But thanks."

Christian nodded. "'Night, boss lady."

"Goodnight, Christian."

He stopped as he got to the door and turned back. "You've been trying to figure out who your father was... Maybe those planners can help fill in some of the missing pieces. Tiffany and Rebecca already know the man."

"Maybe." I looked down at the planner in my hands and shrugged. *Or maybe some things are better left unknown.*

Chapter 8

Bella

"WHAT IS THIS?" Miller picked up the daily planner and plopped down on my bed.

I held a green dress on a hanger against my body. "Is this too sexy to wear to the game this weekend?"

"You own the team. Dress however the hell you like. But when did you get that? I've never seen you wear it."

I tossed the dress on the bed and dug into my closet again. "I bought it for my date with Julian. But I changed at the last minute because it didn't feel like me."

"Who did it feel like?"

"I don't know. Professor Marks, maybe?"

Miller's head bent back in laughter. "That woman was definitely trolling for college boys with her get-ups. Her outfits all looked like they were painted on. There was a reason her classes were seventy-percent guys."

"Oh?" I teased. "Were her well-known outfits the reason you took the class?"

Miller laid back on my bed with the daily planner still in his hands. "Definitely not. Did you not just hear me say the class was seventy-percent boys?"

I chuckled and turned with another outfit pressed against me. This time it was a pair of black pants and a colorful blouse. "Is this better?"

He scrunched up his nose. "That shirt is hideous. Put the dress on. Let me see who wore it better, you or Marks."

"Okay."

"You still didn't tell me what the deal is with this planner." He opened to the first page. "This isn't your handwriting."

I pulled off my sweatshirt and slipped on the green dress. "Oh, no. That's my father's. I found a bunch of them in a drawer in my desk. Or his desk, I mean."

"No shit. What does it say?"

"I don't know. I'm sort of afraid to read it."

"Why?"

I smoothed the dress over my body and held out my arms. "What do you think?"

Miller leaned up on his elbows. "Wow. You look hot. Definitely wear that."

I looked down. "I'm not sure *hot* is the message I want to send. I want to look professional."

"You do. You're not even showing any cleavage, Bella. I'm just not used to seeing your curves."

I walked over to the full-length mirror behind the closet door. The dress did look good on me, but I still thought it might be too much for a game. "Maybe I'll bring this and the other outfit and figure it out when I get there."

Miller frowned. "Translation: you're going to go with the black pants and frumpy shirt. Now tell me why you're afraid to read about your old man's appointments?"

I sighed. "I don't know. What if he's funny and nice?"

"You'd prefer him to be humorless and a dick?"

"Sadly, I might. Everyone I've come in contact with has nothing but great things to say about him. Do I really want to find out they've all been right and it's only *me* he didn't want or care about?"

"How could his not wanting or caring be about *you* when he didn't even get to know you? Any decision he made about having you in his life was about *him*. Not you, sunshine."

"I guess... I don't know. I'll think about it some more. Christian thought I should read it too." I walked back over to my suitcase and took off the green dress to pack it. Then I tossed in the other outfit.

"*Christian* as in Christian, my face is worthy to be chiseled in stone, Knox?"

I nodded. "He's been helping me learn about the team."

Miller sat up and studied my face.

"What?" I asked.

"Bella, do you want to *bone* the hot quarterback?"

"What? No."

Miller pointed to my face. "Liar! Your voice went about eight octaves higher when you answered. That's always been your tell."

"What are you talking about?"

"You squeak when you lie, Bella."

"I do not."

Miller pointed again. "There it is. Did you just hear that? Your voice went up even then. You also turn pink sometimes, too."

"You're crazy."

Miller rubbed his hands together, like a kid waiting for someone to hand him a giant ice cream cone over the counter. "You guys are going to make a super kid, with your brains, his athleticism, the education you two rich bitches can afford to spring for—not to mention you're both pretty as hell."

I bent to grab a pair of shoes from my closet and pointed one at him before packing them into my suitcase. "You're doing it again."

"Doing what?"

"Making up a crazy story in your head that you'll get invested in and will only lead to disappointment."

"We've had this conversation. I told you I don't do that."

"Umm...an hour ago when we went to the diner for breakfast, what did you tell me about the waiter?"

"That his Greek parents own a yacht in Greece and spend their summers sailing around from Mykonos to Santorini to Crete."

"And why did you say that?"

"Because he was clearly Greek and comes from that type of background."

"You were about five seconds from dumping Trent and buying sunscreen to pack for your Mediterranean jaunt."

"And I should be! How else are we going to have two children and a summer home in Amagansett—*not* the Hamptons—if I don't join them on their boat for the summer so he can fall in love with me? By the way, even though I want to be the stay-at-home dad, we're going to use his sperm to make our babies. He's got great bone structure."

I shook my head. "I wasn't going to tell you, because you seemed so happy in your dreamland, but your Greek waiter's name is Jose, and he's dating a woman."

"You're lying."

"I'm not. But my point is, you see things you want to see and wind up disappointed."

"So I daydream a little. Shoot me. I'm a romantic. But you're also deflecting from the truth. You like the quarter-back."

"Not in the way you're fantasizing about. Besides, a relationship with Christian wouldn't be appropriate."

"Why not?"

"He works for the Bruins, a team I now own. His contract is up for renewal this year. Imagine we started dating and the coaches decided to not renew him?"

Miller waved me off. "Excuses. I don't know shit about football, but even I know he's the star of the league, and your coaches will do anything to keep him. Besides, plenty of good relationships start with boning the secretary. It happens..."

I finished packing and zipped my suitcase. "You should leave fantasyland and come to realityworld. You know, the place where I have a second date with Julian."

Miller's eyebrows jumped. "He finally called? I wasn't asking because I figured you'd tell me if it happened, and I didn't want to bring you down. It took him long enough."

"He called the other day, and I called him back this morning. I think he's going slow because he's hesitant to get involved unless he can see a future with me, since we're good friends."

"Did he tell you that?"

"No, but it makes sense."

Miller grinned. "Or you're making up the story you want. Sound familiar?"

I picked up a thong that must've fallen out of my suitcase and tossed it at Miller. It landed on his face. He palmed it to his nose and inhaled deeply. "Do women really smell like fish? Or is that a straight-guy excuse for being too lazy to go down on his woman?"

My face wrinkled, and I ripped my panties from his grip. "Eww...you're gross. My panties do not smell. And neither does my vagina."

Miller laughed. "Okay, but you *are* making up an excuse for a guy who took too long to call after the first date."

"It's a logical one, though."

"So is that he was too busy to call because he's dating four other women."

I frowned. "Don't pee on my parade."

"Tell that to Jose and his girlfriend..."

I smiled. "Anyway, I'm going out with him again next Thursday."

"Maybe he'll go wild and hug you at the end of this date."

I shook my head. "I should never have told you he shook my hand at the end of date one."

"I would bet my entire life savings that the quarterback would do more than shake your hand at the end of a first date."

That bet I would definitely *not* take. I was certain Christian Knox was not shy when it came to women. I was also certain our chemistry would be off the charts. But I wasn't about to admit that and open the door for more talks about something that wasn't going to happen. I shot Miller a look. "So the bet would be for what? A dollar eighty-two, then?"

"Not all of us own a football team, sunshine. Which reminds me, you can fill my tank on the way to the airport."

"Then we better get going. I don't want to be late and miss the team plane."

Miller stood and took the handle to my luggage. "Pretty sure they'd wait for you, princess."

—

"You've got a little drool..." Christian pointed to my cheek. "Right here."

I reached up to my face as I blinked sleep from my eyes and looked around, confused. I'd been sitting next to the team's director of analytics when we took off.

Christian thumbed toward the back of the plane. "Jeff's son is a big fan. I told him I'd stop by where he sat in the stands next home game if he switched seats with me."

"Why did you do that?"

"I wanted to see if you snored. I'm a light sleeper, and that will make things more difficult when you start sleeping over at my place."

"You're not practicing, yet you've somehow hit your head. I won't be sleeping at your place."

His grin widened to a full-fledged smile, drawing my eyes to his dimples. "We'll see."

I forced my eyes from his face. That's when I noticed Christian was wearing a suit, a full, three-piece one, vest, tie, and all.

"You're all dressed up?"

"Gotta look professional when we go on the road."

The navy of his suit brought out the color of his eyes, and his jacket accentuated the broadness of his shoulders. He actually overflowed from his seat, impinging into mine a bit. "Does your suit have shoulder pads?"

He smiled. "No, ma'am. That's all me."

God, he really is sexy as hell.

Christian leaned toward me. "In case you're wondering, I'm evenly proportioned. Big *everywhere*."

I felt my face redden. "Thanks for sharing..."

He shrugged. "Of course. Full disclosure is important in a relationship."

"We don't have that type of relationship."

"Not yet. But we're working toward it."

I laughed. "Is this how you get all your dates? You repeatedly tell them they're going to go out with you?"

"Nah. Just you. Normally, they ask me out."

"That sounds much easier. Maybe you should redirect your focus to one of those women."

"Easy is no fun..."

"Oh." I nodded. "Is that what this is about? You're one of *those*, huh? The kind who likes the chase."

"I'm not going to lie and say I don't enjoy a good chase once in a while. But that's not the reason I'm interested in you. Think I already laid out those reasons. You're beautiful, thoughtful, independent, smart—a hell of a lot smarter than me—down to earth. I could go on. But there's one more reason I can't seem to leave you alone."

I shifted in my seat to face him. "I'm almost afraid to ask..."

Christian looked over his shoulder before moving close. "I'll never live this down if one of the guys finds out I said it, so I'll deny it if it gets around. But I get butterflies in my stomach when I'm with you. First time it happened, I thought I was hungry or something. But I wasn't. It was just you."

Oh.

My.

God.

I thought butterflies were strictly for women—like a menstrual cycle or the ability to put the cap back on the toothpaste. Christian stared at me, waiting for a reaction, which I tried to curtail on my face but clearly couldn't. He tapped the underside of my jaw.

"You should shut this." His eyes sparked hot. "It's making me imagine things you don't want me to tell you about—not yet, at least."

I was still trying to formulate a coherent thought when Jeff walked over. I'd never been so grateful for an interruption.

"Sorry. I think I left my medicine in the seat back." Jeff pointed to the pocket in front of where Christian was now sitting. "I don't mind takeoff and flying, but I need a little something before we land."

Christian reached forward and pulled out a prescription bottle. He held it up to Jeff. "Happy landing."

Jeff chuckled. "Thanks, man."

The exchange was probably only thirty seconds, but I no longer felt like a bug stuck in a web with the spider approaching. "Why don't you have a girlfriend, Christian?"

He smiled. "That's a very good question. I'm trying as hard as I can, but she's not budging."

I laughed. "I don't mean me. I mean a girlfriend in general. You must have a plethora of choices. When was the last time you had one?"

"A girlfriend or...a woman to spend time with?"

"An exclusive relationship, I mean."

"A couple of years ago."

"What happened with that?"

He looked away. "Kerrie drank too much."

I don't know what I'd expected him to say, but it wasn't that. "Oh...I'm sorry."

He shrugged. "It's fine. I'm not against people drinking alcohol just because I choose not to most of the time. But she became a different person after drinking a bottle and a half of wine herself. I picked up a woman I liked and took one home I didn't. She was a lawyer, and after a couple of drinks she would start to interrogate me about what I'd been doing when I was on the road with the team. I never gave her reason to suspect anything, and when she was sober, she didn't seem to have doubts. I tried to talk to her about it, but she wasn't receptive to the conversation at all."

"I didn't realize you didn't drink alcohol. Is it because of your training?"

Christian looked up at me. "My dad's an alcoholic. When I was growing up, he lost most of his jobs because of it. In college, I started partying a little too hard, and my coach dropped me to second string for two games. I realized I was heading down the same path as my dad if I didn't clean up my act. So I stopped drinking. It's not a sobriety commitment or anything. I have a couple of drinks every once in a while. But it's definitely not a regular thing for me."

I nodded. "Well, I'm sorry to hear about your dad. But it sounds like you learned from his mistakes. Are the two of you close? Your dad and you, I mean."

Christian shook his head. "Not really. When I signed my first contract, I paid off my parents' house. It had been in and out of foreclosure a half dozen times over the years when he'd lose jobs. I didn't want my mom to have to worry about it anymore. But my dad got pissed. He saw it as me telling him he couldn't provide for his family. I had to apologize in order to keep the peace for my mom. She and I talk every week, but my dad rarely gets on the phone anymore."

I nodded.

"Anyway," Christian said, "to answer your question, I have had relationships. The one with Kerrie was about a year, and I was with Jessica for almost two years—she and I met during my last year in college. So I'm not afraid of commitment. But it isn't easy when you spend a good part of the year on the road. Not to mention the media likes to make a big deal out of me even talking to a woman. My first year in the NFL, I met a pop singer during a playoff game I went to, as a spectator. The entire interaction lasted five minutes, but there were pictures splashed across magazines and websites for months. The woman I'd been dating had been confident and trusted me, but after that, she grew accusatory if I even went out with the guys after winning a game."

"That must be hard."

He shrugged. "What about you? How many serious relationships?"

"None, actually."

His brows pinched. "But you've dated and..."

"Yes, I've dated and had sex, if that's what you're getting at. I just haven't had any long-term adult relationships that I would dub serious."

"Why not?"

"Talia likes to psychoanalyze me and say it's because I have trust issues. But I think it's more because I haven't met the right person yet."

He grinned. "I think you're right. You were just waiting for me."

I chuckled. "You really are a master at rounding conversations back to you."

"I bet *Julian* doesn't put in the same effort. Bozo didn't even ask for a second date." My face must've given me away, because Christian groaned. "You're going out with him again, aren't you?"

I smiled. "Yeah. He said he'd been busy working on a project."

He frowned. "When's the big day?"

"We're going out next Thursday night."

Christian took a deep breath and blew it out audibly. "Alright. I don't like it, but I guess you're going to have to get past that guy before you find your way to the right one. Just don't tell me about the date." He held up a hand. "Even when I ask."

A little while later, we landed in Colorado. Christian went on one bus with the team, while I went in an SUV with my half-sisters and some other people from corporate. When we arrived at the hotel, people were lined up surrounding the entrance, including at least a dozen young women wearing Christian's jersey number. I felt a pang of jealousy, and I wasn't even his girlfriend. So it was pretty easy to understand why his lifestyle was tough on relationships. I pushed thoughts about Christian Knox aside and walked to the reception desk.

"Hi. Bella Keating checking in."

The woman's nails clacked against her keyboard. "Oh, yes, Ms. Keating. We have your reservation right here, three nights in the Presidential Suite."

"The Presidential Suite? I'm assuming that's a fancy room."

She smiled. "It's our best room. Fourteen-hundred square feet with a view of the city and a beautiful grand piano."

A grand piano? What the heck did I need that for? "Umm...are there any other rooms available?"

"Most of the hotel is sold out because of the team staying, but I can check. What type of room would you prefer?"

"One with a bed, and maybe a TV."

The woman looked like she wasn't sure if I was kidding or not. "You mean a regular room?"

I nodded. "That would be perfect."

"Sure. Would you excuse me a moment?" The clerk disappeared and came back with a guy in a suit. His name tag said *Derrick Knowles, Manager.*

Great. They brought out the big guns.

"Hi, Ms. Keating. My associate tells me you'd like to switch rooms."

"Yes, that's right. I'm sure the Presidential Suite is beautiful, but I don't need all that space."

"I'm happy to lower the price, since this is your first time at our hotel. Maybe that would allow you to experience what we have to offer?"

I shook my head. "I appreciate that, but it's really not about price. I just hate to be wasteful."

The manager smiled, but still didn't look convinced. "Of course. Whatever you wish."

Eventually, I checked into room 709. It was a standard room, but had a beautiful view of the city. Denver was two hours behind New York, so by the time I settled in and got changed and washed my face, it was almost eleven thirty at home, though the time on the clock read only nine thirty. I'd just flicked off the light and was looking forward to getting into bed when I heard a faint knock. I thought someone had knocked on a nearby door, not mine, until it happened a second time. At the door, I pushed up on my tippy toes to look through the peephole. None other than Christian Knox stood on the other side.

I opened the door and held onto it. "Are you lost?"

He shoved his hands into his pockets and rocked back on his heels. "Nope. Just wanted to say goodnight, neighbor."

"Neighbor?"

He motioned toward the door to the left and grinned. "I'm right next door, room seven eleven."

I squinted. "You *happen* to be next door?"

"I'd like to say it was the world colluding for us to be near each other. But I bribed a bellman with two tickets to the game to get your room number, then switched my room with a lineman."

I chuckled. "At least you're honest."

"Just wanted to let you know I was nearby in case you need anything."

I shook my head, but was physically incapable of wiping the smile from my face. "I think I'll be fine. But thank you for the offer."

"No problem. Sweet dreams, boss lady." He winked. "I know I'll be having them."

Two hours later, I was frustratingly wide awake. I liked my sleep, and on the rare occasions when it failed to come to me, I got angry. Turning over as if I was giving my back to a man who'd pissed me off, I ripped the covers down. A minute later, I flipped over onto my back for the tenth time, blew out an annoyed breath, and turned my head to see the time on the combination iPhone charger and clock: 11:58. *Ugh.* And that was Denver time. Back home, it was two in the morning, yet I was wide awake like it was AM and not PM.

I wanted to pretend it was a random case of insomnia—maybe the nap on the plane had messed with my sleep schedule—but the only time I had trouble conking out was when I was frustrated by a problem I couldn't solve. Normally that meant there was a bug in my code, or an algorithm had produced wonky results. But today the frustration was my inability to stop thinking about the man on the other side of the wall. It was as if my body was hyper-aware of how close he was.

When I couldn't sleep like this, I had two choices. One, take matters into my own hands for a quick dopamine surge. Or two, read. Reading late at night always knocked me out since my eye muscles were usually tired from staring at a computer all day. The constant movement back and forth was better than counting sheep. And that was exactly what I was going to do tonight, since I refused to get myself off to thoughts of my team's quarterback. So I climbed out of bed for the book I'd tucked into my bag before I left home. Though I'd forgotten the book I brought was one of my father's planners. I debated putting it back, but since I really needed some sleep, I climbed into bed with it and took a deep breath before opening to a random page—May 14th—and beginning to read the handwritten notes jotted next to the time:

6:45 –E train to Battery Park City. Enters Stuyvesant High School.

What the hell? That's the train I took and where I went to high school... I froze. *Was he writing about me?* It couldn't be. That made no sense and had to be a big coincidence.

So I went back to reading, hoping I'd realize he was referring to some other person who happened to go to my high school. Or maybe my tired eyes were playing tricks on me. I started fresh from the top of the page once again.

6:45 – E train to Battery Park City. Enters Stuyvesant High School.

3:15 – E train back to 42nd Street. PS 212. Picks up a boy, approximately five years old.

The hair on my arms stood up. *Holy shit. It's no coincidence. This is about me.* My father had *followed* me? It felt like the breath had been knocked out of my lungs. PS 212 was where Wyatt went to elementary school, and I often picked him up.

Written underneath that entry was a sentence underlined twice.

Does she have a child?

It dawned on me that if I was picking up Wyatt, this journal entry had been written *after* my mother died. That timing freaked me out even more than the fact that he'd followed me. I flipped back to the cover to check the year, but the gold numbers had been worn away, like so many of the others. So I went back to reading...

3:35 – Enters American Folk Art Museum with boy.

6:00 – Exits museum. Walks to Covenant House on 41st. Still with boy.

I actually remembered that particular day. Talia had gotten a new job, so I'd started picking Wyatt up from school every afternoon. Even though the shelter we lived at allowed kids, it wasn't the best place for them. So I tried to minimize the amount of time we spent there. The shelter had student passes that no one ever used to get into any New York City museum for free, and I thought it would be fun to hit them all. I'd made a list of all 145 museums in the city, and every day Wyatt and I went to a different one. That day, I'd thought he'd probably be bored at the Folk Art Museum, but it turned out they had an exhibit on talismans, and we stayed until the museum closed at six—the time written in my father's planner.

The planner had a few more entries for the day, the last of which was me coming back to the shelter at eleven PM after spending a few hours studying at the library. At the bottom of the page, there was an area for notes, with some blank lines. Two sentences were scribbled:

She's the spitting image of her mother. Doesn't smile much, except when she's with the boy.

What the fuck?

Chapter 9

Christian

THE NEXT MORNING, I spotted Bella sitting alone at a table in the hotel lobby next to the free coffee on my way back from the gym.

"I've been thinking..." I pulled out the chair across from her, spun it around, and sat backward. "What if you made one of those prediction models you like so much, and let it figure out who you should go out with? You know, feed it the facts about me and Bozo and see who it thinks you'd have a better time with. Put in the essentials." I curled one arm and flexed to show her my muscles, which of course were newly plumped from my workout. "Like bicep size, sprint time, ability to travel on your schedule..."

I'd expected a laugh, or at a minimum an eyeroll, but instead Bella just stared. Her eyes were pointed in my direction, but it seemed like she wasn't seeing me.

"Bella? You okay?"

She blinked a few times. "Yeah. Sorry. I didn't get much sleep last night."

I grinned. "Me sleeping so close got to you, huh?"

She shook her head. "I read one of my father's daily planners."

I sat back. "Shit. Did it upset you?"

"No, not upset, I guess. But it left me really confused. He followed me."

"What do you mean he followed you? When?"

"Not long after my mother died."

"You mean he had a private investigator find you?"

"No. He followed me himself—watched me going into and out of the shelter I stayed at for a while. He sort of logged what I did each day, and sometimes wrote a thought or two down. Oh, and I think he might have also built me a library."

"Come again?"

She sipped her coffee. "When I first lived at Covenant House, I went to the library most nights because there weren't any quiet places to study at the shelter. I usually stayed there until they closed and then sat on the steps and read for a while. The walk home wasn't fun because I'd often get harassed by addicts and homeless people who hung out around Times Square. On one of the days John followed me home, he wrote in the notes section of his daily calendar, *Need a closer library—unsafe*. A few days later, he had an appointment on his schedule to go see a building three doors down from the shelter—the building that was turned into the Covenant Annex Library. I think it opened about two months after I moved into the shelter. It was basically a few rooms of books and a big, quiet area with comfortable couches to study. I loved that place. There weren't many people who used it, so it was like having my own private building to do my homework and hang out. Last night I googled the library and found an article that said it was funded by an anonymous donation. I think it might have been John Barrett because he didn't like me walking home late at night."

"Are you kidding?"

She sighed. "Nope. For the last few years, I've been wondering when he found out about me. If he knew I existed when I was fifteen and cared enough to follow me around and build me a safe place to spend time, why didn't he tell me who he was when he was alive?"

That was a damn good question. The John Barrett I knew was a stand-up guy, not one who let a fifteen-year-old live in a shelter. I could *almost* understand if he'd had an affair and didn't want to acknowledge a child because it would hurt his marriage. But his wife, Celeste, had died a long time ago.

I shook my head. "I don't know, Bella. It doesn't make any sense."

"He basically stalked me. And that's just in this planner. I only brought the one. There are more. How long did he follow me?"

I rubbed the back of my neck. "I can't imagine John Barrett having the time to follow someone around for one day, let alone months."

"It's really creepy to realize I had no idea someone was watching me. I like to think I'm pretty alert when it comes to my surroundings. I've been sitting here for about an hour, and I keep glancing around to see if someone is watching me, even though obviously he's gone."

Bella's eyes were rimmed red with dark circles beneath them. "Did you sleep at all last night?" I asked.

She frowned and shook her head. "Reading usually makes me sleepy. But I couldn't stop my mind from racing after I read the planner. My body is exhausted, but my mind feels like it still wants to run sprints."

I eyed the now-empty coffee cup in her hand. "Caffeine and daylight are going to make it worse. Can you sleep today, or do you have meetings and stuff before the game tomorrow?"

"I have a few meetings, but I can reschedule or bow out."

I smiled. "Perks of being the boss."

"Two are with some of our big advertisers that are local here, but Tiffany and a few others will be at those. I'm sure she'd be thrilled if I skipped." She sighed. "What's your day like?"

"Team meeting at nine. Light practice after on the field, which I'll be on the sidelines for. Then team dinner this evening. Rumor has it you're coming to that."

She nodded. "I don't want to miss it. I'm not trying to fill John Barrett's shoes, but the one thing I've heard from everyone in the organization is that he was approachable, so I'd like to establish myself as the same, if that's possible."

"I could just have the team bus drive by where you live on the way home from the airport. That'll dispel any myths that you're an elitist."

Bella chuckled. "You're teasing and you haven't even seen the inside yet."

"We could remedy that. I'll pick up wine on my way over Monday night when we get back."

She smiled, and it finally felt real.

"Thank you," she said.

"For what?"

"For listening. You're really easy to talk to, even with things that aren't easy to talk about."

"Glad to be of service." It was on the tip of my tongue to offer *other services*, but I managed to refrain since I'd already gotten in a little flirting during a time she was feeling pretty somber. "Well, I need to hit the shower before we head over to the stadium for the team meeting. You going back up or staying down here for a while?"

"I think I'm going to take a walk outside and get some fresh air, try to clear my head before going upstairs."

"Good idea."

I stood and tucked my chair under the table. "I'll see you tonight. I hope you get some sleep."

"Have a good day, Christian."

⸺

"Holy shit. I'd think I was looking in a mirror, but damn, I'm better looking," I called as I walked off the field after watching the light practice. My twin brother was leaning against the side of the tunnel that led to the locker rooms.

He gave me a bear hug and lifted me off my feet. "You fucking wish you were as handsome as me."

My teammates all stopped to slap hands with Jake as they passed. "What are you doing here?" I asked.

"It's my bye week. We had an early practice this morning and then I hopped on a puddle jumper to come visit you. Thought maybe you'd have some free time this afternoon. My favorite jewelry store is in Denver, and I need to go shopping."

"Don't you have enough of that shit?"

"Not for me, bro. Buying Lara a special ring."

My eyes bulged. "Special as in an engagement ring?"

He nodded. "It's time. She's put up with my moody ass for two years now. Plus, I want to start popping out some kids. We're not getting any younger, you know. Her thirtieth birthday is coming up soon. I'm throwing her a big surprise bash. Figured I'd pop the question there."

I shook my head and wrapped my arms around Jake for another hug. "Jesus Christ. My big brother is getting married."

He was all smiles. "You know, just because I'm older doesn't mean you have to take forever to follow in my footsteps. I only got three minutes on you, not eight years. When are you going to get yourself a nice girl?"

"I'm working on it."

"Oh yeah? Who's the unlucky lady?"

I put my arm around his shoulder. "Come on, I'll tell you about her on the way to the jewelry store."

———

"You're kidding me? The new owner? Why don't you shoot for Miss America while you're at it?" Jake and I were in an Uber on the way downtown to look at rings.

"Nah." I shook my head. "I went out with Miss Universe. She was too into being pretty for me."

"What's wrong with being pretty? I'm pretty."

"I'm only going to agree with you because you look like me. But I didn't say there was anything wrong with being pretty. I just don't like it when a woman thinks it's the most important thing she can offer."

"I've seen pictures of the new owner on the news. Doesn't look like she falls short in the pretty department."

I shook my head. "No, she definitely doesn't. Bella is gorgeous. But the best part is that she has no damn clue how beautiful she is."

"That's not easy to find anymore. Most girls know it because they post one picture on social media and get thousands of comments telling them so. I hate Lara's Instagram. She's got a half-million followers. I can't even look if she posts a bathing-suit shot because I want to kick the asses of fifty-thousand lonely guys who comment. But she makes good money off of it, and she likes it. It makes her happy, so I don't complain."

I smirked. "Plus, if you told her not to post, she'd tell you to go fuck yourself. So there's that, too."

My brother chuckled. "True. So why doesn't this woman know she's beautiful?"

"Maybe saying she doesn't know isn't exactly the right way to put it. It's more like it's not her focus."

"What is?"

"Right now, doing the right thing by the team. But she's intelligent, so her energy has always gone toward her career and helping friends and family."

"If she's intelligent, what the hell would she be doing with your dumb ass?" my brother teased.

"You do know identical twins usually have about the same IQ, right? So you're insulting yourself."

He shrugged. "Did you ask her out yet?"

"I pretty much ask her out every time I see her. She won't go out with me...yet."

My brother threw his head back in laughter. "Holy shit. She's immune to your charm. I like her already."

"Shut up."

The car pulled up to an office building, and my brother went for the door handle. "This is it."

I looked outside, up and down the street. "I don't see any stores."

"This place is a little different." He climbed out of the back of the car. "Come on."

The Diamond Vault was definitely different. We went into a nice office suite and were handed champagne before our private, one-on-one shopping appointment. Then we got a one-hour lesson on diamond buying before the rocks started to roll out on black velvet displays. I understood why they gave you liquor before shopping once I heard some of the prices. But Jake must've known what he was in for because he didn't flinch. Three hours after we walked in, he'd picked out a diamond and a setting.

"Damn." I shook my head as we walked out. "That's more than I paid for my lake house up in Maine."

He stopped at the curb and leaned over, putting his hands on his knees. "I think I might throw up."

I laughed. "And here I thought you were so calm in there."

"Had to treat it like it was a game to get through it, little bro. Never let the opposing team see you sweat."

I put a hand on his shoulder. "Lara's gonna love it. You did good."

He blew out a ragged breath. "Thanks. I need a drink."

"Where are you staying?"

"Same place as you."

"I'll buy your drink. Pretty sure you can't afford it after what you just dropped in there."

Chapter 10

Bella

"**THANK YOU AGAIN** for letting me join dinner, Coach Brown."

"Of course. Anytime. I might request you attend before some of the big games. It's been a while since these boys were on such good behavior."

"And here I thought they were always such gentlemen." I smiled. "Have a good night, Coach. Good luck tomorrow." I looked around the room for Christian, hoping to catch him before I went up to my room for the night. We'd been seated at different tables on opposite ends of the room and hadn't had a chance to speak. I wanted to say thank you for this morning, for listening. But Christian was nowhere to be found, so I headed out.

On my way to the elevator, I saw him standing at the bar and made a pit stop. "Hey. There you are."

He turned and smiled. I thought it was odd that he had what appeared to be a scotch in his hand after he'd told me how little alcohol he drank, but who was I to judge?

"Bella Keating." He knocked back some of the amber liquid in his glass. "I was hoping I'd see you."

"I just wanted to say thank you for this morning, for listening to me about John again."

"No problem. Do you mind if I tell you some things I'd like to get off my chest?"

Christian seemed a little *off*, and I wondered if he might be drunk, though he wasn't slurring his words or anything... I shrugged. "Of course. What's up?"

He took another healthy gulp of his drink and set the empty glass on the bar. "Ten years ago on Christmas, I kissed my cousin's boob."

I laughed. "What?"

"Yep. She'd had a baby a few months earlier and was cradling the baby in her arms. I bent down to kiss the baby's cheek, but didn't realize she was breastfeeding until the very last second. I turned my head when I figured it out and wound up planting one on my cousin's breast."

"Oh my God."

"Another time, my mother took me shopping for back-to-school shoes, but I didn't like anything, until I found a pair in a box sitting alone on the floor. I tried them on and loved them and begged my mom to let me wear them out of the store. I got as far as the cashier when someone came running after me. They'd been trying on shoes and put their old shoes in the box, which is what I had on my feet. It might sound like an innocent mistake, so I should add that the shoes were really dirty and the person who ran after me trying to get their shoes back *was a girl*."

I laughed. "That's hysterical." *He has to be drunk.*

"Also, growing up, we lived next door to an older couple, Dave and Marie. They'd lived there for at least ten years, and I'd always called Dave, Dave. My parents had a little party before I went away to college, and some of the neighbors were invited. At the end of the night, Dave walked up and shook my hand and wished me luck. Then he told me his name was Anthony, not Dave."

"So you'd called him the wrong name for all those years?"

Christian smiled. "Yep. And to this day, I don't believe his name is actually Anthony, even though my smarter, older brother dragged me over to the mailbox the next day and showed me a piece of mail addressed to Anthony to prove it."

A man's voice came from behind me. "Oh, this can't be good." I turned toward the sound only to find...Christian. My head snapped back toward the man I'd been speaking to. He grinned from ear to ear.

"Oh my, there are two of you?"

Second Christian walked around me and stood next to first Christian. He nodded. "This is my twin brother, Jake. And whatever he's told you so far is definitely not true."

Oh wow. "So you didn't kiss your cousin's boob?"

Christian hung his head and shook it back and forth. "You're such a dick, Jake. That happened like ten years ago. You're still telling that story? Don't you have any new material?"

Jake chuckled and extended his hand. "Jake Knox. Nice to meet you, Bella. Sorry. I couldn't resist the opportunity when it was handed right to me."

I laughed as I placed my hand in his. "Were all the stories true?"

"*All* the stories?" Christian said. "You mean there was more than one?"

"Pipe down." Jake slapped his brother on the shoulder. "I didn't even tell her about the love letter you wrote to Mrs. Swanson in sixth grade, the one she was never supposed to find. You know, where you told her what you think about every time you eat a watermelon."

"And she never would have found it if *you* didn't hand it to her, jackass."

Jake looked to me. "The school made him read a book on the right and wrong way to talk to girls. I think it was written in the sixties and was called *When Boy Woos Girl*."

I covered my mouth as I cracked up.

Christian put his hands on his hips and shook his head. "Are we done now?"

"God, I hope not," I said. "I'm really enjoying Jake's stories."

"Yeah, well...I have a few of my own if he doesn't shut the hell up." Christian narrowed his eyes at his brother, but it was clear he wasn't really mad.

I got the sense this type of screwing with each other was a regular occurrence. "You play for Oklahoma, so you have a bye this week, right, Jake?"

He looked impressed. "I do. Surprised my brother and dragged him shopping. It's top secret, but I bought my girlfriend a ring today. Planning on popping the question soon."

"Oh wow! Congratulations. That must've been a fun day."

He groaned. "Fun, but expensive as hell."

"Well, good luck with it." I looked between Christian and Jake. "I'll get out of your way and let you two catch up."

Christian spoke to his brother. "Just give me a minute. I'm going to walk Bella to the elevator."

Jake tipped an imaginary hat to me. "Pleasure meeting you, Bella. I hope I see you again soon."

"You, too, Jake. Have a good night." I turned away and then thought of something. "Are you staying for the game tomorrow?" I looked back to ask.

"I am."

"I'm not sure where you're sitting, but I have the visiting team's owner's suite, if you'd like to watch the game there."

Jake's eyes lit up. "Hell yeah. Thanks."

"Are you staying here at the hotel?"

"Yes, ma'am."

I nodded. "I'll make sure we get a pass for you and leave it with reception."

Jake grinned at his brother. "Think of all the stories I can tell her during a three-hour game."

"Oh, Jesus." Christian shook his head and put his hand on my back, guiding me to walk ahead. "I'll be back, jackass."

Christian and I walked side by side to the elevator. "You didn't have to do that," he said. "Invite him to the box, I mean."

"I'm happy to have him."

"No, I mean you *didn't have to do that*."

I chuckled. "Your brother is very funny. I had no idea it wasn't you while he was telling me all those stories. To be honest, I thought maybe you were a little drunk."

"That's my brother alright. He's the drunk version of me, even stone-cold sober."

"You two must be close if he flew out here to go shopping with you and watch the game on one of his only weekends off of the season."

"Sometimes too close, but yeah, we're tight."

"That's nice. I always wanted a sibling growing up."

"And lucky you, now you have two who never wanted you."

I held my stomach, pretending I just got punched in the gut. "Ouch. That hurts."

Christian smiled. "Did you get any sleep today?"

"I did actually. I walked for about an hour and then came back to the room and drew the blinds and slept for three hours."

"Good. Feel any better?"

"I do. Though I'm pretty sure I'll be looking over my shoulder for a long time. I still can't get over how someone followed me so many hours a day, for at least a few months, and I had no clue. This might sound weird, but I feel violated—almost like someone took something from me that didn't belong to them."

"Someone did. Your privacy."

"Yeah, I guess so. But at the same time, I'm also very curious to get back and see what's in the other planners now."

"I bet."

We arrived at the elevator bank. I pushed the up button and turned to face Christian. "I walked over to your brother when I saw him standing at the bar because I thought it was you and wanted to say thank you for this morning, for listening to me."

Christian shook his head. "No thanks necessary. That's what boyfriends are for."

I raised a brow. "Boyfriends?"

He patted his chest. "I'm a boy, and I think we're friends, so boy friend. It'll be easier if you think of me that way from the get-go, since that's where we're going to wind up."

"Well, I owe you one, boy friend. If you ever need to talk, I think you know where to find me."

The elevator doors slid open, and I stepped in. Christian put his hands on the return panels to keep them from shutting. "I lost my dog when I was ten. His name was Buddy. It still kind of hurts when I think about it. Maybe I should take you up on your offer and come talk about it. Say five minutes from now, in your room? You can slip into something comfortable, and I'll bring a bottle of wine."

I pushed the button on the panel with a smile and looked at my watch. "You have curfew in twenty minutes."

Christian stepped back. His eyes sparkled. "I won't tell if you don't."

"I'll take a raincheck."

The doors started to slide closed. Christian moved with them to stay visible as the gap narrowed. "A raincheck? That means another time? That's not a no..."

I laughed. "Goodnight, Christian."

Chapter 11

Bella

"**SHOULDN'T YOU BE** on the field with the team?"

It took all my self-control not to roll my eyes. Instead, I displayed my pearly whites. "This isn't Christian, Tiffany. It's his brother, Jake."

"Oh. Wide receiver for Oklahoma, right?"

Jake and I had been sitting on the couch in the guest team owner's suite, waiting for the game to start. He stood and leaned forward to extend his hand. "Jake Knox. Nice to meet you."

"Tiffany Barrett. A *legitimate* daughter of John Barrett." Rather than shake, she put her hand in his like she was a princess and he was supposed to kiss the top.

Jake glanced over at me, his forehead wrinkled. I wasn't sure if it was the way she introduced herself or the handshake, but regardless, I shrugged, and Jake proceeded to shake her wilted hand. Because misery loves company, Rebecca walked in next. She took one look at me, her mouth twisted in disgust, and she sauntered over to the hostess and started rattling off what she needed for the day. I wasn't sure what was worse, Tiffany's vocal disdain for me or the fact that my other sister didn't even think I was worth the energy to speak to.

The two of them set up camp on the other side of the room, and Jake sat back down. He looked over his shoulder at my siblings. "Tiffany seems like a real peach."

"They're not my biggest fans."

He shook his head. "And you have to share the visitor's box with them? Do you share the home one, too?"

I sipped the mimosa the sweet hostess had made for me when we arrived. "Actually, we don't share the suites. They belong to me, but I invited them."

Jake's brows lifted. "Glutton for punishment?"

I chuckled. "Perhaps. But I try to put myself in their place. Their father had a secret child and cut them out of the biggest part of his will. I mean, you can't blame them for hating that I exist."

"Maybe. But someone should remind them it's not your fault that you do. It's the people who made you."

I sighed. "Let's talk about something more fun. Do you have a plan for your proposal?"

"I'm throwing Lara a surprise thirtieth. I'm going to do it in front of all our friends and family."

"Oh wow. Go big or go home, huh?"

Jake smiled. "What about you? Ever been married?"

I shook my head. "Only to my work."

"One of those, huh? Were you always that way or only since you took over the team?"

"Always that way. Even in school, I wanted to do well. And I never had any pressure to get good grades. I just enjoy working hard and achieving things."

"Not me. I prefer a nap under a tree to a day of work."

I laughed. "Well, you must know how to work hard when you want to, otherwise you wouldn't be in the NFL."

"My brother is the reason I made it. He'd wake me up at five o'clock in the morning before school to have a catch. The only reason I got good at catching is because my brother got better at throwing. It's tiring chasing down his bullets."

"I feel like you're exaggerating a bit."

Jake leaned forward and scooped some peanuts from the bowl on the table. He tossed a few in his mouth. "Not really. We were born with the gift of height and speed. Twins start out with all the same DNA, but some of it mutates in the womb after the split. Pretty sure my motivation gene mutated, because while we may look identical, that boy runs circles around me when it comes to drive."

"I think you're selling yourself short."

"Nah. I owe where I am today to my family—both Christian and our older brother, Tyler. Those two kept me in line." He paused and pointed to my empty mimosa glass. "Let me get us both another drink."

"Okay. Thank you."

I'd invited all of the corporate staff to the suite, so a few of them arrived before Jake returned. It didn't seem like I had to make introductions since everyone seemed to know him already. He fell into easy conversations, which allowed me to spend some time with the director of analytics, going over the tweaks I'd made to my model and showing him the predictions it had made.

This week's projections turned out to be the best yet. When the game was over, I'd even nailed the score in three out of four quarters.

A few minutes later, Christian joined us upstairs.

"Thank you for babysitting," he said, with a nod to Jake.

"Your brother is great."

"Did he chew your ear off with more stories of dumb shit I did as a kid?"

"Actually no, not today. He was very complimentary of you."

"Damn. I better make sure he doesn't have a fever." He smiled. "I should get him to start saying his goodbyes. He's got a flight to catch, and I'm going to drop him off."

"Oh, okay."

A few minutes later, Jake came over. "Tough loss today. But thank you for having me."

"My pleasure."

He leaned in and kissed my cheek. "I guess I'll see you at Lara's thirtieth?"

My brows pulled together.

Jake smiled. "I can tell he's crazy about you because he couldn't shut the hell up last night after you left. That determination I told you about earlier? It doesn't only apply to football." He winked, just like his brother, and touched two fingers to his forehead in a salute. "See you soon, Bella."

⎯⎯

I was halfway through my fourth read-through of the planner since I'd opened it two nights ago, when I heard a knock at my door.

Christian was on the other side, once again looking too handsome for his own good. I unlatched the top lock and opened the door.

"Coach just called. MRI results are in. I can resume practice tomorrow morning."

"Oh, wow. That's great news, Christian."

He nodded. "Thought maybe you'd come help me celebrate."

I looked down. I'd already changed into shorts and a T-shirt and washed the makeup from my face. "I'm sort of prepped for bed."

"Is that the only reason you don't want to celebrate with me?"

"Of course."

Christian leaned down and reached for something on the ground off to the side of the door. He held up a champagne bottle and two glasses with a grin. "My room or yours then?"

I laughed. "You tricked me. Besides, you told me you don't drink."

Christian bent to the floor again. This time he held up a small bottle of apple juice. "It's the closest thing they had at the bar that looks like champagne."

"Shouldn't you be celebrating with your teammates?"

"Why would I do that when I have such a hot neighbor?"

I figured it was my obligation as team owner to celebrate good news when I was with the team—at least that's what I told myself as I stepped back so Christian could enter. "One drink."

He grinned. "Yes, ma'am."

As soon as he came inside, his eyes went to the planner. It was open to a page, face down in the middle of the bed. "I was...rereading. Trying to figure out if I missed anything important."

Christian peeled the foil from the champagne. "What's the verdict so far?"

"Still just a weird summary of events that occurred while he followed me, and a note here and there."

The loud pop of the champagne startled me, even though I'd watched him open it. I jumped. "Sorry, reading that thing puts me a little on edge for some reason."

He poured champagne into one flute, then twisted the top off the apple juice and poured it into the other. Passing the first flute to me, he held his up in a toast. "To getting back to work."

We clinked glasses. "To getting the star of the team back," I added. After we sipped, I motioned to the planner. "Would you want to see a few pages? I feel like I've told you how odd it is, but seeing it and hearing about it are two different things."

Christian shrugged. "If you don't mind."

I was kind of curious to get someone else's take. I'd never kept a planner, so maybe this type of thing wasn't that unusual. I picked up the book from the bed, flipped a few pages, and held it out to Christian. "Start here."

Christian took the book and sat down on the edge of the bed. I chewed a fingernail as he read one page and then the other, before flipping to the next.

After two more pages, he stopped and looked up at me. "Did you go to Stuyvesant High School?"

I nodded. "And I was on the math team. Did you see the note that says *Japan donation*? Every four years, the team went to Japan for the World High School Math Olympics. It was expensive, but the team would raise money each year to fund the trip. We used to sell candy. Before my mom died, I would give the order form to her, and people at her work would all place orders. But once she was gone, I didn't know anyone who could afford to waste money on overpriced candy, so I went door to door. But then the following year, we didn't have to go door to door anymore. Someone paid for the entire club to go on the trip. There was a rumor that the donation stipulated that the team couldn't go door to door anymore selling things."

"John made the contribution?"

I shook my head. "I have no idea, but he watched me go door to door. And then there's that note. I think he might have."

Christian thumbed through a few more pages without reading. "The whole thing is like this?"

"Every page."

"Well, now I get what you mean when you say it's creepy. I don't think I could've visualized how weird it is—just line after line of places you went, and you had no idea anyone was following you."

"I know. I really wish I could ask Tiffany and Rebecca about it. But I doubt they know what he did, since they had no idea I existed until the will reading. Maybe they could help me understand why he would do it. They had to know him better than most people—he was their father, and they worked together for so many years."

"Why don't you? Worst that can happen is they tell you to screw off. But it seems like they do their best to tell you that every time they see you anyway."

I shook my head. "They would probably demand that I turn over the planners. I was left the interest in the team and the stadium. My sisters were left everything else that was not specifically bequeathed. They spent three weeks in court arguing whether the furniture, fixtures, and equipment in the corporate offices were part of the team or part of 'everything else.' I'm sure if they knew about the planners, I'd be back in court."

"You're probably right."

"I'm sorry. I made this about me. We're supposed to be celebrating your return. I'm happy for you as your friend and as the owner of the team. Today's loss was not fun."

"Is that what we are? Friends, Bella?" Christian's gaze dropped to my lips, causing my stomach to do a little somersault. He took his time making his way up to meet my eyes again. "Because I'm friends with a lot of guys on the team, and I didn't go straight to any of their rooms to tell them the good news."

I suddenly wished I'd kept the big suite I'd originally been booked in. This room felt very small at the moment. *Where's a grand piano to stick between us when you need it?*

Christian stayed silent, watching me the way a pro poker player sizes up his opponent, trying to determine whether he should bet the pot. He rubbed his chin. "Can I ask you a personal question?"

"What?"

"On the plane you said you'd never had a serious relationship as an adult. Did you have one before you were an adult?"

The man was astute, I had to give him that. I motioned to the bottle of champagne. "Can I have more of that, please?"

"Of course."

Christian poured me a glass, our eyes meeting more than once while he did. After, he set the bottle down and waited for me to continue. But first I drank back half the flute.

"I went out with a guy for about six months when I was seventeen."

"Was he the same age?"

I shook my head. "He was twenty-five."

The muscle in Christian's jaw ticked. "Did he hurt you?"

"Oh gosh, no. Not physically anyway, if that's what you're thinking. I was hurt when he broke things off, but I was a kid who thought we were in love."

"Was he your first?"

I nodded. "Oddly, I've been giving a lot of thought to that relationship lately. Maybe it's one of the reasons I've preferred no-strings-attached in the years after."

"Thank you for sharing that with me."

"We're friends, right? Friends share."

His smile was halfhearted. "I should probably go. It's late, and the team leaves early tomorrow morning."

"Oh, sure. Of course. Thank you for stopping by and letting me know. I'm excited to see you back on the field."

Christian set his glass on the small table. "'Night, Bella."

I followed him to the door. He opened it a quarter of the way, but then stopped and shut it before turning back around. Since I'd followed, we were now toe to toe.

"I don't have too many women friends, except for wives and girlfriends of my buddies. But I'm pretty sure friends hug goodbye." He opened his arms and flashed a boyish grin. When I hesitated, Christian lifted his brows, as if to say, *What are you waiting for, friend?* It felt like a challenge—one I wasn't about to back down from. So I stepped forward and circled my arms around his tree trunk of a torso.

God, he's so...thick. I bet all of him is thick.

On that thought, Christian wrapped his arms around me. I'd been hugging him, but my front was barely touching his body. He corrected that. He pulled me against him so hard that I felt every single bump of his eight-pack press into my skin. I was certain when he let go I'd have inverse abs from the dents he left behind. And he smelled damn good, too. Not that it was easy to breathe with his boa-constrictor grip, but each time my nostrils squeaked in air, it was mixed with the most delicious smell—woodsy, with a hint of leather, and so damn masculine. One hand slid up my back, and his fingers dug into my hair. Goosebumps littered my arms, and even though I could barely breathe through his grip, I felt my body go slack after a few heartbeats. Not until that moment did I realize I hadn't relaxed in a very damn long time—which was ironic since it took not being able to breathe to breathe easily. I'm not sure how long we stayed like that, but definitely longer than the length of time friends would hug goodbye.

When he finally loosened his death grip, I already knew I'd be longing for the way it felt after he walked out the door. Christian pulled back, but didn't release his hold completely. He kept his arms locked around my waist and looked down at me, so I had to tilt my head up to meet his gaze.

"I'm not going to be around as much since I'll be practicing again. I keep a pretty strict routine with extra workouts and an early dinner and bedtime." He reached a hand up and pushed a lock of hair from my face. "But I'll be there if you need me. Just call."

I smiled warmly. "I will. Thank you."

He kissed my forehead. "Goodnight, my not-friend."

My smile went as crooked as my glasses. "Not friend?"

He winked. "You haven't figured out what we are yet, but one thing we both know is that we are definitely *not* friends."

Chapter 12

Bella

I DIDN'T SEE Christian all week, and by Thursday I'd started to feel antsy.

Well, that's not an entirely true statement. I *saw* him plenty. He just didn't see me. Mostly that was because I watched him from my office window. Thank God for one-way glass because I'd spent an inordinate amount of time standing here.

Practice had ended for the day, but Christian was still out on the field with one of his wide receivers, throwing the ball around. The receiver missed the catch and ran after the ball, which skidded twenty yards farther. While Christian waited, he turned and lifted his hand to his face, shielding his eyes and looking up at where I stood. I knew he couldn't see me, but I gasped and jumped away from the window.

My heart thundered in my chest as I stood against the wall, feeling like a peeping tom who'd just gotten caught. *I really need to get a hold of myself.*

I hadn't yet regained my composure when my office door suddenly swung open. Tiffany saw me pressed against the wall, and her face twisted. "What the hell are you doing?"

"I, uh…" I pointed to the other side of the room. "I saw a mouse."

She stepped back through the doorway. "Are you freaking kidding me? I've never seen a rodent here. You must've brought it from home."

Her ridiculousness snapped me back to reality, and I stepped away from the wall. Walking to my desk, I sighed. "Yes, Tiffany. My name is Mary, and he followed me to work one day, work one day."

Tiffany's face wrinkled. "Are you…drunk?"

Guess she didn't get the "Mary Had a Little Lamb" reference. I shook my head. "What can I do for you?"

"Other than deed over the title to the team that is rightfully mine and my *real* sister's? I need you to sign-off on my new lease."

"Lease?"

"Car lease."

"Oh. Why do you need me to sign off on it?"

"Because our annoying CEO doesn't allow any expenses over fifty thousand without a second approval. So I either need the GM's or yours. You know, for a CEO who's also *acting* president, he isn't acting very presidential."

I might not know my sister well, but I was certain she would only walk in here and ask me for something if I was a last resort. I tilted my head. "Did the GM not want to sign off on it for some reason?"

She pursed her lips. "He's a jerk."

I interpreted that to mean he wouldn't sign off. But I wanted to keep the peace, so I held out my hand. "Is that the invoice?"

She marched in and handed it to me with a glare.

Slipping on my glasses, my eyes nearly bulged out of my head when I saw the number at the bottom of the invoice. "Three-hundred-and-sixty-seven-thousand dollars? I thought you said you were leasing it, not buying it."

Tiffany lifted her fingernails for an inspection. "That is the lease price. It's a three-year lease, so they put the total of all the payments."

"You want to spend more than ten-thousand dollars a month on a car? You live in Manhattan and take a car service to work. How often will you even drive it?"

"Just sign the damn thing. No one asked for your opinion."

"Is this what you always spend on a car lease?"

"My last one might've been a little less."

"How much less?"

She shrugged. "I'm not an accountant. I don't get involved in the details. Are you going to sign it or what?"

I wasn't sure how to handle this. If I didn't let it through, she was going to make my life a living hell whenever she could. But if I allowed it, would I be opening the door for her to do whatever she wanted? I looked her in the eyes. "Can I take the weekend to think about it? Twenty-five percent of the team is owned by investors, and we have a duty to them to not pad expenses since we share the bottom line."

She put her hands on her hips. "You're being ridiculous."

"If I am, then I'm obviously not alone if both Tom and the GM wouldn't sign off on it."

Tiffany huffed and stormed out of my office, slamming the door like an exclamation mark at the end of her rant. I sat down, staring at the invoice, still in disbelief. The stated value of the car was one-point-two-million dollars. How much did insurance cost on that type of vehicle? More than my annual rent, I was sure.

I was still looking over the invoice when someone knocked on my door. At least I knew it wasn't Tiffany again because she would never give me the courtesy of not barging in.

"Come in!" I yelled.

Christian opened the door. He wore a backward baseball hat, gray sweatpants, and a T-shirt that stretched tightly across the muscles of his chest—the same muscles I'd been unable to stop thinking about since our hug goodbye on Sunday. And he had a football palmed in one hand.

I smiled. "Hey. What are you doing up here? Delivering a pizza?"

"Just thought I'd say hello." He shut the door behind him and walked to the center of the room. Stopping, he rubbed his thumb to his bottom lip as he looked between the window and me. "Were you looking down at the field a little while ago?"

"No," my voice rose a few octaves. "Why do you ask? Did you see someone? I thought the window was one-way glass and people couldn't see in from the other side."

"It is." He shrugged. "But I thought I felt you."

I laughed nervously. "You thought you *felt* me watching you?"

He looked into my eyes. "So you *weren't* watching?"

Shit. I was a terrible liar, and he was the most observant man I'd ever met. He'd be able to read it on my face. So I pulled my chair in and buried my nose in the invoice

Tiffany had left behind. "Nope. Was in a meeting with my sister. She wants to expense a car lease that costs more than most people's first homes."

Christian didn't take his eyes off me. When I chanced a glance up, it looked like he was still trying to read my face. I smiled. "How was your first week back at practice?"

His eyes sparkled, and I got the feeling he knew exactly what I'd just done. Though if he did, he let me off the hook this time. He leaned against the back of the chair on the opposite side of my desk. "It was good. My knee feels better than ever. How was your week? Did you continue on in the planners?"

I nodded. "I did. I read a few more. But I stopped when I got to an entry about him visiting my mother's grave. It brought up emotions I hadn't felt in a while, so I decided to take a break. Whatever is in there isn't going to change things, and I'd rather be in the right frame of mind when I continue."

Christian frowned. "I'm sorry. I should've checked in with you earlier, but I wanted to give you some space."

"It's okay. I could've told Miller if I needed to talk to someone. I'm actually not sure why I haven't filled him in on the planners yet. It's not like me to fail to report all gossip back to him. But I went to visit my mom's grave the other day, and that helped."

"Good. I'm glad." Christian thumbed toward my door. "I have to run to a five o'clock physical therapy appointment downstairs. They might have cleared me to return to practice, but they're making me stick with these laser light therapy sessions to keep inflammation to a minimum and increase the blood flow."

"Oh, I didn't know about that. I might need to tweak my algorithm if you still need treatment. It's coming out with an aggressive completion percentage."

Christian flashed one dimple. "Only tweak it to increase it, boss lady."

"I hope you're right. We need a win this weekend."

"I'll do my best."

"I know you will."

"Are you hanging around a while? Want to grab something to eat after my therapy?"

"I actually have plans."

Christian nodded. "Bozo?"

I wasn't surprised he remembered. "Julian, yes."

"Going anywhere good?"

"An Italian place down on Bleeker that I've never been to."

"You going straight there?"

I nodded. "We're meeting there."

Christian walked around the desk. I stayed rooted in place, but my face must've looked nervous because he grinned and opened his arms. "Just giving my friend a hug..."

"Oh."

Same as last time, he wrapped me in his arms so tightly I could barely breathe. Yet it caused my body to let out a sigh and relax. He was just so big and warm. His arms felt like the only safe place to allow my guard to slip down, if only for a moment. Not to mention, he smelled damn good again, even after a long practice. I didn't want to let go, but too soon Christian pulled back. He dropped a quick peck on my forehead and looked down at me. "That should do it..."

My forehead creased. "Do what?"

"Coat you up with my scent to keep the other animals at a distance."

I laughed. "You're insane."

He winked and let me go. "See you soon, boss lady."

———

"So how are things with the team? You were working on an algorithm last time we saw each other, right?" Julian sipped his wine.

Our table hadn't been ready when we arrived, so we had a glass at the bar before being seated. Since I hadn't had anything to eat since breakfast, I was already feeling a little tipsy after a glass and a half.

I nodded. "Things are good. I finished writing the code for the algo and loaded all of the stats for the team by player. My first set of results weren't that great, but I made some tweaks with Christian's help, and my margin of error is narrowing."

"Is Christian the head of analytics?"

"No, Christian is a player on the team."

Julian's brows furrowed. "Knox?"

"Yeah, you know who he is?"

"Of course. Everyone knows who he is. Even an AI geek like me."

I refrained from mentioning that I was currently wearing eau de Knox...and that I might've sniffed my shirt on the car ride over. But I'd spent enough hours thinking about Christian Knox the last week or two. Tonight was all about the man who was my perfect match, and I intended to keep that focus.

"Do you mind if we don't talk about the team?" I asked. "It's been so consuming, and I could use the mental break."

"Of course."

I sipped my wine. "Tell me what's going on with you?"

He smiled proudly. "I've been asked to keynote at the Innovative Technology Conference on Artificial Intelligence."

"Oh, wow. That's big. Congratulations. What's your topic going to be?"

"The revolutionization of quantum computing in pattern spotting."

For the next twenty minutes, Julian rattled on about how his latest code rollout was going to integrate multiple databases and search millions of records in seconds, locating similarities in data that would previously have taken years of man-hours. A few months ago, this would have been the type of conversation I lived for, yet I found my mind wandering a little.

"I was thinking of kicking off with a holograph of an artificial neural network computer model, superimposed to look like it's running inside the brain. What do you think?"

I squinted at a couple standing at the bar.

"Bella?"

"Hmm?"

"What do you think?"

"About what?"

"Using a holograph in the opening of my speech?"

I glanced back over at the bar again. The man standing with that woman looked like Christian. Or did he? Was my mind screwing with me?

Julian twisted in his seat to follow my line of sight. "Do you see someone you know?"

The man had shifted so his back now faced me, and the woman he was with laid both hands on his chest and laughed. Yeah, I was definitely seeing things.

"No." I shook my head. "I'm sorry, Julian. I thought I saw someone I knew, but it wasn't."

"Oh."

"You were asking me something. What was it again?"

He frowned. "It's not important."

Shit. I was going to blow this date if I didn't get my act together. I adjusted myself in my seat and leaned forward, giving Julian my full attention. "It *is* important. Your work is important, and I really want to hear about it. I'm sorry if I was distracted."

Julian smiled warmly. My renewed focus seemed to smooth things over. At least for a few minutes until I saw the guy from the bar heading toward our table. I still thought I was looking at Christian Knox's doppelgänger... until the man flashed two canyon-deep dimples and waved.

Oh.

My.

God.

It freaking is Christian!

His gloating smile was brighter than sunshine as he approached. "Bella? I thought that was you."

"What are you doing here, Christian?"

He shrugged. "Getting dinner."

"At *this* particular restaurant?"

"It's one of my favorites."

Could it be a coincidence? I didn't think I'd told him the name of the place I was going tonight, though I'd mentioned it was on Bleeker Street.

The woman standing next to him hugged his bicep. "It's one of his favorites, yet he couldn't remember the name of it. We had to stop in at four different restaurants on the block so he could look around and see if it was the right place." She pointed to her stilettos. "These are made for curbside drop-off and pick-up only."

I tilted my head and squinted at Christian. "What exactly made you realize you were at the right place?"

Christian flashed a shit-eating grin and shoved his hands in his pockets. "I'm not really sure. Guess I saw what I was looking for when I walked in—the tables and all, I mean..."

My eyes narrowed. "Uh-huh."

Christian looked over at Julian and extended a hand. "Hi. I'm Christian Knox."

Julian stood and shook. "Julian Morehouse. I'm a big fan."

Christian's grin widened as he looked at me and pointed to my date. "He's a big fan."

I rolled my eyes.

"That's some grip you got there," Julian said, his hand still encased in Christian's. "But do you think I can get my hand back? I need my fingers to work my keyboard tomorrow."

"Oh, sure. Sorry." Christian's eyes gleamed. "Habit from holding the ball tight all day during practice." He motioned to his date. "Candice, this is Bella Keating, my boss." He made a halfhearted wave in Julian's direction. "And that's Julius."

Julian extended his hand to Christian's date. "It's Julian, actually."

"Oh, sorry. That's right. Bella has mentioned you. You work in artificial intelligence, right?"

"I do."

He pointed to Candice. "Such a small world. So does Candice."

Is he freaking kidding me? He showed up at the restaurant where I was on a date and brought a beautiful woman who would be a good match for *my* date?

"How about if we join you?" Christian asked. "You know, since we have so much in common?"

Before I could say it wasn't a good idea, Julian nodded. "We'd love that." He looked to me. "Right, Bella?"

I put on my best fake smile and spoke through my teeth. "Sure."

Shocker, Christian wound up right next to me, and his date snuggled close to Julian. The two of them immediately started talking about what branch of AI they were in. So I leaned over to Christian and whispered, "What do you think you're doing?"

"Enjoying dinner." He shrugged. "It is my favorite restaurant, you know."

"I'd bet the team that you have never stepped one foot inside here until tonight. You're trying to sabotage my date."

Christian did his best to look offended. "Why would I do that?"

"Because you have no idea how to take no for an answer."

"I absolutely know how to take no for an answer, when the person means it."

"Oh my God. You are so full of yourself."

He leaned closer and whispered in my ear. "I wish I was filling you."

My eyes widened. I should have smacked the jerk. But instead, I was too busy visualizing him...filling me.

I wanted to punch him. Or jump his bones. There was a very fine line between the two at the moment.

"Elliott over there is out of his league with you," he added.

"First of all, it's Julian, and you know it. Second of all, why, exactly, would I be out of his league? You don't even know the man, so you're, what, judging him by his appearance?"

"Wasn't talking about his looks. Guy's got a handshake like a fish. You need a guy with more self-confidence than that."

"Oh, and I suppose since you have an overabundance in that department you could fill the role?"

He grinned. "Or I can fill something else..."

I tossed my napkin on the table and stood, speaking to my actual date. "Excuse me for a moment, Julian. I need to go to the ladies' room."

"Of course."

I moved quickly away from the table. I didn't have to go to the bathroom, but I needed a few minutes to collect myself. Or apparently, talk to myself...

"Julian is perfect for you," I said, looking in the bathroom mirror. "He's smart, kind, a gentleman, and handsome."

I bet he doesn't talk dirty, my reflection answered inside my head.

I squinted at the mirror. "Big deal. You're only into it because it's been a while since you were with a man."

Sure, that's the reason your panties are wet right now. It's your dry spell, not how broad the man's shoulders are, or how narrow his waist is, or the carved lumps of muscle that run between the two. And it's definitely not his cocky smile, or how forward he is about wanting you—

"Julian and I have so much in common."

You own a football team, and Christian lives and breathes the sport.

My lips pursed. "I'm his boss."

Big whoopty-doo. You're leaving all the important staffing decisions to the management team anyway.

I leaned toward the mirror. "Shut up. Just shut up."

I'd been so engrossed in conversation with myself, I didn't even notice the door to the ladies' room open until a woman was standing behind me, looking concerned.

"Is everything okay?" she asked.

"Yeah...I was, uh, practicing my Spanish." *Really? Practicing Spanish? That's the best you could come up with? You were speaking damn English! Ugh.* I took a lipstick from my purse and lined my lips, even though they didn't need it. Once the woman disappeared into a stall, I took a deep breath and shook a finger at the idiot in the mirror before walking out.

Unfortunately, the moments in the bathroom did nothing to screw my head on straight, and I walked directly into someone two steps out the door. I lost my footing as I bounced off of them.

"I'm so sor—" I started to apologize before I'd even regained my balance, but paused when I got a look at the face of the person I'd crashed into. Though I shouldn't have had to see a face since the rock wall of a body should've clued me in.

Christian grabbed my shoulders, steadying me. "*Whoa.* Slow down. Where's the fire?"

"You *are* the fire, Christian. What are you doing here?"

"Fire because I'm hot, right?"

I shook his hands from my shoulders. "I'm being serious. Why are you here?"

"Same as you." He shrugged. "Dinner."

My hands went to my hips. "Look me in the eyes and tell me it's a giant coincidence, and you didn't come here because you knew I'd be here."

Christian met my glare. His beautiful blue eyes bounced back and forth between mine for a few seconds before he lifted a hand to my cheek. "You're so beautiful. Your eyes have little flecks of gold around the iris, and they turn almost gray when you're mad."

Anger transformed into a flutter in my belly. And the stupid hormones that surged through my veins the moment he touched my cheek caused an immediate brain fog. I couldn't even remember what we'd been talking about. But the moment grew too intense to remain quiet. So I said the first thing that came to my head. "It's called central heterochromia. It's genetic and more noticeable when the iris contains low quantities of melanin."

Christian's brows dipped.

"The gold ring, it's called central heterochromia. Usually it shows concentrically, instead of sectoral, like I have. But some people have quadrants of different color."

143

The corner of Christian's lip twitched. "Good to know. Come home with me."

"I'm on a date, Christian."

"Only because you're trying to forget what's going on between the two of us."

"God, you really are an egomaniac..."

He stroked my cheek with his thumb. It felt rough on my skin, and goddamn if I didn't feel it between my legs. "Let's both be honest. I'll go first," he said. "It's not a co-incidence that I'm here. I came looking for you. Definitely not one of my finer moments, but it was driving me nuts thinking of you out on a date with that guy."

The little flutter in my belly turned to full-on mush.

Christian lifted his chin. "Your turn. Honesty time." He slid his hand from my cheek down under my chin and tipped my head up so our eyes met. "Tell me you don't feel anything right now, that it's only me who feels like you're a magnet, and I'm a piece of gold."

I bit down on my lip. "Gold isn't drawn to a magnet— not pure gold anyway. Iron, nickel, and cobalt are. They're called ferromagnetic elements."

Christian's eyes dropped to my lips, and he smiled. "Even the random facts you spit out when you're nervous are sexy."

"Christian..."

He put two fingers over my lips. "Don't come home with me, then. Let me take you for dessert, or coffee, or whatever. I'll drop you off after and be a perfect gentleman, I swear."

My bottom lip was going to be swollen from all the gnawing I was doing.

Christian surprised me when he took two steps back and held up his hands. "Just think about it. Mull it over during dinner. If that guy is really more your Ferragamo element than me, I'll back off."

I smiled halfheartedly. "Ferromagnetic."

"Damn, brains are sexy as hell." He winked. "Who knew?"

I took another minute to compose myself after Christian returned to the table, though I didn't feel any less flustered when I wandered back. Nevertheless, eventually the four of us settled into comfortable conversation. At one point, Julian was talking about his work, and I had this vision of the two of us sitting on my couch, each at separate ends, both wearing matching pajamas. Julian was reading a book, and I worked on my laptop. He looked over and smiled warmly at me before burying his nose back in his nonfiction hardcover.

Coming back to reality, I had no idea what Julian had just said, so I offered a smile at his pause. Luckily, Candice was paying attention. While she babbled on, I finished off the wine in my glass and stole a glance at Christian. There was no way in hell Christian would be sitting on the opposite end of my couch if he were in my apartment the morning after a sleepover. Maybe I'd be trying to work at one end, but when our eyes met, he'd grin and haul me from where I sat to straddle his lap. And definitely no pajamas. A morning after with Christian would be his T-shirt from the day before, sans underwear, likely because he'd ripped the panties from my body.

When I stole another glance at Christian, his eyes gleamed like he knew what I was thinking, and he leaned over to whisper in my ear. "Dead giveaway when you suck on that bottom lip."

A little while later, the waiter came over with a small, leather-bound folder. "Would you like to see the dessert menu? Maybe some coffees or cappuccinos?"

Christian held up a hand. "Nothing for me, thank you. I should call it a night. I have an early day tomorrow." He turned to me and lifted a brow. "How about you, Bella? Dessert?"

A sense of panic washed over me. I looked over at Julian, who was also waiting for my answer, then back to Christian before returning my gaze to Julian. Unlike Christian, Julian would probably not try to get me to go home with him, but what if he kissed me goodnight tonight? Did I want that? I *should* want that...

I glanced back at Christian, who was watching me intently. Did I want Christian to kiss me? My attraction to him was a no brainer, yet the thought of kissing him also scared the shit out of me. I had no idea what I wanted to do, but when I looked up into Christian's eyes, I realized one thing. If I kissed Julian, I would feel guilty. Whether that made sense or not didn't matter; it's how I would feel, and I knew it in my bones. So I sighed. "I have an early morning, too. So I'll pass on dessert. Thank you."

Christian's smile stretched from ear to ear. It was comical how fast he wanted to wrap things up after that. "Just the check," he said to the waiter, completely forgetting there were two other people who might've wanted dessert at the table. Then he insisted on paying the tab for everyone and stood before he'd even put the pen down after signing the receipt. He tossed a wad of cash on the table for a tip.

"Did you drive here?" He lifted his chin to Julian, who shook his head.

"Subway."

"I have a car waiting around the corner. We'll drop you both." He dug his cell from his pocket and typed. "I'll have him pull around now."

"I'm all the way uptown," Julian said. "I wouldn't want you to go out of your way."

"It's no problem at all."

Outside, Christian opened the car door for Candice, then held his hand out for me to climb in next. "Julian, four will be a little tight. Why don't you go in the front? We'll drop you first."

"Oh...okay."

When we pulled up at Julian's apartment, Christian made no attempt to move. He had no plans to offer to let me out so Julian and I could say goodnight in private. Instead, he rolled down the window. Julian bent and waved. "Thank you again for dinner. It was very nice meeting you, Christian." He nodded to Candice before looking at me. "I'll call you."

Christian was already rolling up the window in Julian's face by the time I said, "Okay." He then leaned forward to the driver. "You can drop off Candice next."

The driver nodded. "You got it."

For the first time all evening, Candice looked a little perturbed. "Maybe you can drop Bella first, so you can come up for a glass of wine or something?"

I felt a little nauseous, thinking the two of them had probably already had *or something* before.

Christian shook his head. "First week back at practice really knocked me out, and I have an early day tomorrow."

"Oh...okay."

The backseat of the car was uncomfortably quiet the rest of the way to Candice's apartment. She leaned forward with a forced smile when we pulled up at the curb. "It was nice meeting you, Bella."

"You, too."

Christian caught my eye as she climbed out of the car. "I'll be back in a minute. I'm going to walk her up."

I watched as the two of them walked side by side to Candice's building. When they disappeared inside, my gut twisted.

What are they doing in there? What am I doing in here?

A few minutes later, Christian folded his large frame back into the car. "Dessert?"

"Did you kiss her goodnight?" The words tumbled from my mouth before I could stop them.

Christian smiled and shook his head. "On the cheek, same way I do my mother." He leaned over to me. "*Not* the way I'm going to kiss you when you're finally ready."

My eyes met his. "I don't know when that might be..."

He took my hand, lacing our fingers together. "That's okay. You're here with me and not that other guy. One step at a time."

Chapter 13

Christian

"SO, CANDICE AND Bozo make a cute couple, don't they? Should we help them exchange numbers?"

Bella narrowed her eyes. "Don't push it. You already took over my date, dumped him curbside, and got me to come here with you. What happened to one step at a time?"

I reached across the table and weaved my fingers with Bella's again. I'd done it in the car, and she hadn't pulled away. Sadly, it did more for me than spending the night with the women I'd been with lately. "I'm just fucking around."

She shook her head. "I can't believe you brought a woman who worked in AI with you to crash my date. It's pretty impressive that you were able to come up with one on such short notice. She was gorgeous, too."

I squeezed Bella's fingers. "Doesn't hold a candle to you."

The waitress came over, and we hadn't even looked at the menu yet. She did a double take when she saw me. "You're...Christian Knox, the football player."

I glanced at her name tag. "And you're Francine. Nice to meet you."

The woman's eyes widened. "You know my name?"

I motioned to the tag pinned on her uniform. "It's written right there."

She laughed nervously and patted her hair down. "Oh, right. Of course. Duh. I'm a huge fan, Mr. Knox."

"It's Christian."

"You're the only reason I watch football." She covered her mouth. "Oh my God, I can't wait to tell my boyfriend, Freddy. He's going to freak out. You're my hall pass!"

I glanced over to find Bella's eyes wide. If she found this shocking, I should probably make sure she steered clear of the exit after the games. It wasn't uncommon for a woman to ask me for an autograph, then lift her shirt to flash her tits and hand me a marker.

The waitress turned red. "Oh my God. I can't believe I just said that." She turned to Bella. "I'm sorry. I didn't mean that as an offer. Well, unless you guys are just friends, I guess?" Francine held up her hands and took two steps backward. "I'm going to shut up now. Why don't I go get you some waters?"

I smiled. "That would be great. Thanks."

Bella shook her head when the waitress disappeared. "Does...that type of thing happen often?"

The cocky bastard in me wanted to say it did, but I didn't want to give Bella another reason to be afraid. So I shrugged. "Sometimes I get recognized."

"And offered sex..."

"She wasn't offering. Besides, you could walk into any bar in this city and a man would offer you sex."

Bella snort-laughed. "I've never walked into a bar and been offered sex."

"A man has never offered to buy you a drink?"

"Of course. But that's just buying a drink, not offering sex."

I shook my head. "Buying a woman a drink is never just buying a woman a drink. If you responded, '*Let's skip the drink and have sex*,' the majority of men wouldn't say no."

"So every man who buys a woman a drink wants to get in her pants?"

"Pretty much."

Bella motioned between us. "You bought me, Candice, and Julian dinner earlier. Does that mean you want to sleep with all three of us?"

"I paid the check because I'm a dick and didn't want Bozo to pay for your meal, so it was less like a date."

"Oh." She nodded. "So you didn't want to sleep with Julian, just me and Candice?"

Bella was smarter than me. I had no doubt she could twist anything I said into a pretzel and throw it back. But I knew how to cut a conversation off with her. I leaned in. "You're the only one I want to fuck, Bella. Doesn't matter who offers to spread her legs. I'm waiting to bury my face between yours."

She opened her mouth to respond, then shut it, then opened it again.

I grinned. "You want to look at the menu now?"

She quickly hid her face behind the oversized leather menu, but I could still see her eyes. They had that glazed-over look in them, like maybe she was picturing what I'd just told her I wanted to do. When crinkles formed at the sides of her eyes, I knew she was trying to cover a smile.

Bella liked my crude mouth, whether she'd ever admit it or not.

She glanced up from the menu. "What?" she asked.

I couldn't wipe the grin from my face. "Nothing. Do you know what you want?"

Her eyes scanned the menu some more. "The tiramisu sounds good. But so does the salted caramel cheesecake. Oh, and the brownie sundae." She paused. "What do you feel like having?"

I somehow managed to refrain from describing exactly what I wanted to eat, in detail. "Those sound good."

The waitress came back over with two waters. This time she completely avoided eye contact with me and stared down at her notepad. "Have you decided?"

"We'll have the tiramisu, salted caramel cheesecake, and the brownie sundae."

"Coming right up."

Bella laughed. "I didn't mean we needed to order all three. I'm still full from dinner."

"I'll eat whatever you don't. Food doesn't go to waste when I'm in training. I need the calories."

"God, I wish I could say the same thing. I really need to start exercising. But I don't enjoy running or the elliptical."

"There are plenty of ways to get exercise. What activity do you enjoy?"

"I have no idea."

"What sports did you play in high school?"

Bella smiled. "Sports? I was on the debate team, president of the math club, and played the cello."

I chuckled. "Ever try yoga?"

"I took a class once, but I couldn't keep up. It was a beginner class, yet everyone else seemed to know all the moves already, so I never went back."

"Swimming?"

"I hold my nose when I go in the water. I don't like the feeling of chlorine going up my nose."

"Rock climbing?"

She wrinkled her nose.

"Bicycling?"

"I actually used to love bike riding, but I'd be too afraid to ride in the city. The taxi and Uber drivers are madmen."

"What about a spin class then?"

"I've never tried. But they play loud music, right?"

"Usually."

"Blasting music makes me stressed. I don't like to feel like I can't keep track of my thoughts. The bicycle riding I used to love was outdoors. When I was growing up, my mom used to take me to this campground up in Vermont that her parents took her to when she was a kid—Green Mount Campground. We would go for a week in the summer, and then she'd surprise me a few times a year, and we'd escape the city for a weekend. The campground rented bikes, and all we did was ride around the paved trails from the time we got up until we went to bed. It was my favorite thing to do."

"Do you ever do it now?"

Bella shook her head. "The campground closed a few years back."

I nodded. "What about riding on a track? The stadium obviously has one. It's paved and outdoors. Lots of people from corporate use it before and after practice."

"Maybe I'll try that. Though I'd need to get a bike first, and there is definitely no place to store it in my apartment."

"I'm sure the equipment manager would be happy to store it for you, and I can take you to pick one up, if you want."

The waitress brought our desserts. Bella eyed the tiramisu, and her tongue peeked out to wet her full lips. *What I wouldn't give to run my tongue along those, suck on the bottom one like she does when she's nervous, bite down, and tug...* I bet she'd like that.

Bella picked up a spoon and debated what to try first before settling on the tiramisu. She stopped after scooping up a heaping pile of the cake and looked at me. "Aren't you going to have some?"

I planned to, but right now I was too focused on watching her slip that into her mouth and enjoy the fuck out of it. "I'm going to let you be the guinea pig and see if they're any good first."

"Gee, thanks."

I couldn't peel my eyes from her mouth as she opened it and slid the mound of cake in. Some whipped cream stuck to her top lip, and when she swiped at it with her tongue, I had to shift in my seat to accommodate the tightening in my pants. Christ, this woman was going to make me hard watching her eat. She made me feel like I was in sixth grade again, unable to control my dick when I saw a girl's nipples through her shirt when we came in from the cold after recess. Bella closed her eyes as she swallowed, and I couldn't stop myself from imagining it was my dick she was enjoying. It's a good thing we'd ordered three desserts, because it was going to take a while for my body to come back from this.

She opened her eyes and smiled. "It's sooo good."

I couldn't agree more.

When I still made no attempt to pick up a spoon and join her, Bella cocked her head. "I gave it my seal of approval. Aren't you going to try some?"

I held her eyes and opened my mouth in response.

"You trust me to feed you?" She scooped up an enormous amount of cake. I'm not kidding, it was like three quarters of the big slice wobbling on that spoon. "Lord knows you have a big enough mouth," she said. "You should be able to handle this."

While my mouth was still full, Bella grinned. "What? No I-can-handle-anything-you-give-me comment?"

I pointed to my cheeks and spoke with my mouth full. "You gotta give a guy a chance for a comeback."

She giggled, and we spent the next half hour eating desserts and forgetting all about the fact that she'd been on a date with another guy an hour ago. At one point, a family walked by our table—they happened to have a set of twin boys who were probably about thirteen or so. Bella looked over at them, then at me.

"What were you like as a teenager? I bet the kids in the halls parted like the sea when you walked by. Were you the most popular boy?"

I shrugged. "I had a lot of friends."

"What about girls? I'm sure you were popular with them, too. I mean, you already told me about the twenty-three-year-old girl in Colorado you thought you had a shot with when you were fifteen. So your confidence must've come from something."

I'd learned long ago that when women asked about my past with other women, they didn't really want the answer, not in detail anyway. "I had a few girlfriends. Nothing too serious."

"Did you bring them to your room filled with football trophies to seduce them?"

"Actually, I never brought a girl home. I didn't really bring friends around much either."

"How come?"

"I've mentioned my dad has a drinking problem. Think I skipped that he's an angry drunk. I never knew what kind of a mood he would be in, so I avoided the house as much as possible and hid that he was an alcoholic from most of my friends."

Bella frowned. "I'm sorry."

"Thank you. But it worked out for me. Not wanting to be home made me put in extra time with football in high school. That gave me the edge I needed to get noticed by colleges. Well, that and Coach gave me an advantage. He used to meet me after regular practice ended, and we'd run drills and throw the ball around until it got dark."

"I'm so glad I've had the chance to know him. He really seems like a good man."

"He's the best." For the first time, I looked for a resemblance to Coach in Bella—or John Barrett even. Not finding one, I asked, "Do you look like your mom?"

She nodded. "When I was little, people used to tell me I was the spitting image of her, but I couldn't see it. Recently, though, I was looking for some papers and came across old photos of her. I thought they were of me at first."

The light above caught the gold flecks in Bella's eyes. At risk of sounding like a clichéd Hallmark movie, I could really get lost in those things. "Did she have two-color eyes, too?"

She shook her head. "No, did my dad?"

I thought about what John Barrett looked like. "I'm not sure. I didn't spend a lot of time gazing into them."

"Should I consider myself lucky that you noticed mine, then?"

"Nah. I get to look at yours, so I'm the lucky one."

It was almost midnight by the time the Town Car pulled up at Bella's apartment, yet I still wasn't ready for the night to end. I told the driver to double park wherever he could, since there was no parking anywhere on her street.

"You want to...take a walk around the block or something?" I asked.

Bella looked down at her heels. "These aren't really walking shoes. Besides, this isn't the greatest neighborhood for strolling. It's mostly cracked sidewalks and creatures checking out the garbage at the curb."

"Oh, okay." I rubbed my hands on my thighs.

Bella looked over and grinned. "You're cute when you're trying to be good."

"Oh yeah? Cute enough to kiss goodnight?"

She laughed. "Well, that didn't last very long, did it?"

"Trying not to push with you is physically painful."

"Well, I wouldn't want you to be in pain. So why don't you at least walk me up?"

We were barely out of the car when a paparazzo popped out of nowhere. His flash went off, and Bella jumped back and wobbled. I steadied her before palming the camera, which was practically in our faces.

"What the fuck are you doing?" I roared. "Sitting in front of her apartment at midnight?"

"Mr. Knox, is it true that you and Ms. Keating are dating?" The piece of shit cared more about getting a quote than the expensive camera I had in my hands.

I stepped in front of Bella and yanked the camera around his neck, hard enough that he had to bend, but not hard enough that it broke. "Get the fuck out of here before I choke you with this strap."

"But are you two dating?"

Bella put a hand on my bicep. "Christian, don't hurt him. It's okay."

I shook my head. "It's not okay. You don't sit in the bushes and pop out at women in the dark. That's what robbers and rapists do."

"I know. I didn't mean it was okay that he does this all the time. I just meant we should ignore him."

I looked over at the guy, who was still bent in half since I had the camera strap around his neck in my fist. "You do this to her all the time?"

"I'm trying to make a living, man."

"You can ask the same questions and take pictures of her during the daylight, when she comes to work at the arena, not at her place at midnight." I pulled a little harder on the camera strap. "You got it?"

He nodded, so I let go.

"Will you at least tell me if you're dating?"

I stabbed a finger into his chest. "If you're out here when I get back, we're going to have a problem. Got it?"

I scooped my hand around Bella's waist and pulled her close as we walked toward the fruit stand. "You really need a place with security."

"I know. The other night someone got into the building and came up and knocked on the interior door to my apartment."

I stopped in place. "Are you kidding me?"

"It was fine. I saw the guy had a camera through my peephole and yelled for him to leave, or I was going to call the cops, and he left."

I shook my head. "I'm walking you upstairs to your apartment door."

Bella waved to an older man sitting behind the counter watching TV as we headed for a door next to the refrigerator cases. It wasn't even locked. And the stairway was pitch dark.

"Isn't there a light?" I said.

Bella fiddled with her phone and turned on the flashlight to illuminate the dark hall. "It's broken."

I mumbled half the way up the creaky stairs. When we got to the landing at the top of two flights, Bella stopped and motioned to the only door. "This is me."

I put my hands on my hips and shook my head. "I'm so freaked out about your lack of security that I can't even appreciate that I have you alone in a dark hall."

"It's not that bad..."

"Your security is a frail, eighty-year-old man who's watching soap operas, and some guy just jumped out of your bushes."

She dug keys out of her purse, then had to shine her phone on the doorknob to know where the lock was. When the door opened, she reached inside and flicked on a light, which made it slightly easier to see.

"Thank you for dessert."

I nodded and took her hand. "Are you sorry I crashed your date?"

She was quiet for a moment before shaking her head. "Not really. I like spending time with you."

"Then you should do it more often."

Bella laughed. "Smooth."

I swung our joined hands. "Go out with me, Bella?"

"I think technically I already did. We sat next to each other at dinner, and you paid the bill and drove me home."

"I want a real date. One that's just me and you."

She looked down and was silent again for a long time before meeting my eyes. "Your contract is up this year. What if it's not renewed?"

"Because we started dating?"

"No, not *because* we started dating, but the meeting to decide on all the contracts is only a few weeks away. What if the GM recommends not renewing because of your injury or for whatever reason, and we're already dating?"

I grinned. "That's not going to happen."

"But it could..."

"It won't. But if I got cut because I couldn't perform at the same level anymore, that would be on me, not you."

She shook her head and sighed. "What do you want from me, Christian? Is it only sex or something more? Because I'll be honest, I could deal with a physical relationship, but I'm not sure more is such a good idea. Between my position at the team and me being confused about things with Julian..."

The woman had just told me a sex-only relationship was on the table, and instead of jumping on it, I felt a little offended. "I don't want to just fuck you, Bella."

She sighed. "That would be so much easier for both of us. You're always on the road, and my life is chaotic right now."

In my gut I knew her hesitancy had nothing to do with relationships being hard or even my being on the team she owned. Bella was nervous. Maybe it was because so many people in her life had disappeared on her, or that she was used to her independence. I wasn't sure, but I thought I saw fear in her eyes. "I'm not looking for easy anymore, Bella. I'm looking for real."

She mulled that around for a long time before finally nodding and taking a deep breath. "Okay."

"Okay? Meaning you'll let me take you out?"

She smiled. "Okay usually means yes."

My head fell back, and I looked up at the ceiling. "Fuck, yeah."

She giggled, and I felt the sound in my chest. Using the hand already joined with hers, I yanked her against me. She practically stumbled as I wrapped both arms around her waist.

"Saturday. It's our only bye week this season."

"Okay."

I lifted one hand and stroked her hair. "Thank you."

She nodded. "Let's just take things slow, alright?"

"Not that I'm complaining, but let me see if I have this straight. My choices were, we could be fuck buddies, which is the opposite of slow, but if I want more than that, we take baby steps?"

"I know it doesn't seem to make sense. I guess I compartmentalize things in my life, and sex when it's only sex is simple, but sex when it's more isn't."

I wasn't sure I understood it, but that didn't matter. "I can do slow."

Bella smiled. "I'm not sure that's true. But I'm willing to try."

I kissed the top of her head and forced myself to release her from my arms. "You got it. Though you better get inside."

"Why?"

"Because while my brain understands slow..." I motioned to the hard-on already growing in my pants, after only ten seconds of holding her. "My body doesn't."

She covered her mouth. "Oh my."

"You probably should lock the door, too."

Bella pushed up on her toes to kiss my cheek. "Goodnight, Christian."

"'Night, boss lady. I'll see you Saturday."

Chapter 14

Bella

"IS YOUR BIRTHDAY today?"

Josh carried in a second arrangement of flowers and set them on my desk. This one was three times the size of the one delivered an hour ago and had the most vibrant colors I'd ever seen in flowers.

I stood. "No, my birthday is in March. But wow, those are gorgeous."

He smiled. "Well, then someone must really like you..."

I opened the card pinned to the side. Oh boy. The arrangements weren't from someone who liked me, it was some*ones*. Unlike the flowers Julian had sent, this card was handwritten, and for some reason, I just knew the slashy, bold print was Christian's.

Bella,
Until tomorrow...
X
Christian

My cell rang, and the name that flashed was just what I needed at the moment. *Miller.* I swiped to answer. "How did you know I needed to talk to you?"

"I read about it in the *Post.* And I'm pissed that's how I had to find out. Give me all the deets, woman."

My forehead wrinkled. "What are you talking about?"

"You didn't see this morning's *New York Post?*"

"I don't read the *Post.* It's too much sports."

"Ummm, sweetheart, you own a football team now. But that's another conversation. You and Hunka Hunka Burning Love are on Page Six."

"Still on your Elvis TV binge?"

"Yeah, and I'm pretty sure Elvis was singing about Christian Knox when he sang that song."

As usual, our conversation had gotten off track. "Back up, Christian is in the *Post?*"

"You're *both* in the *Post.* And the way his big hand is wrapped around you, tucking you close to his side, is hot as fuck."

Oh God. That paparazzo from last night. "Can you send me a pic of the photo and what it says?"

"Sure, hang on."

Thirty seconds later, my phone buzzed with a new text. I opened it to find exactly what Miller had described. Christian and I were walking toward my building, his arm wrapped snugly around me. We looked like a couple. But in case people didn't view the photo that way, the caption beneath sealed the deal.

Contract negotiations at midnight?

The New York Bruins' star quarterback's contract is up this year. Are Christian Knox and new team owner, Bella Keating, deep in negotiations at midnight?

Ugh. As if I didn't have enough trouble with people taking me seriously around here. "Shoot. Don't these people have anything better to do?"

"The last time I talked to you, you were going on a second date with Julian last night. Instead you went out with Christian?"

I leaned back in my chair with a sigh. "I actually did go out with Julian last night. But Christian showed up and sort of crashed my date."

Miller cackled. "I fucking love that dude! There is nothing sexier than a man who knows what he wants and goes after it. Except maybe a man who knows what he wants, goes after it, *and has a big dick*, which I bet he does. And oh my God, you better not be a tight ass with information like you usually are. You have to spill on this one. How big is it? I bet it's eight inches, at least. He's circumcised, right? I'm not into a hooded warrior. How was his manscaping? I saw a picture of him on the Internet the other day, and his chest hair is cropped tight. The curtains should match the rug and—"

"Take a breath, crazy man," I interrupted. I probably should've started with the fact that I had no clue how big Christian's dick was, but I was too curious about something else. "You just *happened* to see a shirtless picture of Christian online the other day?"

"Yes," Miller said primly. "I wasn't even looking for it. I went to add something to my kitchen-redecorating Pinterest folder, and my Christian folder popped up instead."

"You have a Christian *Pinterest folder*?"

"Trent started it. We were going to collect them for you, but then we realized it was a fun hobby for us. Looking at pictures of him is better foreplay than watching *The Vampire Diaries* for the eighth time."

I laughed. "You're seriously warped, you know that?"

"Don't change the subject. How big is Hunka Hunka Burning Love?"

"I wouldn't know. He crashed my date, and then we went out for dessert, and he dropped me at home. I didn't sleep with him."

Miller sighed. "God, you're boring."

I leaned back in my chair. "I'm so confused, Miller. Julian is right for me. I know the way I picked him might have been a tad unorthodox, but I was starting to settle into the idea of having a real relationship for the first time. We were such good friends; taking the next step wouldn't have been that hard. But I wasn't even upset that Christian crashed our date."

"Things change."

"But Julian and I are perfect for each other."

"Perfect on paper doesn't always make a love match, sweetheart. I know you'll find this hard to believe, but you can't feed a bunch of data into a formula and decide who you should fall for. Love is illogical."

I frowned. "I hate illogical."

Miller chuckled. "I know you do. You like things to be orderly and sensical. It kills you if something happens that you didn't see coming. But sometimes the best things in life are the unexpected ones."

"Julian sent me flowers this morning," I said. "So did Christian."

"Whose are bigger?"

I looked over at the two vases on my desk. Christian's gargantuan one dwarfed poor Julian's—in size, vibrancy, and even personality. There was a parallel between the flowers and the men.

"Christian can have any woman he wants. You should've seen the waitress last night stumbling over her words when she came to take our order."

"Maybe. But it seems like the woman he wants is you."

I took a deep breath in and exhaled audibly. "I agreed to a date with Christian tomorrow."

"We need to go shopping. I'll be at your office at six. Where are you going?"

"I have no idea."

"Well, you're rich now. We'll buy multiple outfits so you're prepared for anything."

"I have plenty of clothes at home."

"You have plenty of clothes to date Julian Morehouse. Trust me, you have nothing in your closet worthy of Christian Knox."

I should've been insulted by that comment, yet he was probably right. "Make it six thirty. I have a meeting at five, and it might run longer than an hour."

"You got it, sunshine. I'll see you later."

One good thing about this job was that I didn't have time to overthink. After I hung up with Miller, I had to run to a meeting, and then three more after that. By the time I got back to my office, it was almost four. I walked to the wall of windows and looked down at the field. Players were scattered all over the turf, so it looked like practice was finishing up. Christian was in the endzone, throwing the ball to one of his receivers. I watched for a few minutes, in awe of how graceful such a large man could be. He made it seem so easy—like I should be able to throw a ball sixty yards. After a few more minutes, he and the player he'd been throwing with slapped hands, and Christian headed toward the tunnel, talking to the offensive coordinator.

"Why haven't you signed the sponsorship deal I put in for signature last week?" My sister Tiffany's voice made me jump. I turned to find her already in fight mode, her legs spread wide and arms folded across her chest. "And where is my car lease?"

I exhaled. "Hi, Tiffany. How are you?"

"Unhappy. Why isn't the Foreman contract signed?"

As if her unending state of miserableness would be cured if one contract were signed...

"I asked the PR department to do a little digging. One of the companies Foreman owns makes children's clothing, and I remembered reading an article a few months ago about some questionable child labor they might've been using in Myanmar."

"All of our vendors are vetted before we do business with them."

"Okay, but we don't do an annual update on all our business partners. I looked back, and we've been doing business with Foreman for ten years. Their business could have changed a lot since then."

"They're an upstanding company."

"I'm sure you're right. But it couldn't hurt to run another check. I'm sure PR will get back to me with their report soon. I figured it's better to be safe than sorry. We wouldn't want anything to tarnish the Bruins name."

A wicked smile spread across Tiffany's face. "Yes, we wouldn't want anyone *else* to tarnish the team name, not when the lovely new owner is doing such a great job of it on her own."

My eyes narrowed. "How am I hurting the team's name?"

"Getting passed around by the players more than the ball in a game doesn't exactly make us look good."

"Passed around? What are you *talking* about?"

"I saw the *Post*."

I sighed. Of course that's what this was about. "Do you have anything else you need to discuss with me?"

Her answer was to turn around. But she stopped in the doorway. "He'll be done with you by the time we get to playoffs, if it even lasts that long. Just ask Salma in accounting."

And here I'd thought I'd been standing my ground so nicely in today's square off with my sister. But that last comment knocked me for a loop. Salma in accounting? With the big boobs and beautiful, shiny hair? Luckily, my sister was long gone so she didn't see she'd landed a direct hit. Though I suspected she knew it.

Five minutes later, I still hadn't really recovered, but I knew Josh would be knocking at my door shortly to remind me it was time to go to yet another meeting. So I forced myself back to work and called up the agenda on my computer. A few lines in, there was a knock at my door. I looked up to find Christian.

He took one look at the *two* vases of flowers on my desk and frowned. "You have a minute?"

I nodded. "Only that. I have a meeting soon."

Christian shut the door behind him and walked to my desk. He gestured to the flowers. "The florist accidentally sent two?"

I shook my head. "One is from Julian."

It looked like Christian was going to say something, but then he closed his mouth and the muscle flex in his jaw spoke for him. I'd never been a jealous woman, but suddenly I knew what he was feeling. Though I wasn't about to keep quiet like him.

I tossed my pen on the desk. "Did you sleep with Salma in accounting?"

He squinted at me. "Where did you hear that?"

"Does it matter?"

He folded his arms across his chest. "Only because I'm curious to know who's feeding you bullshit information."

"So you didn't sleep with her?"

"We met at the team holiday party two years ago. I had a couple of drinks, which I don't usually do. We talked for a while, and then she caught me off guard when she asked me out. I said yes. The next morning I realized that was dumb, so I planned to talk to her and tell her I wasn't going to go out with her. But I was flying to my brother's for Christmas. By the time I got back, she'd already told half the corporate office we were dating. After I let her know I wasn't going to go out with her, she told everyone I'd dumped her since I'd gotten my fill. I left it alone. Figured I'd embarrassed her by changing my mind, and there was no reason to get into a pissing contest to set the record straight."

"Oh…"

"Are you going to tell me who's trying to sabotage our relationship before it even starts?"

I frowned. "Tiffany. She told me I was going to be just another woman you blew through." I shook my head. "I'm not sure if you saw the *Post* this morning. But they ran one of the pictures the paparazzo took last night with a suggestive headline."

Christian's stance softened. He unfolded his arms and tucked his hands into his sweatpants pockets with a shrug. "I heard about it. You do know your sister is just trying to get in your head. She gets her kicks upsetting you."

I sighed. "I know."

Christian caught my eyes. "So we're good? You believe me about Salma?"

"Of course. Unlike my sister, you've never given me a reason to doubt you'd tell me the truth."

"Good." He smiled halfheartedly. "Is it my turn to be jealous now?" Christian pointed his eyes to the roses he hadn't sent. "Did he ask you out again?"

"He wrote that he had a good time and hopes to do it again soon, just the two of us." I gestured to the card. "You're welcome to read it yourself."

"Thanks, but I don't need to." Christian looked down for a moment. "Do you want to go out with him again?"

I shrugged. "I'm confused about my feelings toward Julian. I thought he was exactly what I needed."

A cocky smile stretched across Christian's face. I was waiting for a matching cocky response, but then there was a knock at my door. Josh cracked it open and peeked his head in. "Oh, sorry. I thought you were alone. I was coming to give you the five-minute warning before your next meeting."

"Thanks, Josh. I'll be there."

"Good enough." He nodded to Christian. "Knox."

Christian lifted his chin. "Sullivan."

After Josh closed the door, Christian picked up a petal that had fallen from the roses. He rubbed it between his fingers. "You're busy, so I'll get out of your way. I was just coming up to ask if eight AM tomorrow is okay?"

I'd assumed we'd be going out in the evening. But it didn't matter. "Sure."

"I'll pick you up."

"Okay."

"Wear something comfortable."

"Oh...what are we doing?"

"It's a surprise."

I wrinkled my nose. "I'm more of a planner than a surprise-type person."

Christian smiled. "You also thought Bozo was exactly what you needed. Keep an open mind." He winked. "See you tomorrow, beautiful."

Chapter 15

Bella

I CHANGED FOUR times.

Not to mention before putting on the outfit I currently wore, I'd actually googled *comfy clothes*. The range of photos that popped up went from yoga pants, to cute little dresses, to ripped jeans and sneakers. The written definition I'd found wasn't any better: *clothing that when worn makes you feel relaxed.* Relaxed? Are they crazy? Clearly they had no idea who I was. That word didn't make a frequent appearance in my vocabulary during a normal week, but now it was fifteen minutes before *Christian Knox* was picking me up.

Or so I thought...

Knock. Knock. Knock.

Shoot. I looked at my reflection in the mirror. I had on a long-sleeved, smocked dress Miller had made me buy last night, and I really wanted to change again. But it was going to have to wait until after I let Christian in.

At the door, I took a deep breath before opening. "Hey..." My face fell when I saw Christian's outfit. He had on a pair of black sweats and a form-fitting thermal. "I'm overdressed, aren't I?"

Christian's eyes drifted up and down my body. "You look beautiful. But you might want to put pants on."

I sighed and stepped aside. "I knew I was overdressed. Come in. I need to change. And I'm warning you, it'll probably be more than once."

Christian looked around my tiny apartment, stopping at the couch, which had a pile of clothes strewn all over it, most of which still had tags on it from my shopping trip.

"I take it this isn't the first wardrobe change you've made."

"*Comfy clothes* covers a wide spectrum of options."

"Do you have any of those yoga pants women wear to exercise?"

"I do. Is that what's appropriate for today?"

Christian shrugged. "They'll work. Plus, I'd like to see your ass in them."

I chuckled. "Let me see what I can do." I walked over to my dresser and opened the drawer where I kept my rarely used exercise clothes while Christian looked around.

He peered down at the bookshelf. "What are all these?"

"Those are antique metronomes. I collect them."

"The timing things musicians use to stay on tempo?"

"Yep."

"Do you play an instrument?"

I shook my head. "Not since high school. When I lived at the shelter, I played in the orchestra, and my teacher gave us each a metronome to use when we practiced. She said learning to play while it clicked was good training for following the hands of a conductor. I didn't really use it for practicing, but the clicking sound had a way of relaxing me. After my mom's death, I struggled with panic attacks a lot, and I found that putting the metronome on, and focusing on it, was soothing. One day I passed an antique store and saw one in the window. I went in and bought it, and that started me collecting old metronomes, I guess."

Christian flicked the switch on one, and the rhythmic clicking started. He kept it on for about ten seconds before turning it off. "That would drive me fucking nuts."

I laughed. "Miller says the same thing."

I held up a pair of Lululemon leggings, a cropped top, and a zip-up matching jacket. "Is this good?"

He grinned. "Definitely. That's sexy as shit. I can't wait to see it on you."

"But is it also appropriate for where we're going? Better yet, why don't you tell me where we're going since I'm going to find out soon anyway. Then I can make an informed decision on what to wear."

"Nah." Christian shrugged. "We're working on you learning to go with the flow."

"Oh we are, are we?"

"Yep. Go get changed."

I squinted before heading to the bathroom. "Bossy."

When I came out, Christian was sitting on the couch, which was more of a loveseat to fit in my tiny apartment. He took up more than half of the thing. My eyes shifted to the neat pile next to him. "Did you fold my clothes?"

He nodded. "You seem like the type who wasn't going to leave until they were folded, so I figured I'd get it done so we can get on the road. We have a long drive."

That was oddly sweet, and also very true. I held my arms out to display my current outfit. "So this works for today?"

Christian held up his pointer and motioned in a circle. "Turn. Let me see the full thing."

I did a 360-degree pivot. "Well?"

He stood. "You have a great ass."

"Thank you. But is the outfit good for today?"

"Yeah, you can wear anything."

"If I can wear anything, why did I have to turn so you could see the outfit?"

"That was for my benefit."

I followed him out, and Christian had a dark SUV parked down the block. Once inside, I fastened the seatbelt and looked around. "This thing has as much square footage as my apartment. Where do you keep it?"

"In a lot across from my place."

"Do you get to drive it often?"

"I have a bike, too. I use that most of the time because it's easier to get around in the city."

"You ride a bicycle around the city?"

Christian started the engine. "A motorcycle."

"Oh. Isn't that dangerous?"

"My brother Tyler lives in Jersey. He stayed with me for the weekend at Christmas last year. A cab popped the curb and broke his toe. This city is a warzone however you take it."

We drove north on I-95 for hours. Christian still refused to give me any hints about where we were going, but I'd begun to suspect he might be taking me to his cabin up in Maine—at least until he got off the interstate and started heading west on a different highway. When he eventually got off at an exit in Vermont, I recognized it. "God, I haven't been out here in years. We're near the campground I told you about where my mom used to take me bike riding."

Christian smiled. "I know. We'll be there in five minutes."

"We're going there?"

He thumbed over his shoulder. "Bikes are in the back."

"Bicycles?"

"Yep. Got you a twenty-six inch. Took a guess on the size you'd ride."

"But the campground closed down."

"It did. But we have use of it for the day."

"How?"

"I looked up Green Mount Campground. The property is actually for sale. I called and told the realtor I wanted to check it out. She offered to show it to me, but I said I'd prefer to do it on my own. She was hesitant. Then I told her who I was and gave her two tickets to next week's game. We should have the place all to ourselves for the afternoon."

I stared over at him.

Christian felt my eyes and looked over. "What?"

"I can't believe you're taking me bicycle riding at the campground. This is not how I thought a date with you would be."

"How did you think it would be?"

"Oh, I don't know. You would take me to some overpriced restaurant and then try to get me to go back to your place so you could feel me up."

Christian smirked. "Now you just ruined part two of the date."

I laughed. "Seriously, Christian. This is the sweetest thing anyone has ever done for me. The fact that you listened to me the other day when I told you the story about the campground says so much about you."

"Don't build me up too much in your head. Otherwise, you'll be disappointed when I spend half the day behind you, watching your ass go up and down."

I would never have taken Christian Knox for modest, but there was a layer of it just beneath the cocky surface he wore on the outside.

We made a left, and the entrance to the campground came into view. The big wooden welcome sign I remembered had been replaced by a thick chain that blocked passage and a *Private – No Trespassing* sign. Christian pulled up and put the SUV in park.

"The real estate agent gave me the combo to the lockbox. I'll be right back."

I watched from the SUV as Christian jumped out and fiddled with the lock at the center of the chain. He laid the chain on the ground, then came back and pulled in before going back to replace the chain so no one else could enter.

"Do you remember where the bike path started?"

I pointed up ahead to the right. "I do. It's probably about a half mile in, up that way."

We parked at a grassy area at the start of the path. Unfortunately, it had seen better days. Tree roots had broken up the pavement, and tall weeds decorated what had once been a neat, clean place to ride. Christian surveyed the area. "I think we're better off riding on the street rather than that thing. At least there shouldn't be any cars."

"Yeah, that's perfect."

Christian opened the back of his SUV to reveal two bikes packed inside. He unloaded the bigger one on top, then set the white one next to me.

"Looks like it'll fit," he said.

"It does. Whose bike is it, though?"

Christian shrugged. "It's yours. I bought it last night."

"You *bought* this bike?"

"You said you wanted to find an activity to get more exercise. Figured maybe you'd get some use out of it."

I looked down at the bike and shook my head. "I don't know what to say."

Christian pulled a duffle bag from the SUV and took out two helmets and water bottles. He handed one of each to me. "You wanna give me a tour of the place?"

I smiled. "I'd love that."

For the next hour and a half, Christian and I rode around the campground. It was overgrown and beat up, but it didn't matter at all. The sun was shining, the wind blew in my face, and I had that warm feeling in my chest that coming here with my mom had always given me. It felt like I didn't have a care in the world. I couldn't remember the last time I'd been able to say that. When we got to an area with picnic benches, Christian pointed.

"You want to take a break for a few minutes?"

"Sure."

We parked the bikes and sat with our asses on the table and feet on the seat. I let out a content sigh. "This is the best day I can remember in a long time."

Christian smiled. "Good. I'm glad you're enjoying yourself."

"I don't think I realized how tense I've been. Living in a constant state of stress made me forget what being relaxed feels like."

"Exercise is good for more than just the body. It's good for mental health, too."

He was right, of course. But it wasn't only the exercise that had me feeling this way. It was the man sitting next to me. And I wanted to show him what he did to me. So I stood on the bench seat and lifted one leg to climb into Christian's lap. Facing forward, I straddled him and wrapped my hands around the back of his neck. "It's more than exercise that's making me feel this way, Christian."

He wrapped his arms around my waist. "Oh yeah?"

I nodded.

Christian's eyes dropped to my mouth, and we both moved at the same time, closing the distance between us. The minute our lips fused, my entire body lit up. Slow lasted all of five seconds. One of Christian's hands slid up to my neck and squeezed, while the other hoisted me closer to him. Neither one of us seemed to be able to get close enough. We'd taken too long and had so much pent-up frustration to let loose. My hands curled into the back of his T-shirt, bunching the material into my fists as Christian used the hand at my neck to tilt my head and deepen the kiss. *Oh God.* We'd definitely waited too long. *Way, way too long.* I wanted to strip the man naked right here in the outdoors and climb him like a freaking tree. Christian groaned, and the sound traveled through our joined lips and straight down between my legs. His body hardened beneath me, and I knew it would only take sliding back and forth a few times for the friction to set me off. And I was considering doing it, until Christian wrenched his mouth from mine.

"No..." I panted. "Don't stop yet."

Christian's breathing was harsh. He leaned his forehead against mine. "Someone's coming."

"What?" I glanced around to find a car pulling over next to the picnic table we were making out on. I hadn't even heard them coming. "Shit..." I went to climb off, but Christian hauled me back. Instead, he turned me and positioned me to sit between his legs.

"You need to stay right here, sweetheart," he whispered. "Or we're about to greet whoever this lady is with an extra arm."

A blond woman parked and got out of the car. She had on a pair of high heels and dangled a purse from her forearm, walking toward us like she was Elle Woods. "Hi. I'm sorry to interrupt. I'm Cat Block, the real estate agent you spoke to."

Christian's head dropped, and he groaned quietly. "Great."

I stood and reached out my hand. "Hi. I'm Bella, and this is Christian."

Christian stood and did the same, but was careful to keep his body positioned behind mine.

She looked over at the bicycles. "Are those yours?"

Christian nodded. "I wanted to see the entire property, including the areas the car can't make it to."

Cat smiled. "Smart. Well, I just thought I'd stop by and see if you have any questions. How do you like the property so far?"

He squeezed my hip. "I like it a lot."

"Great. I'll let you finish your tour and give you a call tomorrow to see what you're thinking."

Christian nodded. "Thank you."

We waved as she pulled away.

"Did she say her name was Cat Block or Cock Block?" Christian groaned.

I laughed. "I didn't even hear her pull up."

I turned around and rested my palms flat on Christian's chest with a sigh. "That was some kiss."

Christian smiled warmly and stroked hair away from my face. "I've wanted to do that since the first time I met you."

"Uhh, the first time you met me, I lectured you about sexually harassing women."

He grinned. "I know. You were so cute and serious. And your glasses were crooked. Sort of like they are now again."

"Are they?" I reached up and righted them, or at least I attempted to. "I fall asleep with them on all the time, and then they get a little bent. I should just wear contacts."

"Nah." Christian leaned in and dropped a sweet kiss on the tip of my nose. "They're like you, a little warped."

We spent another hour riding bikes before we ventured back to Christian's car. As we got on the highway and headed back to the City, Christian entwined our fingers and lifted our joined palms to his lips, dropping a sweet kiss on the top of my hand. "Are you hungry?"

"I'm actually starving."

"Would you want to come back to my place? We can order in? I liked it being only the two of us today, and I'm not ready to share you with people yet."

How could I say no when he asked like that? Plus, I didn't want to share him either, and there was a good chance that would happen based on how often he got recognized when we went places. I looked over and smiled, doing something I never do—answering without any internal debate. "I'd like that."

Chapter 16

Bella

CHRISTIAN'S BUILDING WAS nothing like mine. He lived in a modern high rise with a doorman and lobby that had thirty-foot ceilings. We'd walked in at the same time as a guy about our age wearing a suit. It wasn't lost on me that the staff called him Mr. Waxman, while I noticed Christian was just Christian.

Inside the elevator, Christian inserted a keycard into the panel, and thirty-four illuminated without needing to push any buttons. When we arrived on that floor, Christian put his hand on my back so I'd walk in first. I'd expected to enter a hall, but the foyer we stepped into was actually part of his apartment. And it opened to a jaw-dropping view of Manhattan.

"Oh my God." I laughed nervously. "What must you think of my place if you live here?"

Christian tossed his keys on a round table. "It makes me think a lot of you. I love that coming into a shitload of money didn't change you. Though I do think you need a place with some security at this point."

He led me through the kitchen and into the living room, which had floor-to-ceiling windows. I shook my head, looking out at the City. "This doesn't even look like the place I grew up. It seems so sparkly and clean."

"Most things look better at a distance. You can't see all the tiny cracks and grime."

"The same could be said about a lot of people."

"True." He stepped behind me and bent to kiss my shoulder. "Except you. The closer I get to you, the more I like what I see."

The thump of my heart seemed to grow louder. I tapped my nail to the glass. "Did you know that one in thirty-eight people in the entire United States lives down there? Our little thirteen-by-two-mile-wide City is pretty jam packed."

A smile teased at Christian's lips. I got the feeling he recognized what I was doing—rambling on about some fact because I was nervous—even before I did. He tilted his head toward the kitchen. "Menus are in there. I'll give you a tour after we order. What are you in the mood for?"

"Do you like Thai food? You're only a few blocks from my favorite place. The owner used to have a food truck downtown near the water for years, but last year he opened a small restaurant."

Christian's brows drew together. "Are you talking about Uncle Moon's Thai House?"

I smiled. "I am."

"I freaking love that place. John Barrett actually turned me on to it. When we had a good week, he'd invite a bunch of food trucks to come after practice. That was always my favorite one."

"Really?"

"Yep."

"Wow. That's so funny."

"Guess you and John had a few things in common." Christian's dimples made an appearance. "He did like me, after all."

After we placed our dinner order, Christian poured me a glass of wine and took me on a tour of his apartment. The first stop down the long hall was an office on the right. It looked like a smaller version of my office at the stadium, with similar bound playbooks and team photos on the wall. After that, there were two spare bedrooms across from each other, each with en-suite bathrooms, and a half bath on the left. At the end of the hall, Christian opened the door and held his arm out for me to enter. "My bedroom."

I hadn't thought anything could rival the view from the living room, but apparently I'd been wrong. His bedroom faced west, and the sun was mid-set, casting orange and purple hues across the sky. I walked straight to a double set of French doors that led to a balcony, staring in awe. "I don't think I'd ever leave this room."

"That could be arranged…" Christian was behind me, but I could hear the smile in his voice.

Out on the balcony, I noticed a long stretch of grass and smiled. "There's your happy place. Do you keep a stock of Chipwiches in the freezer at all times?"

"I do."

I spent another minute taking in the view before turning to check out the rest of the room. I'd figured Christian was somewhere nearby, but I found him leaning against the doorway.

"Why are you all the way over there?"

"Admiring the view."

It was clear he wasn't talking about the one I'd been appreciating.

I looked over at his enormous bed. "That's a very big bed you have..."

"I'm a very big man."

I bet you are...

He still hadn't moved from the doorway. I cocked my head. "Doesn't my tour include the master bath? You showed me the other ones."

Christian motioned with his chin. "It's right over there."

I squinted. "You're not going to show it to me?"

"I think it's better if I stay right where I am."

God, he was even sexier when he was coy. Something about the way he leaned casually against the doorway, the sleeves of his shirt pushed up, and followed me with his eyes, was titillating. It was like he had to control the distance he put between us because he wasn't able to control his desire.

"If you say so..." I walked to the bathroom with a little more sway in my hips. But I'd already lost interest in the huge walk-in shower, double-sink counter, and clawfoot tub. I was too distracted by the tingling throughout most of my body. Remembering that kiss from earlier made me want to break the willpower Christian was currently showing. So I walked back through the bedroom, stopping at the foot of the bed. "Is it comfy?"

Christian swallowed. "Try it out for yourself."

Don't mind if I do...

I sat down on the edge and bounced up and down a few times. "Feels nice." I sipped the wine in my hand and patted the spot next to me. "Come sit with me."

He shook his head slowly. "I'm trying to give you what you asked for...slow."

I bit my bottom lip. "Slow sounds good..."

Christian groaned. "You're killing me, Bella."

I leaned over and placed my wine glass on the nightstand, then patted the bed. "Please..."

I watched the internal feud play out on his face before he looked to me for confirmation. When I didn't back down, he blew out a breath, walked to the bed, and sat down next to me. It felt like we were playing chess, and it was my turn.

So I climbed over to his lap and straddled him. "Now isn't this nice?"

"It is. And so was today."

I scooted forward so I was sitting right on his crotch and wiggled my hips a few times as I settled in.

Christian let out a string of curses beneath his breath. "You keep moving like that and this isn't going to end up nice *or* slow."

"Maybe that's what I want..."

He shook his head. "I'm not gonna be your fuck buddy, Bella, if that's what you're trying to do. I want the whole thing, spending the afternoon doing shit together and then taking you home to my bed and stripping you naked."

"Isn't that what we'd be doing?"

"That's what I'm doing." Christian lifted his chin. "But what are you doing? You wanted to take it slow."

I grinded myself back and forth a few times and bent to kiss Christian's neck. "I'm doing this."

But Christian's jaw was still clenched tight. So I moved my mouth to his ear. "Don't you want me?"

"I want you more than I've ever wanted anything." He groaned. "But you asked for slow, and if I start, I'm not going to be able to stop. You need to be good with that."

My answer was bold. I reached down and slipped my hand between our crotches to cup his dick, giving it a good, firm squeeze.

That did the trick. With a roar, Christian fisted the back of my hair and pulled my mouth to meet his. It was miles from gentle and sweet, and exactly what I needed. His free arm wrapped possessively around my waist, bringing me flush against him, while his tongue pilfered my mouth. There was a desperation to the way we clawed at each other, like nothing I'd experienced before. Christian used my hair to yank my head back, then worked his way from my lips down my neck to suck along my collarbone.

"Need this off..." We separated only as long as it took him to yank off my zip-up sweatshirt. He used his thumbs to push down the fabric of the top underneath and drew one of my nipples into his mouth. Christian swirled his tongue and sucked, finishing off with my hardened bud between his teeth and a not-so-gentle tug before moving on to the other breast. "Need to taste you..."

I was about to say "Isn't that what you're doing?" but the words turned into a yelp when I was suddenly in the air. Christian stood with me on his lap, one hand sliding down to cup my ass so I didn't fall, and then he set me back on the edge of the bed and dropped to his knees on the floor in front of me.

Oh God.

He peeled my pants down my legs and frowned when he realized my panties hadn't come with them. "Sorry. I'll buy you new ones."

One flick of the wrist later, I was bare assed on his bed. Christian nudged my knees open and licked his lips. "You're glistening, you're so wet."

He settled between my legs and wasted no time sucking my clit into his mouth. My back arched off the bed. It felt so damn good, and my body had yearned for Christian's touch for so long. It wasn't going to take much for me to fall over the edge.

Christian licked up and down my opening, then buried his face deep in me. His nose pushed against my clit while his tongue thrust in and out of me. But it was the scruff on his cheeks creating friction that made me whimper.

"*Oh God.*" I writhed as he ravaged me. Christian reached up and used one hand to pin me to the mattress. I responded by digging both hands into his hair and yanking hard. But it didn't deter him at all. His tongue, teeth, nose, and face were unstoppable.

And then he pushed a finger inside me.

"*Christian!*"

"Keep calling my name, baby. I've been dreaming about that sound."

The vibration from his words added a new kind of ecstasy, and it all became too much.

Too much.

Yet I wanted so much more.

Oh God.

Oh God.

My orgasm ripped through my body, and I moaned in greeting.

Like barreling over the edge of a rollercoaster.

Free falling.

"That's it, sweetheart, come all over my tongue. You taste so good..."

Just when the wave I was riding was about to crest, Christian crooked his fingers inside me and pumped harder. "Oh my God...yes...yes."

I felt spineless as I came down from the high, panting and unable to feel my legs. I thought I might even fall asleep, at least until I heard a man's voice speak.

"Christian?"

I bolted upright with wide eyes, but Christian only smiled and held a finger to his lips.

"Intercom on. Yeah, George?"

"I have a delivery from Uncle Moon's Thai House. Would you like me to send it up?"

"No thanks. I found something better to eat here. Keep it. It's paid for. Tip, too."

"You sure?"

Christian looked down at my half-naked body. "Positive. Thanks." He paused. "Intercom off."

"That scared the crap out of me," I said. "I thought someone was in the apartment."

Christian reached back and tugged his thermal over his head. "Trust me. I wouldn't let anyone see what I'm getting to see right now." He rose from his knees, but then bent and put two fingers under my chin, tipping my head to meet his eyes. "You good?"

"My heart is still racing a little from hearing an unfamiliar voice, but yeah."

"I meant are you good with what's happening between us."

I smiled goofily. "Oh, yeah. That was amazing."

"Do you want to stop?"

"Oh my God, no. I might cut you from the team if you do."

Christian chuckled. "Good." He reached into the nightstand and pulled out a long strip of condoms, tossing them on the bed.

My eyes widened. "Overconfident much?"

"Not at all, sweetheart." He looked down and wrapped his fingers around an intimidatingly thick bulge in his pants. "I think it's going to take a while to get this to go down. You don't realize what you do to me."

Christian was a handsome man with an incredible body, and clearly the parts I hadn't yet seen were going to live up to the hype of the rest of him. But it was the way he looked at me and the things he said that made my heart thud in my chest. Sex didn't normally scare me, because I knew exactly what it was—two people enjoying a physical connection. But with Christian, there were emotions involved, whether I wanted to admit that to myself or not.

My internal ruminations were interrupted when the hand wrapped around Christian's bulge started to move up and down. *Oh, Jesus.* Here I was wasting time being anxious about the intimacy, when I should have been wary about *that thing.* Christian stroked himself a few more times, then hooked his thumbs into the waistband of his boxer briefs and bent to peel them down his legs. When he stood again, my jaw went slack. It was long. And it was thick. Rigid hard, it bobbed against his equally firm belly, reaching almost to his navel.

I licked my lips, and Christian groaned. "Fuck, Bella. I need to get inside of you now."

He ripped a condom from the strip and grasped it between his teeth to tear it open before sheathing himself. Then he cradled me in his arms a moment before gently placing me in the center of the bed. When he straddled my body and entwined our fingers, lifting them over my head, I felt my belly flutter again. He settled on top and took my mouth in a kiss—at first soft and sweet, but quickly grew hard and desperate. And I loved it. I loved that he was incapable of going slow, because I felt the same way. And I loved that I tasted myself on his tongue.

Christian broke the kiss and pulled back to look into my eyes as he pushed inside of me. I was wet and ready for him, but it had been a while, and his girth would've been a snug fit even if it hadn't. Something that was almost relief washed over me as he filled me, and my eyes fluttered closed.

"Stay with me, sweetheart." Christian's voice was a hoarse whisper. "Be right here in this moment with me."

I opened and held his gaze. But the intensity sparking between us was too much, and tears prickled at the corner of my eyes. "Can you...go faster?"

Christian smiled. "So you can get it over with and turn it into just sex? Not a chance, babe." He stroked my cheek as he glided in and out of me. "I'm crazy about you. I promise I'm going to fuck you hard and fast later, probably with you up on all fours while I hold your head in the pillow. But right now, I want you to feel it." He leaned down and kissed the spot above my heart. "I want you to feel it here."

When his eyes returned to mine, everything else in the room faded, except the current running between us. We stayed that way a long time, our gazes locked while

Christian moved rhythmically in and out. But eventually, he started to lose his control. His arms shook and jaw flexed. Gentle gliding became hard thrusts. And going easy became angling my hips so he could drive deeper into my body. When I moaned, Christian smashed his lips against mine. I wrapped my legs around his waist and scraped my nails along his back. My heart raced to the finish line along with my body.

"Christian..." My second orgasm built faster than the first, and my body began to shudder in anticipation.

"Right here with you. Come around my cock, baby."

That did it. Sweet and dirty, the combination detonated the bomb inside me. My body pulsed as I cried out his name over and over. Christian went into overdrive, quickening his pace and thrusting deep. Finally, with a groan, he buried himself to the hilt and stilled. I could feel his cock jerk inside of me as he released.

Spent, I waited for the moment he would collapse on top of me or roll off. But it never came. Instead, Christian smiled down at me, gliding in and out at a leisurely pace and kissing me until he had to get up to deal with the condom. He came back with a warm facecloth. When I tried to take it, he insisted he be the one to clean me up. That just added to the intimacy we'd shared.

"Thank you," I said.

Christian leaned over me and tossed the facecloth. It flew through the bedroom, slipped through the partially open bathroom door, and landed somewhere inside.

"Well, there's a perk of having a quarterback's arm I'd never thought of."

Christian scooped me up and repositioned me so my head was on his chest. He lay on his back, stroking my damp hair. "Thank you."

I turned to look up at him, resting my chin on my fist, and smiled. "I think I should be thanking you."

He pushed a lock of hair from my face. "I meant for giving me more than just your body. You stuck with me when you wanted to run the other way, so to speak."

I nodded. "It's easier for me to give someone my body than my trust."

"I know. But I promise I'm not the guy you dated in high school, or any of the people you loved who weren't there for you, or even your old man. I'm not going anywhere."

I felt a prickle of unease somewhere deep inside. "For how long?"

Christian's brows dipped. "You mean how long am I sticking around?"

I nodded again.

"I'm not going to break a promise to you and say forever. Because it's too soon for that. But I will promise not to vanish without an explanation. Or leave you wondering what *you* did, when you didn't do anything wrong. We're adults, and we'll communicate if things ever go off track."

I took a deep breath and let it out. "Okay."

"Plus, I'm pretty sure if one of our hearts gets broken in this, it's going to be mine, not yours."

Chapter 17

Christian

"I LOVE WHEN you say my name when you come." I brought the hand towel between Bella's legs for the second time in as many hours and gently wiped her clean.

She rolled onto her side. "Because it's not enough that millions of people wear your name on their back and chant it every Sunday."

I chucked the towel in the direction of the bathroom, and it sailed straight inside. "It's different. When you do it, I feel like it comes from a place that's uncontrolled. That's not a side you show too often. And maybe it gives me a little validation, because my feelings for you are definitely uncontrollable."

A growl came from the vicinity of Bella's stomach. I raised a brow. "Was that you?"

She covered her mouth in a demure laugh. "Well, what do you expect? You gave my dinner to the doorman. Are you going to ever feed me or what?"

I reached for her. "Oh, I'll feed you alright..."

Bella pointed to my bottom half. "That thing... It's a little intimidating to think about...you know."

"No, I don't know. What are you referring to, Bella?"

She squinted at me. "You know exactly what I'm talking about."

I rolled us so she was on her back, gathered her hands in one of mine, and yanked them high above her head. My other hand went to her waist. "Say it. What action is a little intimidating to you? If you don't say it, I'm going to tickle you until you do."

"My God, you're an egomaniac."

I tickled her, and she squirmed beneath me. "Stop... Christian, stop! You're going to make me pee."

"Say it."

"No!"

I tickled her harder.

"Stop!" she cried.

"Say it!"

"Fine," she spat. "It's a little intimidating to think about sucking your cock."

Was it demented that I started to harden just from hearing her say the word *cock*? Maybe, but I didn't give two shits. I traced the outline of her lips with my finger. "Say *suck your cock* again."

She rolled her eyes, but she was smiling ear to ear. "Will you let me up to pee if I do?"

"Yes."

"Fine. I'm never going to *suck your cock* if you keep making me say *suck your cock*." She laughed. "You didn't specify that I couldn't add to my statement, so let me up to pee, you big oaf."

While Bella was in the bathroom, I grabbed my phone and reordered the same food we'd requested hours ago.

Can't have my girl's stomach making noise. When she strutted back in, buck-ass naked, my cock twitched to life, as if it hadn't just been inside her ten minutes ago. I cleared my throat, trying to ignore the urge so I didn't make her sore. "I placed a duplicate order for the food we never got earlier."

"Oh good. I'm starving."

"Me too." I tossed my phone back on the nightstand. "Do you have plans tomorrow?"

She shook her head. "Just some work stuff to catch up on."

"Think you can do that on a plane?"

"On a plane? Where would I be going?"

"To Oklahoma. Tomorrow night my brother is throwing a surprise party for his girlfriend."

"Oh, that's right. He's going to propose at the party, right?"

I nodded. "I'm flying out in the early afternoon."

"His team is playing San Francisco tomorrow at one, right? I'm surprised he's having a party on a game day."

"Lara will be, too. That's why he picked Sunday night. She'd never expect him to plan anything on a game day. According to him, she has no clue the party or the proposal are coming."

Bella smiled. "That's exciting."

"So you'll come?"

She seemed to debate for a moment. "I'm not sure it's a good idea, considering our professional relationship. I know we haven't talked about it, but maybe we should keep our relationship private."

Unlike her, I didn't have to debate shit. I sat up. "No."

Bella's forehead creased. "What do you mean no?"

"I'm not hiding who you are to me. What are we supposed to do, stay inside all the time?"

She flirted a smile. "I can think of worse things."

I got up from the bed and pulled my underwear on, since it's difficult to stand your position with your limp dick out. "We're not just fucking, Bella."

"I know. That's not what this is about." She got up on her knees on the edge of the bed and locked eyes with me. "It's really not. This is about my struggle to get people to treat me professionally within the Bruins organization. It's all still so new, and I don't need gossip to derail whatever progress I've made. People are already talking about us from the *Post* picture."

I looked into her eyes. She was telling the truth. Which, of course, made me give in. "Fine. We'll keep things private...for now. But there's no reason you can't come with me to the party. I can't risk missing practice on Monday morning, so I'm flying private, not commercial, and coming back the same night. And the party isn't that big, just some close friends and family. I'll make sure everyone knows to keep their mouths shut about us."

She still didn't look convinced, but she nodded. "Okay."

I smiled. "That's my girl."

She reached out and ran her fingernail along the outline of my cock through my underwear. "Thank you for being understanding about the rest."

"You might want to keep your hands to yourself, or we'll miss eating again."

Bella sucked that pouty bottom lip into her mouth. "How long do we have until the food comes?"

"The app said thirty minutes."

"Plenty of time to make *you* come before the food does." She leaned forward and took hold of my hips, then pressed her mouth to the head of my cock through my underwear, dropping a sweet kiss.

Oh fuck. I hardened the rest of the way. "Thought you were afraid of doing that."

"I'm feeling brave and want to show you my appreciation for understanding why I want to keep things quiet." She pulled my boxer briefs down to my thighs and looked up from under her lashes. "Will you feed it to me slow?"

Feed it to me.

Fuck me.

A man could be eighty and need Viagra to get a hard-on, but when a woman tells you to *feed her your cock*, we all turn to steel.

I swallowed and nodded, unable to form words.

Bella wrapped her hand around my dick and her pretty pink tongue peeked out, licking the precum off the top of my head. She looked up, showing it to me on her tongue before closing her mouth and her eyes and offering a sated smile.

I immediately envisioned spurting all over that inviting tongue.

Slow.

Fucking slow.

Tell that to my heart, which was already going nuts in my chest.

She opened her eyes again, made sure I was watching, and took me into her hot little mouth. Her fingers wrapped around the base, and she kept sliding down until she reached her hand. Then she pulled back, flattening her tongue along the underside as she made her way to the tip. Bella looked up at me again, her eyes sparkling as she took my hand and placed it on the back of her head. My fingers curled into her hair, and she didn't have to guide me to add the other hand. She went back to work, bobbing up and down, pumping me with her hand as she sucked my cock. But her motions were too slow for the way I was feeling. So I balled a wad of hair in each hand and took over the rhythm, going faster and deeper, until I was fully fucking her face.

Before long, I felt the rush coming. My balls drew tight, my limbs started to tingle, and I quickly realized the point of no return was coming faster than usual. So I forced myself to let go of her head and tried to pull back, but Bella had my hips gripped tightly.

"Babe..." My voice strained. "I'm gonna... You gotta move."

Bella's response was to look up at me again, let me know she'd heard, and suck me in even deeper.

Oh fuck. She's going to let me come down her throat.

My head lolled back, my neck no longer able to support the weight as I lost my last ounce of control. I groaned her name as I bucked one last time and stilled, filling her throat with what seemed like a never-ending stream.

After, I barely had enough strength to open my eyes, and I panted as if I'd just run down the entire field, even though Bella had done all the work.

"Holy shit." I shook my head. "That was..."

Bella wiped her mouth and filled in the blank. "Good?"

"No, babe. Good doesn't come close to what that was. That was running the winning touchdown in with two seconds left in the game—spectacular. Screw the grass and the ice cream. That hot little mouth of yours is my new happy place."

She smiled. "I'm glad. But we should probably keep ten feet away from each other for the next twenty or so minutes. Otherwise we might miss our food again."

I ran my finger along her collarbone. "Not sure that's possible."

She giggled. "I think we need to put on some clothes. Do you have a T-shirt or something I can borrow? I don't want to put back on the clothes I wore all day."

"Sure."

I walked into my closet with the intention of getting her a tee, but then I saw the stack of my jerseys. I pulled one of those out and tossed it to her instead.

"A jersey?" She unfolded it and looked at the back, where my name was emblazoned. "Is this your signature move? Giving the ladies your jersey after? Do they get to take it home as a parting gift?"

I leaned down and kissed the top of her head. "Your grandfather, Coach, always told me it was bad luck to let a girl wear a jersey with your name on the back, unless you were sure she was going to be your wife and take that name."

Bella chuckled. "Athletes and their superstitions. I'm surprised you didn't buy into that one."

I winked as she pulled the jersey on. "Who says I didn't?"

The next day, we went to Bella's apartment before the flight so she could get ready. It was pretty unbelievable that I'd picked her up only twenty-four hours ago to go bike riding. It felt more like a year had passed, at least in terms of our relationship. Maybe that's the way it was when you were friends with a woman before becoming more. I wouldn't know, since that wasn't how it had worked for me in the past. But I liked it. It was like we were already close, so adding the sex part only brought us closer.

Bella opened the door to her bathroom and exited wearing a skimpy robe, her hair wet and slicked back from the shower. She had on a different pair of glasses than normal—tortoise shell, rather than matte black. She looked like a walking wet dream.

"Those new?"

She looked down at her robe. "This?"

I pointed to her face. "The glasses. I like 'em."

"No, they're not new. But my regular ones were extra crooked today. I didn't want to get teased, so I changed them."

I stood. "I *really* want to fuck you with those on."

Bella held out her hand. "Stay right where you are, Knox. You've already only left me forty-five minutes to get ready, and I had to spend fifteen of those scrubbing sticky maple syrup from my body after this morning."

We'd made pancakes together for breakfast, but she looked so damn sexy wearing my jersey in the kitchen that I wound up lifting her onto the island and pouring the syrup all over her so I could lick it off. I smiled and licked my lips. "If there's any left between your legs, I can take care of that for you."

"I think I'm good."

"Shame."

Bella went about getting things out of her drawers in her bedroom. But since her apartment was a studio, her bedroom was also her living room and kitchen. It was just one big area. I sat down on the couch and watched her.

She pulled a pair of shoes from a closet and looked over. "Are you going to watch me get ready?"

I shrugged. "Nothing else to do."

"Well, you're making me nervous. So you need to find something else."

"Okay." I looked around. "Where's your TV?"

"I don't have one."

My face wrinkled. "You don't have a television?"

"I don't watch much, and clearly I don't have much room. So when my last one broke two years ago, I never bothered replacing it."

"So you've watched *no* television for two years?"

"Miller and I watch movies at his place sometimes. And we watched all the Bruins' games there during the two years of the inheritance appeal, before I officially became the owner. Other than that, if there's something I want to see, I watch it on my laptop."

I glanced around again. "So what exactly would you like me to do?"

She pointed. "There are books on the shelf."

I smiled. "Think I'll play with my phone."

A few minutes later, Bella was in the bathroom blow-drying her hair. I got bored with my phone, so I went to check out her books. I wasn't much of a reader, except for playbooks and the occasional biography, but I figured I'd see what she was into. There was a full shelf dedicated to what I thought was computer programming languages, but I couldn't even be sure. Then she had a few shelves of legal thrillers and various other novels. On the bottom was more of the same, except for one book on the end that stuck out. It had a gold-ringed binding, and I thought it might be a photo album, so I slipped it out. Sure enough, it was. The front cover had a small, square cutout window with a picture inside of it. I lifted the book closer to get a good look at the little girl in pigtails and crooked glasses. Yep. That was definitely Bella.

I carried the book over to the bathroom door and knocked.

"Come in!"

I opened the door. "Hey. I found a book I'm interested in after all. You mind if I look through it?"

She spoke to my reflection in the mirror. "Of course not. Go ahead." But my smirk must've tipped her off because then Bella turned around. "Hang on a second. What book is it?"

"Don't know. Doesn't have a title."

She cocked her head. "What book doesn't have a title?"

I grinned. "The kind that has a cute little girl with pigtails on the cover."

"Oh gosh." She chuckled. "I forgot that album was on the shelf."

"Is it alright if I look?"

"Sure. But we won't discuss any photos from the age of ten to twelve. I went through a Hypatia phase."

"A what?"

"Hypatia. She was an astronomer and mathematician. I did a book report on her in fourth grade and made my mom style my hair like hers for a while."

"What was her hair styled like?"

"Oh, you'll see."

I planted myself on the couch again. The first two pages of the album had baby pictures of Bella. She was a tiny little thing with big, green, alert eyes and a smile that seemed perpetually on her face. When I turned the next page, I was momentarily confused. It looked like a recent picture of Bella, but her hair was darker and something about her seemed different. Then I realized Bella was the baby and the woman holding her must've been her mother. *Damn, she really looks like her mom.*

I watched Bella grow up as I flipped the pages. When I got to about age ten, there was a photo of her standing in front of a classroom, holding up a picture of a woman with an old-fashioned hairdo that was back in style with the bohemian crowd today. Her own hair was piled on top of her head in a loose bun, with a gold band placed near the front, sort of like a Greek goddess might wear. The quality of the photo wasn't great, but Bella had the same retro hairdo for the next few pages, so I figured the woman in the picture she'd held was the mathematician she did her book report on. I couldn't help but chuckle as I went through the next two years.

I was having fun until the photos abruptly stopped only halfway through the album. A hollow ache formed in my chest as I realized why. There was no one to take the pictures anymore. No one to pay for them to be printed.

No one to care if Bella even came home at night. I turned back to look at the last picture of a young teenage girl. Bella was probably in early high school. Just like most of the other pictures, she wore a bright smile to match her bright eyes. It made me feel a little sick to think she'd had no idea what was coming.

Since the photos had left me feeling uneasy, I thought seeing pictures of her and her mother might bring Bella down, too. So I got up to put the album back on the shelf before she finished in the bathroom. As I did, a newspaper clipping slipped out. It must've been tucked in the back or folded into one of the blank pages somewhere. I picked it up and read the headline.

Woman, 34, killed by hit-and-run driver outside Bruins Stadium.

And I thought I'd felt like shit because the pictures stopped...

The blow dryer was still running, so I let curiosity get the best of me.

Police in East Rutherford, New Jersey, are looking for a hit-and-run driver who fatally injured a thirty-four-year-old woman. According to Bergen County police, the woman was an employee of the New York Bruins and had been walking east on Tremont Avenue, approximately fifty yards from the west entrance to Bruins Stadium. She was struck by a westbound vehicle and pronounced dead at the scene. The ac-

cident occurred at approximately one o'clock in the morning, after the employee had completed her shift following the Bruins' evening game. According to one witness, the car, which was described as a red, antique, collectible-type vehicle, possibly from the fifties, sped off and got away. Anyone with information is asked to contact the Bergen County Police Department at 201-557-9999.

Wow. Bella had said her mother died, but I hadn't realized it was a hit and run. I'd still been living in Indiana, finishing my senior year at Notre Dame at that time. Guess it hadn't made national news, or I was too wrapped up in myself to pay attention. But damn... Bella didn't even have a face to hold accountable for her loss. That had to make it worse. The sound of the blow dryer stopped, so I tucked the newspaper article back into the album and returned it to the shelf before going back to the couch.

Bella came out wrapped in a towel a few minutes later. She looked around. "I thought you were going to look at my old photo album?"

"Started playing a game on my phone and got sucked in," I lied.

"Well, that saves me some embarrassment." She picked up a jar of moisturizer on her nightstand and headed back to the bathroom. "I need about fifteen minutes to do my makeup and get dressed."

"Sounds good."

Twenty minutes later, Bella emerged in an emerald green slip-type dress that draped a bit at her cleavage and a pair of silver strappy sandals. It was simple, but damn, she looked phenomenal.

"What type of a place is the party at?" She looked down at her outfit. "I'm not sure what to wear. Am I over-dressed?"

"You look gorgeous." I stood. "But does that wrinkle easily?"

"I'm not sure. I've never worn it before. Should I change?"

"Nah. We'll just take it off."

"Take it off?"

"When I try to fuck you in the car, and the plane, and probably the bathroom of the restaurant where the party is. You can't look like that and expect me to keep my hands off of you for too long."

She smiled. "I guess you like the dress?"

"I like the woman in it in anything. But you look amazing. Are you leaving the glasses on?"

"I was going to. You said you liked them."

"I do." I looked her up and down and shook my head. "You are most definitely getting fucked before we get there…"

Chapter 18

Bella

"THERE'S MY MOM and my brother Tyler." Christian started walking, but I didn't. We'd arrived at the restaurant twenty minutes ago, though it had taken us that long to get inside since everyone had swarmed Christian to say hello. When he felt the resistance at our joined hands, he turned back. "What's the matter?"

"Your mom is here?"

His forehead wrinkled. "Yeah. Why?"

"I...I guess I just didn't think about your parents being here."

"It's only my mother. My father wouldn't come to a thing like this."

"But your mother is here."

"Is it a problem?"

"No, except that I'm going to *meet your mother*."

Christian's lip twitched. "Yeah, that's usually how it works. Two people are in the same room, sometimes they meet."

"That's not funny, Christian."

"Considering that most of the color seems to be gone

from your face, I take it meeting my mother makes you nervous?"

"I've never met anyone's mother, Christian."

"Like ever? You've only ever met young people?"

I narrowed my eyes. "You know what I mean."

Christian stepped back toward me and rubbed my shoulders. "Alright, talk to me. What makes you nervous about meeting her?"

I shook my head. "I don't know. Everything?"

"Do you think you could be a little more specific?"

"Well, what if she doesn't like me?"

"Stop overthinking it. She's going to love you."

"How do you know that?"

"Because I like you. And my mother wants me to be happy. Plus, I've never introduced her to a woman I was dating before, so she's going to be excited to meet you."

My eyes bulged. "Do you think you're making me feel better by telling me you've never introduced anyone to her before? That's even *more* pressure. What if she says hello, and I dive into a diatribe about the advances in cryptography algorithms?"

"Why would you do that?"

"Because you know how I get when I'm nervous."

Christian grinned. "Yeah, I do. You're adorable."

"Christian..." I glanced over his shoulder and saw his mom walking toward us with a big smile. "Oh my God. She's coming..."

Christian turned, and his mother held her arms out. "There you are!" She hugged her son for a long time, then looked at me. "You must be Bella?"

I glanced at Christian, and he read the confusion on my face. "I texted her while you were getting ready to let her know I was bringing someone."

I gave him a sugary smile that did not match the evil eye I also gave him. "Oh. I'm glad she knew." I held my hand out to his mom. "It's very nice to meet you, Mrs. Knox."

She opened her arms and brought me in for a hug. "It's Priscilla, please. I'm so excited you're here. Christian usually keeps his personal life so quiet. Do you do that? I feel like girls probably share more with their moms."

Since I probably looked like a deer in the headlights, Christian intervened. He put his arm around his mother's shoulder and lifted his chin to the man standing next to her. "Before Mom smothers Bella, let me introduce her to Officer Knox."

Christian's brother had a warm smile as he extended his hand. "Tyler. Nice to meet you, Bella."

"So, Mom, what's the deal with the proposal? Is it going to be before dinner or after?"

She shook her head. "I'm not sure. Why?"

Christian looked at his watch. "Because it's almost six now here, but it's already almost eight back in New York, and I have practice in the morning."

His mother frowned. "Can't you skip that just once?"

He looked over at me. "I would, but the new owner's a tyrant."

Priscilla's frown deepened, but then she caught the joke. "Oh." She laughed. "I forgot you said Bella was the new owner. But doesn't that mean she can give you permission to stay a little longer and miss one practice?"

"That's more of the coach's decision, Mom. But I need to be at practice. I've missed too much being out with my knee already."

A woman in a white shirt, black slacks, and a black vest walked over. "Mrs. Knox, a guest has arrived who is on the guest list, but we can't find a seating card for him. Would you help us figure out where we should put him?"

"Of course." She turned to us. "Duty calls. I'll be back. Your brother is running a little late. He should be here in about fifteen minutes. Tyler, come help me with the seating chart, please?"

"Sure, Mom."

I let out a sigh of relief as they walked away.

Christian lifted a brow. "Was she that bad?"

"No, not at all. She was very sweet. I'm just...nervous."

Christian took my hand. "Come on, let's go get some air before Jake gets here, or someone else cramps us, and you wind up high-tailing it out of here."

We walked down a hall at the back of the restaurant, and Christian opened the door at the end. He slipped something out of his pocket and stuck it between the lock and the doorjamb to keep it from closing, and suddenly we were in a small, covered courtyard.

"Is that the card you brought your brother stuck in the door?" I asked.

"Yep."

"It's getting all wrinkled. Why don't we find a rock or something?"

Christian waved me off. "He won't give two shits if it's wrinkly with a little lock grease. At least not after he sees the gift I got him. Knowing what a wuss he is, he'll probably cry."

Christian hadn't brought a present or anything with him from the plane that I'd noticed. "What did you get him?"

"A dollar."

I chuckled. "A dollar is going to make your brother cry?"

"It's a special dollar."

"What makes it so special?"

"It's our victory dollar. When we were eleven or twelve, we were number one and two on the middle school track team. Any given week, we'd beat each other's records. We're super competitive and physically pretty similar, so the number-one spot flip-flopped a lot, based on heart. One day, when we finished track practice, we both saw a buck on the grass at the same time. We dove for it and wound up ripping it in half."

I smiled. "I could see you two doing that today..."

"Oh, no doubt." Christian shook his head. "Anyway, we fought over who should give who the other half of the dollar for a few days, until I came up with the brilliant idea to race for it. The victor gets the loser's other half. I won, and he had to sit at the table and watch me tape the two pieces back together that night. But I never spent it. We both played volleyball in the spring, and Jake won team MVP at the end of the season, so I gave him the dollar back. It's been going on twenty years, and that buck has been passed a few times. Neither one of us is very good at complimenting the other, so giving the buck is our way of saying, *I'm proud of you. You done good.* But until now we've only ever given it to each other for sporting events."

"Awww...that's so sweet."

Christian tried to play it down. "Eh. I'm just cheap."

I put my arms around his neck. "You are not, Christian Knox. You might be a man of steel on the outside, but you're a big mush on the inside."

He rubbed my arms. "Lara's a great girl. Definitely out of that numbskull's league."

"Mush," I teased.

"I'll show you mush..." Christian pressed his lips to mine in a hot and hard kiss. His hand cupped my cheek as he deepened it, and by the time he pulled back, my *brain* was mush.

He looked back and forth between my eyes. "You want to get married and have kids someday, boss lady?"

My heart did a somersault. "I honestly never gave it much thought. My relationships don't usually last long enough to start daydreaming about dresses and what we'd name our kids."

"Not sure the length of the relationship is what makes you think about a future with someone. Seems it's more about when it feels right."

His words and the look on his face hit me hard, and when I swallowed, I tasted salt.

After a moment, Christian smiled. "I want a tribe of them—kids, I mean." He winked. "Since you asked."

"How many are in a tribe?"

He shrugged. "Maybe six or eight?"

My eyes bulged. "You want to have *six or eight kids*?"

He grinned. "Nah. Two or three should do it. But now that doesn't seem so scary, does it? You see? I'm learning how to manage you."

I play-smacked his abs. "You're a jerk."

Christian laughed. "Come on. We'd better get back inside so we don't miss when they get here."

Jake Knox's hands shook as he got down on one knee. There was something so endearing about seeing such a big, tough guy nervous. Toward the end of dinner, he'd called Lara up to the front of the room to make a toast to the birthday girl. She was clearly shocked when the moment became something more. But she jumped into his arms while he was still down on one knee and knocked the large man over. The ring went flying, and he had to scramble to find it. Everyone hooted and hollered and laughed, and I looked over to find Christian's eyes watery.

"You're crying!" I said.

He swiped at his eyes. "No, I'm not. Too much fresh pepper on my pasta."

I chuckled. "Sure."

He put his arm around my shoulder and squeezed. "He did good."

Not too long after that, we had to head back to the airport. Local time was only nine, so the real party was just getting started when we left, but it was eleven in New York, and we still had to fly home and be at work in the morning. At least if I was dragging, I wouldn't be getting tackled by a three-hundred-pound lineman.

The small private plane Christian had chartered had wide, lie-flat seats. We sat facing each other as we took off, but once we were in the air, Christian reclined his seat and crooked his finger at me. "C'mere."

"Where?"

He tapped his chest. "Lie on top of me."

I pointed. "I am not having sex with you on that chair. Or anywhere on this plane, for that matter."

He smiled. "I just want to hold you."

The man was irresistible when he showed a vulnerable side. So I unbuckled and snuggled on top of him.

Christian stroked my hair. "Thank you for coming with me."

"I had a good time. And I still can't get over how much you and your brother look alike. It was sort of weird watching the man I'm sleeping with get down on one knee to propose to another woman."

Christian's hand on my head stopped moving. "Think we can use boyfriend?"

My nose wrinkled. "What do you mean?"

"Instead of *guy you're sleeping with.*"

"Oh."

He caught my gaze. "In case it's not clear, that's what I'd like to be...your boyfriend."

"What does that mean to you?"

"It means we spend time together on a regular basis. Maybe stay at each other's places sometimes. We're honest with each other and take care of each other's needs. It also means we don't sleep with other people. Or date anyone else." Christian paused to make sure he had my full attention. "Especially Julian."

I shook my head. "I haven't thought about Julian since you showed up and crashed our date."

"I'm afraid to ask too much and scare you off. But I need to be realistic, too. I'd lose my mind if you were dating someone else at the same time. And it's not because I'm a possessive guy. I've been in casual relationships where there was no commitment. But I feel possessive when it comes to you. So can you handle that?"

I thought about it before nodding. "I wouldn't want you with anyone else, either."

Christian kissed my forehead. "Good, so it's settled."

I didn't actually feel *settled* about any of this. But I hoped that would come with time.

"You know what my mom said while you were talking to Jake, and I said goodbye to her?"

"What?"

"She said it was the first time she could remember me using *we* so much."

"I don't understand..."

"She'd asked if I was going to come visit her in Florida in the offseason this year. I said, 'Yeah, *we'll* figure something out.' She also asked why I needed to leave so soon, and my response was, '*We* have an early morning.' I guess I've been an *I* guy for so long, she noticed when I started using *we*. The fucked-up thing is, I didn't give it any thought. It came out that way because I see you in my future."

I'd been afraid to believe in a future with anyone, because people in my life hadn't exactly been reliable, but I wanted to believe it was possible with Christian. I smiled. "You should get some sleep."

"You, too."

"Yeah, I should. You know how some people only re-quire four hours of sleep and they're chipper? I'm not one of them." I started to climb off Christian, but he held me in place.

"Where are you going?"

"I need to tie my hair up before I go to sleep."

He released me from his grip, and I found a tie in my purse. Christian watched as I pulled my hair back and bundled it into a high pony. Then I snuggled back into the chair bed with him, and he covered us with a blanket.

"You should do pigtails." He smiled. "Like you did when you were in elementary school. And maybe a school uniform..."

I lifted my head to look at his face. "I thought you didn't look at my photo album?"

Christian closed his eyes. "Sorry. I lied. I did look at it."

"Why would you lie about that?"

He shook his head. "I don't know. It was dumb. But it just ended so abruptly when you were a teenager, and it made me sad. I thought it might make you feel down if you came out and I was flipping through the pages."

"That does kind of make me sad when I look through it."

"Full disclosure? I read the newspaper article, too. It slipped out when I was putting the album away."

I shook my head. "I'm not even sure why I keep that."

"I didn't realize it was a hit and run. Did they ever catch the driver?"

"Unfortunately, no. The investigation was active for a year, but they never were able to figure it out. The accident

218

was near one of the stadium entrances, which has a camera to record all the cars coming in and out, but it wasn't working at the time."

"What about witnesses? The article said there was at least one."

"There were two. They both said it was some sort of a classic car. But when the police showed them pictures, their memories were very different. One picked out a blue Ford Thunderbird from the fifties, and one picked out a red Jaguar. I remember the detective in charge said eyewitnesses who see a traumatic event actually make the worst witnesses. The police found a broken headlight at the scene. Based on the material it was made of, the only thing they knew for sure was that the car had been made before nineteen fifty-seven."

Christian's brows dipped. "A blue Thunderbird from the fifties was one of the cars they described?"

"Yeah, why?"

He was quiet for a minute. "No reason."

I settled my head over Christian's chest. "I'm really tired."

Christian kissed the top of my head and tightened his arms around me. "Get some sleep."

Chapter 19

Bella

"GO, GO, GO, go, go!"

Talia looked over at me and smiled. "You get really into the game."

Miller was seated on the other side of me, in the outdoor seating section of the owner's box at Bruins Stadium. He leaned forward. "She's banging the quarterback."

Talia's eyes widened. "Really? You decided to go out with him?"

I nodded. "Christian and I started seeing each other recently. I was going to mention it to you today, but this is the first time we haven't had twenty teenagers around. And then of course..." I thumbed to Miller. "This one couldn't wait to spill the beans."

Miller leaned over me toward Talia. "I can't get her to tell me how big it is. But I have a Pinterest board with lots of shirtless pictures, if you want."

Talia chuckled. She knew Miller well.

Today was the first game Christian was back on the field, and I was also hosting Wyatt's birthday party. Thankfully, the suite hostess and Miller and Talia were doing most of the work, so I was able to focus on the game.

"So are you just fooling around?" Talia asked. "Or is it more?"

Again Miller leaned forward. "She wanted to just fuck him, but he wouldn't accept that. Now he's her boyfriend. Can you believe our baby has a boyfriend? I'm calling it right now. *I'm* the maid of honor." He pointed to Talia. "You're merely a bridesmaid."

I shook my head. "I think you're getting a little ahead of yourself."

"Uh, no, I'm not. You should see the way he looks at her. He was up here earlier, a few hours before the game. Princess here doesn't want people to know, so he doesn't touch her in public. But he looks at her like he wants to eat her alive. Speaking of which..." He turned to me. "Will you tell me if he at least does that well?"

I ignored him and opened my three-ring binder to mark down that we hadn't converted on third down.

Miller stood. "Change places with me. You and that stupid notebook are in the way of gossip."

I narrowed my eyes, but switched seats with him—so I could pay attention to the game and jot down the stats I wanted to record, not to facilitate Miller's incessant need to talk about my relationship. During a commercial break, he went to the bathroom, and I noticed Talia holding her right side.

"Are you okay? You're holding your side. I saw you do that earlier."

"Yeah, I'm fine," she said. "Probably a little gastro inflammation. Wyatt had me take him out for birthday breakfast tacos this morning. The ranchero sauce always kills me."

I put my arm around my friend. "I've missed you. I feel like I haven't seen you in forever."

"I'm not sure how you can miss me, if you're getting cozy with Christian Knox." She leaned her head on my shoulder. "But I've missed you, too."

"What's new with you?" I asked.

"Same old—oh! But I almost forgot to tell you. Wyatt got two more invitations from coaches to visit schools— Michigan State and Ohio. When I told the coach from MSU that I wasn't sure when I could bring him out, he offered to have an alum do it—some kicker who also played in the NFL for a while. I forgot his name."

"That's awesome!"

"It is. And it's all because of you bringing the media to Wyatt's game."

"I can't take credit for that. It was Christian they followed."

"Well, hopefully I'll get a chance to thank him in person. I'd like to meet the guy who got you to become a full-fledged girlfriend."

I smiled. "You will. He said he's going to come up when he can after the game to hang out with Wyatt and his teammates."

"Oh my God. They're going to flip out."

My cell phone buzzed from my pocket. When I pulled it out, Julian's name flashed on the screen. He'd left me two messages this week, and I hadn't called him back yet.

Talia noticed who was calling. "I was going to ask you about him. Is that over? You liked him, right?"

"I do think we're very compatible. I mean, polynomial algorithms don't lie. We have similar likes, interests, temperament, relationship and life experiences, values, and beliefs—Julian and I would be a ninety-nine percent match on Hinge, and Christian and I would probably be at opposite ends of the spectrum. Julian and I make sense. Christian and I don't."

"Love doesn't always make sense, Bella. It can be irrational."

"Irrational gives me hives."

Talia laughed. "I know. Do you remember when I was dating that guy Rory?"

"Of course. You were together for almost a year."

"I wanted to love him in the worst way. He loved and accepted my son, and he was so good to me. I even sat down one night and wrote out a list of reasons I loved him. When I was done, I realized everything I'd written was reasons I *liked* him. Love isn't something easily put in words. It's a feeling, more abstract than concrete, and often you wind up loving someone who not only didn't check the boxes on your ideal-partner checklist, but someone who added boxes to your checklist you didn't even know you wanted."

I nodded. "Like feeling safe. I never in a million years would have added that box to a checklist of things I wanted from a partner. I've been on my own since I was fifteen and take pride in being independent. But when Christian wraps his arms around me, that makes me feel safe, and it's more than just physically. I feel like I can trust him to protect me in ways I didn't know I needed protecting."

Talia hugged me. "I'm so happy you found someone."

Miller came back from the bathroom with a bottle of wine and three glasses. He held them up. "I could get used to this life. The hostess brought these over for us."

I smiled. "You two enjoy. It's almost halftime, so I'm going to run down to visit my grandfather before everyone gets out of their seat for beer and bathroom trips."

"Why isn't he up here?" Talia asked. "Did he think twenty teenagers would be too much to deal with while trying to watch the game?"

I shook my head. "He loves his seat behind the home team bench. It makes him feel like he's part of the action."

"Alright. Well, go do your thing," Miller said. "But no promises there will be anything left in this bottle when you get back."

"That's okay. The hostess noticed you brought Mike's Hard Lemonade last time you were here, so she stocked the fridge with some."

I went down and sat with my grandfather until the start of the third quarter. I would have stayed longer, but today a woman from the community he lived in was with him. I felt like maybe I was crashing a date, though he'd never say so.

After the game was over, we had birthday cake for Wyatt, and Talia let him dig into all of the presents the kids had brought. A little while later, Christian walked in and the boys swarmed him. He stood just inside the door, surrounded by teenagers shooting questions at him and congratulating him on the win. It wasn't until he told the boys he needed to grab some water that I even got to speak to him.

I introduced him to Talia, and Miller said hello while I got him a water bottle.

"I think I have a little something in my eye," Christian said when I returned. He motioned toward the bathroom.

"It's probably a piece of turf. That happens a lot. Would you mind taking a look to see if you see it? The lighting is better in there."

"Oh sure."

Christian and I went into the bathroom. He closed the door behind us, and suddenly he swung me around, pinning my back against it. The gasp of surprise I let out got swallowed in a kiss, an epic one—the kind that made your brain shut down and your legs wrap around a waist. It even made me forget that twenty kids were right on the other side of the wall.

Then Christian groaned. And I felt that groan go from our joined lips to shoot down my body and spark between my legs. By the time we came up for air, I was so needy, I probably would have let him have me up against that wall. But thankfully, one of us hadn't lost all sense of shame.

Christian leaned his forehead against mine. "Hi."

I smiled. "I like the way you say hello."

He used his thumb to wipe under my bottom lip. "You should see the way I'm going to say *I missed you the last few days* later."

"Is that so?"

Christian's eyes glittered. "Come home with me. We can order in and celebrate the win together."

I'd completely forgotten about the game. "You were amazing today. Congratulations on winning your first game back."

"Thank you. You and your friends plan on taking all those kids home the same way you got 'em here? On the trains?"

I nodded. "We told their parents we'd get them safely back to Wyatt's neighborhood. They'll all walk or take the subway from there."

"How about if I drive you? I told the PT guys I was going to use the team van to take Coach home again. But Coach said his lady friend drove. By the way, who is she?"

"She lives in his community."

"Was today a...date?"

I shrugged. "I don't know. I was wondering the same thing. When I go visit him this week, I'll sniff around."

Christian nodded. "So what do you say about me driving the kids?"

"I think they would love it. But will it hold all of them?"

"There are six rows of bench seats on two sides. Players sit one to a bench, but they can fit two, so it'll hold twenty-four, plus the driver and front passenger."

"Oh, that would work. There are twenty boys and Talia. Could we give Miller a ride too?"

"Of course. Will you come home with me after?"

"Is it a condition of driving the kids?"

Christian's face fell. "No."

I smiled. "Then yes."

"Such a pain in my ass..." he grumbled. "Now give me that mouth again before I let you go back out there."

Christian kissed the crap out of me a second time. When it broke, he gently set me back down on my feet and smoothed my hair. "You better go out first. I need a minute." He looked down.

My eyes followed. "Oh boy. It looks like you need about an hour."

He kissed my forehead. "I'll be out in a few."

Talia's eyes lit up when I walked out. She hooked arms with me and whispered, "I know what you were doing in there. It's all over your face."

I touched my cheek. "Oh my God, really? It's noticeable?"

She smiled. "You're flushed, and your eyes have that glazed-over look."

"All we did was kiss, I swear."

"Must've been some kiss..."

My eyes lost focus even remembering it. "He's such a good kisser."

Talia bumped shoulders with me. "Okay, I said I was happy for you, but now you're just making me jealous."

An hour later, we loaded the boys into the van. They got to go into the underground parking lot beneath the stadium where the PT van was parked, which they were really excited about. When we arrived at Talia's building, the kids unloaded and took turns shaking hands with Christian while I said goodbye to Talia.

"Thank you again for everything. This was the best birthday he's ever had." Talia winced, and she grabbed her right side again.

"Are you okay? That pain is back?"

"Yeah. I just ate and drank too much."

After maybe twenty seconds, her face went back to normal, and she seemed fine again. But I didn't like that it had happened more than once today. "If it keeps happening, do you promise to call me? Or go to the ER and then call me?"

She lifted her purse to her shoulder and waved me off. "Yes, Mom."

I shook my head and kissed her cheek. "I'm calling you tomorrow to see how you're feeling."

"Thank you so much." We looked over at Wyatt, who was now talking to Christian. "He seems really great. Don't run from this one. Give it a chance. Something about the way you two look at each other makes me think he could be the one."

I watched as Christian and Wyatt did some handshake slap thing, then looked back at Talia. "I think you might be right. He might be the one. It just remains to be seen if he's *the one* for me, or *the one* who will break my heart."

Chapter 20

Christian

"IT'S YOURS." I leaned over, unplugged the vibrating cell, and passed it to Bella. She'd been sound asleep, but when I said it was Talia, she bolted upright.

"Talia would never call at three in the morning if something wasn't wrong." She quickly swiped to answer. "Hello?"

I listened to one side of the conversation.

"Oh no." She pulled the covers off. "Where are you?"

Quiet.

"Is Wyatt with you?"

Quiet again.

"Okay. I'll be there as soon as I can."

Bella hung up and rushed out of bed.

"What's going on?" I stood and started pulling on my underwear before knowing why I was getting dressed.

"Talia's appendix burst. She needs to have emergency surgery." Bella scrambled around the room, looking for the clothes I'd stripped off of her hours ago.

I picked up her bra and held it out. "Where is she?"

"Lennox Hill with Wyatt."

I grabbed my cell. "I'll call an Uber. It'll be faster than going to the garage and getting the truck out."

"Thanks."

A half hour later, we found Wyatt waiting in the emergency room. His head was in his hands as he sat in an orange plastic chair. Bella rushed over. I stood behind her with my hand on her shoulder.

"Wyatt? What's going on? Where's your mom?" she asked.

Wyatt stood and hugged her. "They just took her up to surgery. They said she has a blood infection." He pulled back and raked a hand through his hair. "It's my fault. She's had pain the last four days, ever since my party. I should've made her go to the hospital."

Bella shook her head. "It's not your fault. It's mine. I was supposed to call her Monday to check in, and I got sidetracked and never did. I'm so sorry."

I squeezed Bella's shoulder. "It's neither of your faults. Did they say how long the surgery would take?"

"They said it's usually only an hour or two."

I nodded. "Alright, good. Is this where we're supposed to wait? Usually there's a special waiting room near the surgery area."

"They said I should go up to the fourth floor. But I told Bella we were in the ER, so I figured I'd wait here for her."

"Okay," I said. "Let me ask the security guard how we get up to where we need to go."

Luckily, the guard didn't recognize me, and the three of us were able to go straight upstairs to a quieter waiting area. We spoke to the nurse at the desk and told her we were waiting for Talia Kane, and she said she'd check on how things were going in about a half hour and come let us know.

Wyatt sat back in his chair and spread his long legs wide. "Did you know you get me if something happens to her?"

"Nothing is going to happen to her," Bella said. "But yes, I did know that. Your mother and I talked about it years ago."

"What's a medical proxy? Mom also told the nurse you had one of those."

"A medical proxy is a legal document where you name someone to make medical decisions for you, in the event that you're unable to make them yourself."

"Mom's not going to be able to make decisions after this?"

Bella shook her head. "No, honey. I'm sure she will. She filled out that form years ago, at the same time she made me your legal guardian in the event of any emergency. These are just things adults do as a way of planning for the worst-case scenario. But that's not what this is. An appendectomy is a very routine procedure."

"Do you have a healthcare proxy?"

Bella frowned. "I actually don't. But I should."

Wyatt looked to me. "What about you?"

"I do."

"Who makes your decisions?"

"My brother Jake." My eyes met Bella's, silently acknowledging how nervous Wyatt was.

She walked over and sat next to him. "She's really going to be fine. Have I ever lied to you?"

231

Wyatt shook his head. "No. Except for that time in sixth grade when you told me the Crocs mom bought me with my back-to-school clothes were cool. I got made fun of the minute I walked into the building."

Bella mussed his hair. "That's not a lie, kiddo. That's my taste. I have two pairs of Crocs myself. Perhaps next time you want style advice, you shouldn't come to a computer geek."

Twenty-five minutes later, the nurse from the ward desk poked her head into the waiting room. "I spoke to the nurse in the OR. Everything is going great, and they should be done in about forty minutes."

Wyatt let out an audible exhale.

"Thanks so much for letting us know," Bella said.

She smiled. "I'll let you know when she's in recovery. It's usually another hour before she'll be moved to a room after that."

After the nurse left, I took Wyatt down the hall to raid the snack machine. We wound up spending eighteen bucks on chips and chocolate, and the kid downed three quarters of that on his own. Then he fell asleep across three chairs until we woke him to say his mom was done, and he could go see her soon.

Wyatt rubbed his eyes. "I'm going to find a bathroom."

"Okay, honey," Bella said.

Once he was out of the room, she turned to me. "You should go. It's almost five already. You have practice in a few hours."

"I'm good. I'll either go a little tired, or I'll text Coach Brown and tell him I'm going to miss today."

"Won't you get fined?"

"It's the coach's call whether to excuse an absence or fine a player. If he fines me, he fines me."

"I don't want you to get fined."

I shrugged. "I don't miss often, so I think he'll let it slide. But if he does, he does. It's just money. I want to be here for you."

Bella's face softened. I leaned over and kissed her forehead.

When it was time to go in and see Talia, the nurse told us only two could go in at a time. I told Bella and Wyatt to go ahead, but then the doctor came out and recognized me, and suddenly they could bend the rules. So the three of us went in together.

Talia was groggy, but she smiled, and Wyatt dropped the cool cloak all teenagers seemed to wear and ran to her bedside and hugged her. The three of them talked until the doctor came over and asked if it was okay to discuss Talia's condition with all of us present. Talia looked at her son, who immediately shook his head.

"I'm not leaving."

Talia smiled at the doctor. "I forget my son is almost a man these days. It's fine to discuss things with everyone here."

The doctor told us the surgery had gone smoothly, but that Talia had a blood infection, left behind by her sick appendix, which needed to be treated. Normally a patient stayed in the hospital only a day or two after an appendectomy, but he thought we should plan on two to four days because they wanted to be sure they got rid of the infection.

Bella assured her friend that she had nothing to worry about, and she would take care of Wyatt. I promised to pitch in and help out. Then a nurse came over to take Talia's vitals and suggested we wrap up our visit because she needed her rest.

So we said goodbye and left with Wyatt. Talia didn't live far from the hospital, so we walked the couple of blocks to their apartment.

"You didn't get much sleep last night," Bella told him. "Why don't you take the day off from school?"

Wyatt shook his head. "I can't miss. I'm going to jump in the shower right now so I won't be late." He disappeared into the bathroom.

"My, how things have changed," Bella said. "I remember when he hated school and used to pretend to be sick all the time to avoid going. Now he doesn't even want to be late."

I smirked. "If you miss school, you can't go to practice. And if you're late and get detention, you can't go to practice."

"Oh." She laughed. "I should've known better."

I looked around the apartment, which was similar in layout to Bella's. "Is there another room?"

She shook her head. "No. Wyatt used to sleep with Talia. But now she sleeps on that couch. The apartment is rent controlled, so it's a great deal and allows her to pay his tuition at the private school."

"Are you going to stay here while you're keeping an eye on him?"

"I hadn't given the logistics any thought. I could stay on the couch, but that might make Wyatt feel weird to be in the same room with a woman who isn't his mom, and my apartment is no better." She paused. "Maybe I'll take him to a hotel. I'm sure there's a fancy one with two bedrooms somewhere not too far from here."

"Why don't you guys stay at my place? I have three bedrooms, and I'm leaving tomorrow to go to California for Sunday's game."

"Oh gosh. I didn't even think about the game this weekend being away. I'll either have to watch it on TV, or I suppose I could bring Wyatt after his game on Saturday. But I don't want to impose on you. We'll just stay at a hotel. Thank you for the offer, though."

"It's not imposing at all, Bella." I put my hands on my hips. "It's what couples do—they help each other out, rely on each other."

She didn't look sold. So when Wyatt walked out of the bathroom, I figured I'd go at it another way. "Hey, kid?"

"Yeah?"

"Would you rather stay at a hotel for the next couple days or at my place? I have three bedrooms, an eighty-inch TV, and the Eastern Conference MVP trophy you can take selfies with."

Wyatt's face lit up. "Your place."

I put my hands in my pockets and smiled at Bella. "Sounds like Wyatt prefers to stay at my apartment."

She gave me the evil eye.

I lifted my chin to Wyatt. "Pack a few days of clothes. What time does practice end tonight?"

"Usually by five."

"Mine is over by four. I'll pick you up and take you to see your mom before going over to my place after."

"Awesome." Wyatt smiled, grabbed some clothes, and went back into the bathroom.

Bella was still staring at me. "Umm... I'm perfectly capable of picking him up from practice and taking him to visit Talia."

I put my hands on her shoulders. "Of course you are. There's probably not much you aren't capable of handling by yourself. But you're not by yourself anymore. You have me. Plus, you don't get out of the office before six or seven usually. So do what you need to do, and I got this. Besides, you'll be on your own tomorrow when I have to fly out."

It looked like she was considering arguing, so I dipped my head and kissed her until the fight was gone from her face.

"We good?" I stroked her cheek with my thumb.

She nodded and sighed. "Thank you for having us."

"No thanks needed. But I do *have you*, Bella. You just need to accept it."

———

Later that night, Wyatt and I rolled into my place after his practice and our stop by the hospital. I'd told Bella the doorman would give her a keycard to let her in if she arrived first.

I found her standing in the kitchen at the stove, and the apartment smelled freaking delicious.

"Dinner is almost ready. I thought you guys were going to be home an hour ago," Bella said.

Wyatt answered. "We would've been, but Christian got mobbed by a bunch of women nurses."

Bella's eyes narrowed. "Is that so?"

"Uh-oh." Wyatt looked at me. "I got you in trouble. Sorry, man."

I chuckled. "I'm not in trouble. Bella knows I was just being polite. Why don't you go wash up for dinner? Your room is the first one on the left."

Wyatt tossed his bookbag and wallet on the counter and took off running down the hall. Bella was back to stirring something in a pot on the stove. I wrapped my arms around her waist, pushed her hair aside, and kissed her neck. "It smells good in here. I could get used to this—coming home to you making me dinner."

"Or you could have one of the nurses make you something..."

I turned her in my arms to face me. "Is that *jealousy* I hear in your tone?"

"No, but you could've called to let me know you guys were going to be late."

I nodded. "You're right. I should've. I lost track of time. I apologize. Now give me a kiss."

She was still talking when I sealed my lips over hers. I loved that I could feel her melt into me after only a few seconds. After a minute of getting my fill, I let her go before I started mauling her and the kid came back.

Bella cleared her throat. "I was thinking, I should sleep in the other guest room tonight."

My eyes narrowed. "What are you talking about?"

"Well, Wyatt's here, and, you know, we just started dating. I don't want to give him the impression that you should jump into bed with someone so fast. I don't think he's even had a girlfriend yet. He's impressionable."

I'd seen the girls on the bleachers waving at him with googly eyes when we were leaving practice, not to mention, a few of the young nurses had been friendly to him, and he'd been chatting them up.

"He's seventeen, Bella."

"So? He's a young and innocent seventeen."

"The boy is getting laid, sweetheart."

Her eyes widened. "He is not."

Wyatt's wallet was on the counter, so I lifted it and spread the leather on one side tight. I'd been guessing, but sure enough, there was the familiar ring from a condom inside. "Hate to break it to you," I said, holding it up. "But he's not innocent. You're sleeping in my bed."

Wyatt came back down the hall, so Bella stepped back, and our conversation was momentarily tabled.

"Dinner is going to be ready soon," she said. "Why don't you two set the table?"

A few minutes later, we sat down to eat Bella's fettuccine alfredo with chicken.

"How long did it take you to buy this place?" Wyatt asked with his mouth full. "I mean, did you buy it the first year you made it to the pros?"

"No, I bought it about three years ago."

"But you could have afforded it then, right?"

"Wyatt," Bella scolded. "It's rude to ask people what they can and can't afford."

I shrugged. "It's alright. I had some good advice on how to spend my money when I first got started, and it should be passed along. Wyatt's got a great leg. If he makes it, maybe he'll remember what we talked about. Yes, I could've afforded to buy a place like this my first year, but I didn't. You know why?"

"Why?"

"Because someone I'd been close to for years, he actually coached my pee-wee football team, told me that forty

percent of all NFL players have their careers ended pre-
maturely by injuries. And more than sixty percent have
surgery that changes who they are as a player. He told me
never to expect my career to last more than the current
season. So I used fifty percent of my first-year salary, after
the government took their piece of the pie, to buy an annu-
ity. You know what that is?"

Wyatt and I both scooped out second helpings. He
shook his head.

"You give your money to a company today, and they
agree to pay you more money than you gave them over a
long period of time. So if my first year was my last, I knew
I'd at least have a paycheck I could live off of for twenty
years, if I had to."

"Oh..."

I grinned. "Not so exciting, is it?"

"Not really."

"I used the rest of the money to pay off my mother's
house, rent a decent place, and buy a flashy car I didn't
need, which I've since sold."

Wyatt finished off his plate. "Is it okay if I take some
selfies with your MVP trophies to show to my friends?"

"Help yourself. I might've taken a few selfies with
them back in the day, too."

Bella and I cleaned up dinner together, and then Wyatt and I watched reels of the team the Bruins were playing
this weekend to look for bad habits among the defensemen
that I might be able to take advantage of. Bella caught up
on some work on her laptop, and before we knew it, it was
almost eleven.

"You ready for bed, Wyatt?" Bella said.

He nodded and turned to me. "Can you pick me up from practice again tomorrow?"

"Sorry, buddy, I can't. We leave for the west coast in the afternoon. When we have to travel a long distance and there's a big time change, we sometimes fly out on Friday so we have Saturday to adjust before the game."

He frowned. "Oh, okay."

"What about Monday?"

Bella turned out the light in the living room. "Your mom will probably be home by then, Wyatt."

"Oh, right."

"You have a game next week?" I asked.

Wyatt shook his head. "It's our bye week. Next game is a Friday-night game, two weeks from tomorrow."

"I'll try to make it to that, okay?"

He smiled, but then tried to play it cool. *Such a teenager.* "That would be a'ight. I mean, if you can..."

I mussed his hair. "Get some sleep, and have a good weekend. There's a great gym downstairs, if you want to check it out. I'll tell security to leave you some guest passes at the desk."

In the bedroom, Bella started to get ready for bed. She'd brought an overnight bag and unpacked a T-shirt and sweats, but I stripped out of the T-shirt I was wearing and tossed it at her, then swiped the sweats from her pile.

She gave me a look. "Uh, you know, I feel like you're trying to tell me something. But we use words for that, so you couldn't be."

I smirked and walked over, locking my hands around her waist. "Bella, would you please wear my T-shirt, preferably with no bra and panties?"

She laid her hands flat on my chest. "I can do that. But...no hanky panky. Wyatt's right in the other room."

"He's at the other end of the hall. I intentionally gave him the farthest room from ours."

"Still, I don't want him to hear us."

I grinned. "You are kind of loud."

She smacked my chest. "Not unless you're making me be loud, which you won't be."

I pouted. "But I'm leaving for California tomorrow. I'm not going to see you for at least a few days."

She laughed. "I'm going to go brush my teeth."

After she finished, I took a turn using the bathroom. When I came out, she was sitting on the edge of the bed wearing my T-shirt. I walked over and lifted her legs up onto the mattress and guided her to lean back. Then I climbed on top of her and kissed her neck. "I figured out a solution."

"Let me guess, you're going to quickly soundproof the room?"

"No, but that's a thought for the future, in case anyone else ever stays over."

She chuckled. "I'm almost afraid to ask. What's your solution?"

I shrugged. "Long arms."

"Long arms?"

"Yeah, I have them."

"Okay..."

I kissed her lips before climbing down her body 'till my face hovered between her legs. Then I reached up and clamped my hand over her mouth.

Bella's eyes widened, and she started to say something I couldn't make out because the sound was muffled. I

241

lifted my pointer to my lips in the universal *shhh* sign, then lifted the hem of the T-shirt she wore and dove in without warning, licking and sucking every inch of her. When I was done and unclamped my hand, she looked drugged. Her eyes were hazy and hooded as she smiled drowsily.

"Thank God for long arms," she breathed.

I moved in next to her and flipped us so I was on my back, and she was on top with her head against my chest. "Get some sleep," I said. "It's been a long twenty-four hours."

"What about you?"

I nuzzled her closer. "I'm good. I have everything I need right here."

Chapter 21

Bella

THE DAY I'D been anxiously awaiting—yet at the same time dreading—arrived two weeks later.

Things were going great. Talia was home from the hospital and recovering well, Wyatt now had three schools actively pursuing him with talks of football scholarships for college, and Christian and I had settled into a routine of staying at each other's places a few nights a week without it terrifying me. I'd even called a real estate agent to begin looking at new apartments.

But today was the team's contract-planning meeting—the day when coaches presented their plans for player renewals and cuts to corporate. Once approved, offers went out to the players' agents within a few weeks.

When I arrived, at least twenty people were seated around the conference table in two rows, including the CFO, the GM, his offensive, defensive, and special teams coaches, the head of scouting, the director of personnel, the senior team doctor, our CEO and acting co-president, my sisters, our lead counsel, and a bunch of VPs and senior-level directors. The head of the table had been left open for me, but I thought it was important to show people I hadn't been kidding when I'd said I planned to watch and learn this year. So I stood behind the chair and pulled it out for our CEO and my co-president. "Tom, why don't you sit here so everyone can see you?"

Tom had been seated to my left. He smiled and stood with a nod. "Thanks, Bella."

I sat listening and taking notes for the first few hours, none of which contained any surprises. The GM had recommended renewing three contracts that were up, putting one player on the trade list, and extending an option to another they wanted to keep, but he was considering retiring. Then we came to the one I'd been waiting for, the one most people had been waiting for—Christian's contract extension.

As we'd done for the other players, the team doc first gave a health overview, followed by the CEO reviewing the current salary and bonus structure. After, the coaches would normally talk about other teams who'd expressed an interest in the player, as well as where the player himself might've voiced that he wanted to be in the future. This round was a little different.

"When it comes to Christian Knox," the GM said, "I think we could save time by talking about the teams that *aren't* interested in him. Now that he's healthy again, I have no doubt he's got another five years left, if not more. So I'd like to lock him down for that long." He pointed to the binder. "If you look on page thirty-four, I'm proposing a number that will make him the second-highest-paid quarterback in the league, but he'd have the biggest guarantee number, which we know is important to the more senior players. His last contract had him as the eighth-highest paid, and I think he'll be happy with the offer."

Everyone around the table looked down and studied the numbers. I watched to see if anyone looked unhappy, but most hadn't even flinched, though the number was bigger than I'd predicted. When I got to my sisters, Tiffany was staring right back at me.

An evil smile spread across her face as she raised her hand. "Tom, I have a question?"

He nodded. "Okay..."

Tiffany pointed down at the page while looking straight at me. "Does this bonus include payment for personal services to the owner?"

I closed my eyes.

"Excuse me?" Tom said.

"Oh, and Larry..." She turned to the team's lead counsel. "How does that work? Since paying for sex isn't legal in New York state, is the contract even enforceable?"

I felt like reaching over the table and smacking her, but I wasn't about to stoop to her level. Though I needed to say something before my lovely half-sister continued. So I stood. All eyes shifted to me.

Clasping my hands together, I took a deep breath. "I think what my sister is not-so-subtly referring to is my relationship with Christian Knox. While I prefer to keep my personal life personal, perhaps it's best that it come out." I looked at my sister. "Christian and I are dating."

"*Pfft*," my sister sneered. "He's using her so he can get a fat contract renewal. I see it worked."

Tom cleared his throat. "I wasn't aware of Christian's involvement with Bella, but I'll have you know that Bella and I have not discussed any of the recommendations I'm presenting today." He looked at the coaches. "Have any of you discussed Christian's contract with Bella or been influenced by her in any way?"

They all shook their heads.

"With all due respect to Bella, I can see how a personal relationship between a player and an owner might look bad when it comes to undue influence on contracts. But the first time Bella and I spoke, she said this year was for listening and learning, and it was my team to run." He nodded. "She's kept to that word. So my recommendation does not change after learning about her relationship with Christian Knox."

"Thank you, Tom." I looked at Tiffany. "Can we continue?"

She rolled her eyes, so I sat down and looked at Tom, who took the hint and picked up where he'd left off.

When the meeting finally wrapped, hours later, I caught my sister as she walked out. "Tiffany, can we speak for a moment?"

She pursed her lips and folded her arms across her chest, which I took for a yes.

I closed the door behind the last person leaving the conference room, so it was just the two of us. "You know, I've tried hard to put myself in your place. How would I feel if I grew up in a very privileged life and found out, after my father passed, that he'd had a child out of wedlock and left that child a substantial inheritance? I'm sure I wouldn't be happy either. I've tried my very best since I arrived to remember that and always take the high road. But maybe it's time you remember something, too. I'm from the street, not the penthouse like you. I may be sitting up here with you now, but I'm still the little girl from the homeless shelter." I stepped closer. "So if you ever speak negatively about Christian in my presence again, I will kick your ass."

Tiffany's mouth dropped open. "You're so trashy."

I offered an ear-to-ear smile and opened the conference room door. "And don't you forget it."

My body tingled as she stormed out. It felt good to finally say my piece. And even though I hadn't wanted my relationship with Christian to be public, part of me was relieved people knew. Tiffany had tried to hurt me, but it had backfired. I felt unstoppable.

As I returned to my office, my cell phone rang. I thought it might be Christian, but instead Julian's name flashed on the screen. That brought my headspace down, but as long as I was clearing the air and feeling empowered, I guessed I should have a conversation with him, too. He'd called twice in the last couple of weeks, and I'd never called him back. Julian didn't deserve my disrespect, so I needed to be honest.

Taking a deep breath, I swiped to answer. "Hey, Julian."

"Oh, hey. I figured I was going to voicemail again."

"No, you got me. I just got out of a meeting, though. That's why it took me so long to answer."

"How's everything going? You must be pretty busy. I called you a few weeks ago and hadn't heard back."

I shut the door to my office and sat down at my desk. "Things have been pretty hectic, actually. I'm sorry I didn't call. I should've."

"It's fine. I get it. I was just sitting at my desk working on the presentation I'm giving at the AI conference, and I thought of you. We hired a new coder. He sits at a cubicle not too far from my office and has terrible allergies."

"Okay..."

"I was thinking if he worked for you, you'd probably be passed out from lack of oxygen. He never stops sneezing."

I laughed. "Oh my gosh. I'd be passed out, but you must be walking around that office pissed off all the time."

"I'm thinking of promoting him just so I can move him to a private office on the other side of the building."

"You would do something like that. What else is new?"

Julian and I talked for a while, mostly about his work stuff. When the conversation came to a natural lull, he cleared his throat.

"I was hoping maybe we could see each other before I left for the conference next week," he said. "Maybe have dinner Friday night?"

"Yeah, umm...about that..." *God, I really hate letting nice people down.* "I want to be honest with you... I think we're better off as friends."

"Oh..."

"I love our friendship, and you're one of the smartest people I've ever met, but I realized during our date last time that there just isn't a romantic spark. I really thought there would be. Plus, I've met someone."

"I see..."

"I hope we can still be friends."

"Sure. Of course."

Even as we said it, I knew it was unlikely that we'd be the type of friends who spent time together. Our contact would probably be limited to liking each other's posts on social media once in a while.

During the awkward silence that followed, there was a knock at my office door, and Christian poked his head in. I smiled and waved him inside, then held up a finger and pointed to my cell.

"Alright, well, I know you're busy," Julian said. "So I'll let you go."

"Okay."

"I'll give you a call soon."

"That sounds good."

"Bye, Bella."

"Bye, Julian. Good luck with your presentation at the conference."

Christian's face fell as I swiped to end the call and set the phone on my desk.

"Hi."

"Did I interrupt something?" he asked.

"You did, actually."

The muscle in Christian's jaw ticked, but he said nothing.

"Julian had called me twice over the last few weeks, and I hadn't called him back. So when he called this time, I thought I should answer."

"Did he ask you out?"

I stood and walked around my desk. "He did. And I said no. I told him I thought we were better off as friends and that I'd met someone."

Christian's shoulders relaxed. "Oh yeah? You met someone, huh?"

I grinned. "He's really cute. I'll introduce you to him, if you want."

Christian hooked an arm around my waist and hoisted me against him. "Funny."

I tapped a finger to his thick chest. "You should've seen your face. It looked like you might crack a tooth, your jaw was so rigid."

One of his hands slid up my back and gripped my neck, not so gently. "I'll show you rigid."

I laughed as he kissed me. But somewhere along the line, the playfulness disappeared, and my fists had his shirt bunched into two balls. Christian pulled back, tugging my bottom lip between his teeth as he let go. "Missed you."

It had been a busy week, and we hadn't seen each other in four days. "Missed you, too."

He stroked my cheek tenderly. "How was your day?"

"Oh my God, I almost forgot! Tiffany decided to out us in the middle of the meeting today—with Tom, the GM, all of the coaches, and the entire executive team."

"What happened?"

I shook my head. "It doesn't matter. But I admitted we were seeing each other, and then when I got Tiffany alone after the meeting, I threatened to kick her ass..."

Christian's brows jumped. "Really?"

"Yep, and it felt good."

"Which part? Telling your sister off or admitting we're together."

"Both."

He smiled. "Yeah? So you're okay with it being public now?"

I nodded. "I actually feel relieved that it's out in the open."

Christian pulled my hands from his shirt and brought them to his lips for a kiss. Then turned and abruptly headed for the door to my office.

"Where are you going?"

His answer was the loud clank of the lock on my office door. "Nowhere." He stalked back with a predatory look in his eyes, lifting me off my feet and depositing me on top of my desk. He pulled the glasses from my face and chucked them over his shoulder.

"What are you doing?" I giggled.

"Celebrating..." He buried his head in my neck. "Do you know how freaking sexy you are when you don't put up with people's shit?"

He sucked along my neck until my eyes fell closed and my head lolled back.

"Does that mean you'll be happy when I don't put up with your shit?" I asked breathlessly.

"Don't ever put up with my shit."

He captured my mouth in a passionate kiss, and I wrapped my legs around his waist. All of the emotions from today fed into our frenzied connection, and my need to touch his bare skin grew desperate. I slipped my hands under his T-shirt and scraped my nails along his warm back. Christian groaned and pushed my blouse up. His thumbs reached into my bra and pushed down the material, freeing my breasts to spill over. Cool air met my already-peaked nipples, and they hardened at Christian's touch. "I have fantasized about you sitting up on this desk with your legs wide open since the first day we met."

He leaned down and captured a nipple between his teeth, biting before soothing it with his tongue. I felt a jolt between my legs and nuzzled against him.

Christian slipped his hand up my skirt and fingered the edges of my underwear. "Fucking love skirts."

He pushed the material to the side, and his thumb went right to my clit. I was already wet, so his finger slipped easily inside. He thrust in and out a few times before pulling all the way out and pushing back in with two fingers. It didn't take long before it was too much. I needed him inside me.

"Please..." Reaching for the waist of his pants, I couldn't wait any longer.

Christian grabbed my hand. "I don't have anything on me, sweetheart. Just let me make you come."

He pumped his fingers in and out again. There was no doubt he could get me there, but I wanted him so damn bad.

"Christian," I panted. "I'm on the pill."

His fingers froze. "Are you saying you want me bare, baby?"

I nodded. "I'm clean, and I trust you if you say you are."

He looked up at the ceiling. "Today is just all the gifts from you."

Christian removed the hand that had stopped mine at his waist. I was grateful he'd come after practice, and we didn't have to waste time with a zipper and button. I smiled and reached into his easy-access pants. "Fucking love sweats."

He chuckled, but his face grew serious as I freed his cock and lined him up at my entrance. "I can feel how hot and wet you are already. This isn't going to be pretty."

I pushed my hips forward so his crown dipped inside. "It's okay. As long as it's hard."

Christian grumbled a string of curses as he pushed inside in one rough thrust, burying himself deep. It was exactly what I needed.

"Oh my God. Yes!" I yelled. "Like that."

He clamped a hand over my mouth before pumping again. And again. And again. I knew he liked it when I maintained eye contact, but by the fourth hard thrust, I lost the battle and my eyes rolled back in my head. When I began to whimper into his palm, Christian tilted my hips and hit the perfect spot. Each thrust milked my orgasm more and more. After I started to level out, he unclasped his hand from my mouth.

"Hold on to the sides of the desk," he grunted.

If I'd thought it was hard before, I had another thing coming. The desk shook, my body shook, and I didn't just need to hold on to the desk, I had to white knuckle as he increased the intensity of his thrusts. Christian fucked me like it was the Super Bowl of all fucking. His eyes lost focus as he planted himself one last time and let go.

It took a few minutes for our breathing to return to normal. "Wow." I shook my head. I'd never experienced an earthquake before, but I imagined when it was over, it felt a lot like I did at the moment—aftershocks rippling through me and not quite certain what had just happened.

Christian brushed damp hair from my face and smiled. "Yeah. That's all I got too." He kissed me softly. "I don't want to move. But if I don't get us something, you're going to be wearing me all over the skirt that's still under your ass. Stay here."

I found the command not to move amusing, considering my legs felt like Jell-O, and I barely had the energy to speak.

Christian went into the bathroom and came back with a towel. He thumbed over his shoulder as he pressed the cloth between my legs. "I've never been in there. That bathroom is bigger than your apartment."

I smiled and took the towel from him to finish cleaning myself up. "Not for long. I called a realtor. I'm going to look for a new apartment with a little more space."

Christian studied me.

"What?"

"You told Julian you weren't interested, outed us, let me have you bare, and you're going to find a new apartment. Not that I'm complaining, but what brought about all the change?"

I finished righting my disheveled clothes and shrugged. "I'm not sure. I guess it was just time."

"Time for what?"

I thought about that for a minute, then held out my hand to Christian. "Time to start trusting again."

Chapter 22

Christian

"HEY, WHAT ARE you doing tonight?"

I'd called Coach as I walked out of practice. I hadn't been to see him lately, between being busy back at work and spending time with Bella. So I'd asked if she minded if I brought him to Wyatt's game later. After he stopped coaching, he still loved going to watch the young kids play, but he didn't get to do it often since the stroke.

"Big plans," he said. "Gonna decide between the Stouffer's baked chicken with mashed potatoes or the Marie Callender's chicken pot pie. Why? You want to come have the other one?"

I chuckled. "As tempting as that sounds, I think I'll pass. But I have something better for you. I'm going to a high school game at St. Francis in Queens. So is Bella. A kid on the team is her friend's son. He's really good. You want to come?"

"Are you gonna feed me?"

"Does a hot dog and pretzel from the snack stand count?"

"Now you're talking my language. What time?"

I smiled. "I'll pick you up around six. Kickoff is at seven thirty."

"Sounds good. I'll see you then."

I got to my truck and tossed my bag in the backseat before typing out a text to Bella.

Christian: Coach is in.

Half the time she was in meetings, so I didn't expect a response right away. But my phone dinged as I put the key into the ignition.

Bella: Great! I'll meet you guys there.

———

"So are you ever gonna tell me that you're schtupping my granddaughter? Or just gonna keep that to yourself?"

I glanced over at Coach and back to the road. "I was actually going to talk to you about that."

"Sure you were..."

"I'm serious. We haven't had a chance to talk in a while, and Bella wanted to keep things on the downlow at first. She's trying to earn credibility with the team, so she didn't want people focused on her dating one of the players, especially me. You know how it is—I take a woman to one event and the media's either got me married or cheating on her within a week."

"I guess credibility takes a hit when you're dating a clown..."

"Bite me, old man."

Coach chuckled. "Do you and I need to talk about what she's been through? She's a strong girl with brains, but I don't think I need to tell you that people have had a tendency to disappear on her. That means trust issues, and when a person with that baggage gives their trust to someone and it's broken, it's like re-opening a gaping wound, not just the little new one."

I was quiet for a while as we drove, letting that sink in. Eventually, I nodded. "I hear what you're saying, but I'm crazy about Bella. She's not some woman I'm spending time with because I'm bored or need to get lai..." I caught myself and shook my head. "Sorry, but you know what I mean."

Coach looked out the window. "Alright then."

I merged onto the highway from the entrance ramp, and just as I entered the right lane, a car from the center moved over without looking. I swerved onto the shoulder and avoided a collision but had a few choice words for the idiot. "Are you fucking kidding me?" I waved my right arm as my left hand sat on the horn. "Try looking before you change lanes!"

Coach pointed. "Fifty-three Buick Skylark. That car was popular when I was a kid. The guy probably shouldn't be driving. He looks old enough to be the original owner."

I shook my head. "Someone should tell him that."

I merged behind the old car. It was only going about forty miles an hour, though we were on a fifty-five road. So as soon as it was safe, I moved into the middle lane to pass him. Of course, since I was a guy, I had to first pull up next to him and take a look at the moron while making a face. The driver looked about seventy-five, which made me feel like a bully, so I hit the gas without making eye contact.

Coach looked back in his rearview mirror. "They don't make cars like that anymore. John had a 'fifty-seven in his collection."

That reminded me of something. "Didn't he also have a blue Ford Thunderbird from the fifties?"

"Sure did. A nineteen fifty-four. A real beauty."

"Whatever happened to it?"

"I got the entire collection when he passed. He meant well, because those old cars were always something he and I enjoyed, but I don't really have a use for eleven antique cars. I can't even drive one. We used to go to swap meets and car shows on Friday nights when he was growing up. We still went a few times a year up until the end."

I remembered being invited to John Barrett's home the first year I joined the team. He'd had a garage that held more than a dozen cars. We'd smoked cigars, and he took me to look at them all.

"He drove them occasionally, right?"

He nodded. "Usually to the store or around town. You're supposed to drive a car at least once a month so its seals don't dry out and get leaks."

"Did he...ever drive them to the stadium?"

"Once in a while, if it was nice out. Why do you ask?"

I wasn't about to even hint at what was on my mind because it was a ridiculous thought to begin with. Yet...still something niggled. I shrugged. "No reason. Just curious." I tapped the steering wheel, lost in thought for a while. "You still have the cars?"

"Sure do. Probably should give them to charity or something, since they're just sitting around collecting dust."

"Where are they?"

"One of those public storage places. They have a climate-controlled garage for cars attached to the main building. The manager starts 'em and lets 'em run once a month for a little extra cash, but they really should be driven, not just let the engine run idly."

I pondered that for a few exits. "Maybe we can go see them sometime."

"The cars?"

I nodded.

"Sure. I'd like that. It's been a few years."

"I'm leaving tomorrow afternoon for Sunday's game. Maybe next Saturday? We'll only have a morning walk-through, not a full practice."

"Let me check my calendar." Coach scratched his chin. "Yep, looks like I'm free."

Traffic was heavy, so we arrived at the football field a few minutes late. I helped Coach settle in his chair, and we headed to the bleachers to look for Bella. She wasn't hard to find since she was standing at the fence, screaming her head off.

"What'd I miss?" I called.

She turned and smiled. "Oh hey! They called back Wyatt's field goal for a penalty, but the defense had too many guys on the field, and the ref didn't notice." Bella leaned down and hugged Coach but then hesitated, seeming like she wasn't sure how to greet me. I settled her internal debate by hooking a hand around the back of her neck and giving her a quick kiss on the lips. After, I moved my mouth to her ear. "He knows."

"Oh..." She nodded with an uneasy smile. "Okay."

I could see this being-out-in-public thing was going to take some getting used to for her, so I didn't push it. "Wanna go up on the stands? Coach can see easier."

"Yeah, sure. I wasn't sure you'd want to sit with the crowd. It's pretty packed tonight."

"It's fine."

The three of us settled into the first row of the bleachers and watched the game. By the time the ref blew the whistle at the end of the first quarter, it was almost dark and the field lights were on. That brought back a ton of memories. I looked around, not realizing I was smiling until Bella elbowed me.

"What's going on in that head of yours? You're smiling like a cat who ate a canary."

"Nothing. Just remembering the good old days. I used to love Friday-night games under the lights in high school." I wiggled my eyebrows. "And under the bleachers after."

She shook her head. "You know what I did on Friday nights in high school?"

"What?"

"I read books on combinatorics."

"What the hell is that?"

She grinned. "It's the branch of math that interested me most."

Coach was sitting on the other side of Bella, but his wheelchair was positioned in front of the bleacher seats. He leaned back to get my attention. "Where's that hot dog and pretzel you promised me?"

I smiled and looked at Bella. "You want something?"

"Definitely. A hot dog with the works, please."

"I'll take the same," Coach said.

I stood. "Be back."

It was mid-second quarter before I returned.

"It's about damn time. I'm starving," Coach said.

I handed him and Bella each a box with a hot dog, pretzel, and soda before sitting down. "I had to wait in a long line."

"Awww..." Bella bit into her hot dog and covered her full mouth with her hand while she spoke. "Did no one let the superstar cut the line, and you had to wait like a mere mortal?"

"Wiseass..."

At halftime, the game was tied. I took a run to the men's room, and when I came back, Bella was on the phone. She hung up as I sat.

"Everything okay?" I asked.

"Yeah, fine. I was just giving Talia an update on the game."

"How's she feeling?"

"Really good, though she's anxious to be back to work and her regular routine. The doctor said she can go back Monday. Wyatt's been invited to Ohio State by the football coach to see the school and come to their game next Saturday."

"Oh yeah?"

She nodded. "I told Talia I'd take him since she's had to miss so much time from work with her appendix."

"He's gonna love it. Those fans are wild. They make the stadium shake."

"We can probably fly out late Friday evening or early Saturday morning, do the tour and stay for the game, and then I could bring Wyatt with me to the Cincinnati game. It's only about a two-hour drive." Bella shook her head. "Oh shoot. I told my grandfather two minutes ago that I'd come with you guys next Saturday."

"Next Saturday?"

"He said you were going to see a car collection my father left him. He thought I might be interested."

Fuck. Pretty sure I was out of my mind for thinking what I'd been thinking, but it still wasn't a good idea for her to come.

"You won't be missing much." I leaned close to her so Coach wouldn't hear. "I'm just trying to get him out more."

"Oh, okay."

The rest of the game was a nail-biter. The teams battled it out until the last ten seconds, when the game hinged on a long field goal attempt.

Bella and I stood as Wyatt jogged out onto the field.

"God, this is so stressful," she said. "I can't imagine what he feels like right now."

I smiled. "This is the moment you live for playing this game."

She covered her heart. "I couldn't do it. I'd fall apart under the pressure."

"Nah. You'd kill it. You find out how strong you are at times like this. But even if he doesn't make the shot, it's coming back the next day to work harder so you have a better chance of making it next time that counts. Like you walking into that corporate office on day one only to have your sister screw with you the first hour. You kept coming back. That's what makes you better at what you do."

Years of pep talks from a dozen coaches had definitely influenced what I'd said, but when Wyatt reared back and punted the ball, I'm not going to lie—I held my breath.

"He made it!" Bella jumped up and down, while I stuck two fingers in my mouth for an ear-splitting whistle.

The bleachers went crazy, and I might've gotten a little choked up when the team lifted Wyatt onto their shoulders and paraded him around the field.

"Damn," Coach yelled. "That was some game!"

Between the after-game celebration and people asking me to take selfies and sign autographs, we didn't get out of there for almost two more hours. Then we dropped off Coach and Wyatt before going back to my place.

"I had a really good time tonight," Bella said.

"Me too. It was a great game." We were sitting on the couch, and I lifted her feet onto my lap and rubbed as she sipped the wine I'd poured her.

"It was. But it was more than that. It felt like I spent the night with family."

I looked back and forth between her eyes. "Yeah?"

She nodded. "It's been a long time since I felt something like that. Ever since I found out about my father and got to know my grandfather, my visits have mostly been learning things about him and the family I never knew. And while that's great, and I love listening to his stories, it was really nice to just hang out tonight. I realized I'd spent my time with him over the last two years trying to fill in missing pieces, but while I was doing that, I wasn't moving forward and enjoying who he is today."

"What changed?"

She looked into her wine glass for a while. That was one of the things I loved about Bella; she didn't fill airspace. She thought about her words carefully, which made them so much more meaningful. "I think I changed. I've spent the last fourteen years afraid to get attached to anyone new because it hurts so much when they leave me."

Bella looked into my eyes. "It's not that I'm not afraid anymore, but I finally found people who are worth the risk."

I took the glass from her hand and set it down on the coffee table before cupping her cheek. "I'm glad you feel that way. Because I'm fucking crazy about you, Bella."

Her eyes filled with tears, but they were happy ones. "I don't want to look back anymore. I want to go forward and appreciate what I have."

I stroked her cheek with my thumb. "That sounds like a good plan."

And it was, a damn great one. Too bad I didn't follow the no-looking-back rule the next weekend...

Chapter 23

Christian

I FELT LIKE I was doing something wrong.

The following Saturday after practice, I took Coach to the storage building as planned. I'd debated all week whether I should cancel, mind my own business, and leave things be since Bella seemed determined to move forward and not look back anymore. Yet here I was, watching the garage door inch its way up. Aside from the feeling that I was sticking my nose in a place it didn't belong, I also had no idea what the hell I was looking for—other than the blue 1954 Ford Thunderbird that sparkled from the far side of the room the minute the door finished opening.

Coach shook his head. "Damn, I forgot how these old things bring back memories." He pointed to a white Chevelle at the front. "Got my first hickey from Nancy Woodrow in the back of one of these."

I wheeled him over and opened the driver's side door so he could see inside. He leaned in and inhaled deeply. "She even smells the same."

"Nancy smelled like leather? I like my women to have a more feminine smell, maybe floral or something."

Coach chuckled. "Knucklehead."

I took a lap around the Chevelle, checking it out, but couldn't stop myself from glancing over at the Ford a few times. At least I'd managed to not make a beeline for it the minute we'd walked in.

The next car we stopped at was an old Jaguar.

"This is a nineteen fifty-five D-type," Coach said. "One of these sold at auction for more than twenty million a few years back."

My brows shot up. "Twenty million? Are you shitting me?"

"That one won the Le Mans and had all her original parts. This one wouldn't fetch a fraction of that. It has high mileage, an aftermarket paint job, and the underbelly is full of rust. John bought it a few months before his diagnosis. He'd planned to restore it and try to find as many original parts as possible. But that never happened."

"Is that what makes old cars valuable? Having all the original parts?"

Coach nodded. "Partly." He pointed to a red Corvette. "That 'Vette is all original, and so is the Ford Thunderbird in the back. John was offered a pretty penny at car swaps for both of those, but unlike new cars that lose ten grand in value the minute you drive them off the lot, these appreciate. They're a good investment. Plus, he loved to drive them."

I noticed the Chevelle didn't have any plates on it, so I looked around at the others. I couldn't see all the fronts and backs, but none of what I could see had them either. "Do you not need license plates to drive antique cars?"

Coach smiled. "You do. Though John just used one set of dealer plates for them all. All the cars are owned by a corporation that he had registered as a dealer, since he bought and sold often. It's probably not exactly legal, but he didn't go too far when he drove them."

I grew more and more anxious as we went around from car to car. When we finally got to the Ford, I still had absolutely no idea what the hell I was looking for.

"This one was John's favorite," Coach said.

"Oh yeah?"

"Bought it when he signed his first contract as a player."

"So he'd had it a long time then?"

He nodded. "Every few years, he got them appraised by an auction house for insurance purposes. They told him to drive this one less to keep the mileage down. But that never stopped him."

"Did he...ever take this one to the stadium?"

"I'm not sure. He was always there before me and stayed long after I left."

I walked around the back and took my time perusing the sides. When I got to the front, I noticed there was a slightly bigger gap on the left side of the hood than the right. It was barely noticeable, but it was there, and I knew that was a telltale sign a car had been in an accident.

"Do they sell for less when they've been in an accident?" I asked.

"Sure. Usually that's because they have to get bodywork done. But this one is cherry. All original, no accidents, no bodywork."

I bent down in front of the car, looking closely at the headlights. On the left, I noticed two tiny bubbles under the paint, yet on the right, the paintjob was totally smooth.

I was far from an expert on cars, but it made me think the paint might've been touched up. Not wanting to raise suspicion, I moved on to check out the inside. Nothing jumped out at me as peculiar there. And honestly, I wasn't even sure the small things I'd found were peculiar. The car was seventy years old, for Pete's sake. Maybe it was normal for the hood to shift a little and the paint to have a few miniscule bubbles from natural weathering. What the hell did I know?

I stood and looked around. "You still thinking about donating the collection to charity?"

"They're just collecting dust. I don't need the money, and neither do any of John's kids, who'll get whatever I have left when I kick the bucket. So I suppose I might as well."

I nodded. "You got one in mind?"

"I was always a big supporter of that Camp for Kids foundation that pays for camp in the summer for parents who can't afford it. Got John to support it, too. He donated and always had his players visit the camps."

I smiled. "We still do it. I went two years ago. It's a great program."

"I think the camp could use the money more than me. I spoke to my financial guy a while back about donating, and he suggested I get the cars appraised. John used to do that often, to increase the coverage on the insurance. But I didn't bother, so they haven't been appraised in a few years. Apparently, I might have some tax due if they're worth more. I've been meaning to get that process started, but it's not so easy getting around anymore. Simple things like getting down here to meet someone to do an appraisal means asking for help. Which isn't my strong suit."

"Well, you don't have to ask me. I'm volunteering. If you want me to, I'll deal with getting the appraisals done."

"Are you sucking up because you're seeing my granddaughter now?"

I shook my head with a smile. "Does it matter?"

"Guess not. It's not like I have any other applicants for the job of lackey."

"I feel so wanted..."

Coach looked around the garage one more time. "It's hard getting rid of something your kid loved so much. But I think it's time to move on."

I glanced at the blue Ford one last time. *Everyone seems to want to move on, so what the hell am I doing?*

———

A week later, my cell rang while I was on my way to practice. The caller ID flashed a number I didn't recognize, so I let it go to voicemail. After, my phone buzzed with a message, so I hit play.

"Hi, Christian, this is Aaron Winkleman. I received your number from Frank Quinn at Quinn Financial who works with Marvin Barrett. Mr. Barrett is looking to get an antique car collection appraised and provided your contact information so I could get in to see the vehicles. If you could please give me a call back at your earliest convenience. Thank you."

I'd managed to leave my crazy thoughts at the storage center that day, and I worried they'd come rushing back if I returned. But I did want to help Coach, so I saved the information to my contacts, then hit *Call Back* on my car's display and spoke through the speakerphone.

"Aaron Winkleman."

"Hey, Aaron. This is Christian Knox returning your call."

"Hi, Christian. Thanks for calling back. Before I start, I gotta ask...am I speaking to *the* Christian Knox? As in the quarterback?"

"That's me."

"Wow. I'm a big fan. Sorry if that's unprofessional to say, but I can't help myself."

I smiled. "Thank you. I appreciate that."

"Anyway, I was calling because I was given your number to arrange an appraisal on some cars. I take it you know about this?"

"I do. When are you looking to do it?"

"Considering it's football season and your schedule is a heck of a lot more important than mine, I can work around you."

"Thank you. Can you give me an idea of how long the appraisal will take?"

"It takes an hour or two to go through each vehicle, but I'll bring a few guys with me, so it won't take all day. With classics, you have to match up part numbers and record which are originals and which are replacements, because it tends to make a big difference in the valuation."

"Just out of curiosity, can you also tell if a car's been repainted?"

"Usually. Even if you match the paint color perfectly, the undercoating used today and years ago are different, and we also have tools to see what the naked eye can't."

I was quiet for a moment. "Could you do an evening appointment?" I asked.

"As long as you have good lighting."

"The garage is pretty well lit. Would Thursday work? Maybe around five?"

"I'll have to reach out to the team I'm going to bring, since I don't know their availability after hours. But give me about a half hour, and I'll get back to you."

"Alright, great. Would you mind texting this number? I'm probably not going to be able to answer in a little while."

"Sure, no problem."

"Thank you."

I drove the rest of the way to the stadium lost in thought. Right as I was about to lock my locker and head out to the field, my phone buzzed. So I opened the door back up and checked it.

Aaron: Thursday evening at five works for my team. Text me the address when you have time. See you then.

—

"What's that thing for?"

Aaron and his team had been working on the cars for about forty-five minutes. He currently had a palm-sized gadget pressed to the hood of the Corvette, which he had done in several other spots before I walked over.

"It's a paint meter. It tells me the thickness of the paint. A factory paint job is typically one-and-a-half mils, but a repaint is generally heavier—anywhere between two and eight. I run this along anywhere that's often repainted to cover damage—the hood, quarter panels, bumpers—to confirm if the paint is all original."

"Damn... That's pretty high tech just to see if a car's been repainted."

He smiled as he walked to the wheel well and moved the meter along various places. "It catches ninety-five percent of the undisclosed paint jobs. Insurance companies and police departments love this little thing because most people don't know it exists and think a cover-up can only be detected with the human eye."

"What about the other five percent?"

"Gotta feel around the edges of a car. Like this..." He slipped his hand into the back of the wheel well and felt around. "There are a few body shops that can get paint to factory-level thinness. But the factory applies their paint electrostatically, which leaves a smooth surface everywhere you touch. Even the best shops can't replicate that around edges. There are always a few bumps. That catches the other five percent."

A few bumps... "I'll give you some space. But let me know if there's anything I can do."

Over the next two hours, Aaron and his team moved from car to car. Because the Ford was in the back, it was one of the last to be examined. Finally, Aaron himself started that inspection. Just like he'd done with the others, he began on the inside, jotting down various notes on his clipboard before lifting the hood. Again, he checked parts and made more notes, before eventually starting the car and listening to it run. He was really methodical with his examinations, so I knew after he killed the engine and shut the hood, it would be time to check out what I'd been waiting for all day.

It didn't take long for his attention to snag on the gap I'd noticed along the hood. He studied it for a moment and then began to place his little paint-meter gadget all around. At the left front quarter panel, he stopped and made a few notes, then ran his hands all over the edges and underside. I'd been watching the entire thing from twenty feet away, so when he looked up, our eyes met.

"The paint meter strikes again."

I walked over, trying to seem casual. But inside I was anxious as shit. "Oh yeah? Something's been repainted?"

He pointed. "Gap in the hood was a tip-off that something had happened. But the paint's too thick to be factory applied. Plus, it's not smooth like it should be." Aaron squatted down in front of the headlight. He took a small flashlight out of his pocket and shined it in. "New headlight, too. The ones produced after nineteen eighty-three have a different level of clarity. They changed the technology, so even the ones that are supposed to replicate the older ones have it."

"Is there a way to tell when it was replaced?"

"Not when it was replaced. But I can usually tell when the part was made by the component number. You want me to look it up for you?"

"Umm...if you can. These cars are driven by someone to keep them in good condition. I wouldn't know if the damage you found is new or not. But just in case it is, it might help to get a sense of when it happened."

"No problem. Give me a few minutes, and I'll jot down the ID number and then look it up on my iPad."

Finding out the car had been damaged at some point didn't prove anything, but I was still going to feel a hell of a lot of relief if he came back and said the headlight had been made years after Bella's mother's accident, since any cover-up would have been done right away.

But of course, it couldn't be that easy.

A few minutes later, Aaron walked over with his iPad. "Looks like that headlight was made between fourteen and sixteen years ago."

Great. Bella's mother died fourteen years ago, so there went my peace of mind.

Chapter 24

Bella

"WHAT'S GOING ON with you?"

Christian looked over. He'd been sitting on the couch while I got dressed to go out to dinner, staring blankly out the window. His eyes came into focus for the first time in ten minutes. "What do you mean?"

"It seemed like you were lost in thought."

He took a deep breath and let it out. "Sorry. I'm just tired. I haven't slept so well the last two nights."

"Is something bothering you?"

He hesitated before shrugging. "Just a big game Sunday, I guess."

"You're worried about the Phoenix game? They're two and five and we're five and two."

"Every game counts when we're getting closer to play-offs."

"True. But you've beaten them the last seven times you've faced them—nine if you look only at the games played in their stadium. And Joe Rexon is out, Assad Fenton is in the middle of a divorce, and their head defensive coach is probably getting ousted at the end of the season."

Christian smiled. "Someone's been doing her people homework."

"I've actually started googling the top ten players on the teams we play for internet gossip. Then I factor it into my model, which, by the way, has you coming out fourteen points ahead this week."

"I've been replaced by Google."

"Never." I smiled and picked a pair of earrings out of my jewelry box, putting them in as I spoke to Christian's reflection in the mirror. "Did I tell you I'm doing a quick turn for this week's game? Wyatt has a game Saturday night, so I'm not flying in until Sunday morning. And I have an early meeting on Monday, so I'm leaving as soon as the game is over. I know you guys take a few hours to do the post-game wrap up and talk to the press." I walked over and straddled his lap with a flirty smile. "Is there anything I can do to help relieve your stress?"

He smiled back, but it didn't quite reach his eyes. "How about I take you up on that after dinner? We're going to miss our reservation if we don't get going."

It was unlike him to pass up sex to go to a restaurant, but I didn't press. Instead, I gave him a quick kiss and finished getting dressed. The sushi place where we had reservations was across town, so we grabbed an Uber.

"I think I might've found an apartment," I said once we were seated at our table.

"I didn't even know you went to see any."

"Just online viewing. I mentioned to Josh that I was going to look around, and he had a list of apartments in my inbox by the end of the day, even though I hadn't asked him to look into it. I really liked one of the places."

"Where is it?"

"It's in Kipps Bay, close to the PATH train, so I can get to New Jersey for games and practices pretty easily. The building has a twenty-four-hour doorman, a gym, and a rooftop space open to tenants. The unit has a small walk-out balcony off the living room, and it's only about six blocks from Talia and Wyatt."

"That sounds great."

"I think I'm going to go see it tomorrow. If I made the appointment for late afternoon, would you want to come with me?"

"Sure. We only have a walk-through tomorrow, so I should be done by one."

The waitress came and took our drink order, leaving us with menus. I'd been here before, so I knew what I wanted and didn't need to look. "I went to visit my grandfather this afternoon, and he said you've been helping him. Something about getting an appraisal of the cars he wants to donate?"

Christian nodded. "Yeah, it's hard for him to get around, so I went while they did the appraisals."

"What kind of cars are they again? Like sports cars?"

Christian shrugged. "I'm not much of a car guy. Just the old and expensive kind, I guess." He set the menu down. "What are you getting?"

"The Amazing roll."

"I'll have the same."

I laughed. "Do you even know what it is?"

"Nah, but I'm not picky."

I sipped my water. "Are you selling the cars and giving the money to the charity, or donating the cars themselves?"

"Coach is going to talk to Camp for Kids and see what they want to do when the appraisal comes in. They might want to hold on to some since they tend to appreciate over the years."

"Camp for Kids? I read about that program in the team's charity log. Two of the players went to visit the camps in upstate New York this summer... Tyrell Pough and Randall Emory, I think."

Christian nodded. "The team's been sponsoring the program for as long as I've been around. Coach was always a big donator and supporter, and he got John involved."

I shook my head. "It's just another thing that's difficult to reconcile in my mind. My father cared for at-risk kids enough to donate money so they could get off the streets and go to summer camp, yet he watched me live on the streets and in a shelter. How does a man care more for kids he's never met than his own child's well-being?"

Christian traced his finger around the top of his water glass. His face was somber. "I don't know. I'm starting to wonder if I knew the real John Barrett myself."

"I'm sorry." I shook my head. "I'm killing the mood. Let's change subjects. I have some good news."

"Oh yeah?"

"Wyatt got an offer from Ohio State today—a football scholarship equivalent to a full ride!"

"That's great. I bet he gets others. He's really good."

"He is. But he might've gone unnoticed, like many other talented kids do." I reached across the table and weaved my fingers with Christian's. "Thanks to you, he didn't."

"Schools would have found him eventually."

"Maybe. But they didn't have to find him, because you led the way. I'd planned on putting some money aside for Wyatt to pay for college, but I'm certain Talia wouldn't have been happy about it. She worked for everything she has and thinks it's important for Wyatt to do the same. But kids come out of college these days with so much debt. Anyway, I know I've said thank you before, but I was thinking maybe after dinner I'd thank you by showing you how appreciative I am."

Christian smiled, but yet again I felt something lurking in the background.

"Are you sure it's just the game coming up that's bothering you?" I squeezed his fingers. "Or maybe it's the prospect of getting another year older since your birthday is coming up."

He looked down at our joined hands. "It's just the game."

I don't know why, but my gut didn't necessarily believe him. Though I chalked it up to my wariness with trusting people and tried to put it out of my mind for the rest of the evening.

It wasn't too hard, not with the incredible hours we spent in bed following dinner. I had promised Christian I'd thank him properly, but in the end I was pretty sure I was the one who'd been thanked...*twice*. Either way, the week had been long, and the combination of wine at dinner and a pair of amazing orgasms had tuckered me out. I fell asleep in Christian's arms, but woke up at three AM thirsty, only to find Christian staring at the ceiling.

"Why are you up?" I whispered.

He kissed the top of my head. "Go back to sleep."

"I'm thirsty. My dinner was delicious, but salty. I'm going to grab a water. You want one?"

"No thanks."

I snuggled back into him after chugging half a bottle. "You're the first man I've ever stayed the night with, you know."

Christian had been stroking my shoulder. His hand froze. "Really?"

I nodded. "I liked to be the one to leave. So I did it before the other person had a chance to."

Christian was quiet for a moment. "Yet here we are. Staying together at one of our places half the nights of the week."

I turned and propped my head up on my fist, leaning on his chest. "I trust you."

Christian closed his eyes. "I know what that means to you."

"God, I must come across as some kind of sad commitment-phobe."

"Not sad. Cautious."

I smiled. "You want to know a secret?"

"What?"

"You scare me more than anyone I've ever met, yet I don't want to run away from you."

"I'm glad. And I have a secret, too."

"What?"

Christian leaned his head closer and whispered, "I'm scared of you, too. And you know what else?"

"What?"

"If you run because it gets to be too much, I'm going to run, too. Right after you. And I'll catch you eventually."

My heart felt so full. "I'm going to hold you to that, Knox."

Christian took my hand and brought it to his lips. "I'm counting on it."

"You should get some sleep," I said.

"You, too. Sweet dreams."

That night, for the first time in my life, I drifted off to sleep wondering how my dreams could get any sweeter than the reality I was experiencing. I'd never believed dreams could come true, but maybe they could.

Chapter 25

Christian

MY CONSCIENCE EVEN screwed with me at practice.

Or maybe it was the lack of sleep last night because I was hiding something so potentially big from Bella. But either way, it affected everything I touched—my relationship with her included.

She was too smart to miss that I was distracted, and I was scared as shit about the ramifications of her finding out I'd suspected something and hadn't told her. But I also couldn't bring myself to say, *Hey, I think your father killed your mother* without having some concrete proof. There was still a pretty good chance I was wrong, and the car was just a big, fat coincidence. She'd said herself that she didn't want to look back anymore, so I needed to be sure. Or at least surer than I was today.

So after the coach had laid into me about my head being up my ass at practice, I decided to make a phone call.

Sitting in my car in the parking lot of the stadium, I called my brother Tyler.

"Someone die, or do you need to be bailed out?" he answered.

"What? I can't call my big brother and check how he's doing?"

"Of course you can. But you don't. So which is it?"

"Neither. I need some advice and maybe a favor. Do you have some time to talk?"

"Yeah, I'm off today. What's up?"

I sighed. "Is it alright if we talk in hypotheticals? It's a legal issue, and I don't want to put you in a weird position, being that you're a cop."

"Uh-oh. So you *are* in trouble?"

"No, it's not me. I swear. But I'd like to get a copy of an old case file. Is that possible? Like, does the public have access to that stuff?"

"What kind of a case is it?"

"A hit and run."

"What's the status of the case?"

"Closed, I think. The accident was fourteen years ago, and the investigation hasn't been active since the year after it happened, at least that I know of."

"So it's a cold case. Probably then. Most government records are obtainable under the Freedom of Information Act, unless it's going to interfere with an investigation or a court proceeding. But if it's that old and gone cold, chances are that's not the case. Is it a New Jersey case?"

"It is."

"My precinct?"

My brother worked in southeast Jersey, nowhere near the stadium. "No."

"And you want this case file...why?"

I sighed. "I might've stumbled on something relevant to the case."

"So why not take it to the police and let them decide? What's with all the cloak-and-dagger shit?"

"Because if I'm wrong, it's gonna re-open a lot of wounds for no reason."

"Do you know what you need from the case file?"

"Not a clue. I have no idea what I'm looking for."

My brother laughed. "That's helpful."

"Sorry."

"You want me to see what I can get my hands on? I can reach out and do it off the record. It's definitely not you who could be implicated by whatever relevant information you've found, right?"

"No, definitely not. It has nothing to do with me. I was still in college back at Notre Dame when the accident took place."

"Alright then. I'll reach out, if you want—save you the trouble of doing a FOIA request and keep things private for you. The FOIA request itself is public, and your name is pretty well known. Could get leaked that you even made it."

I raked a hand through my hair. That was a good point. "As long as it won't get you in trouble."

"Not at all. But you're going to have to give me the name."

I was silent for a moment, kicking around my choices. "The name is Rose Keating."

"Keating...why is that name familiar?"

"Because you met her daughter at Jake's engagement party. Rose was Bella's mother."

"Oh shit. I didn't realize her mother was killed in a hit and run. So what's with all the secrecy if you're looking into something for your girlfriend?"

"Long story. But she has no idea I'm looking into it."

—

"What do you think?" Bella asked.

I looked around the small apartment. "It's a nice building, in a good location. Has decent twenty-four-hour security and all the basic amenities. What do *you* think?"

She grinned from ear to ear. "I love it."

The woman owned a team worth more than a billion dollars. There weren't too many apartments in the city she *couldn't* afford. Yet a simple, eleven-hundred-square-foot place made her happy.

I wrapped my arms around her waist. "You know, it was never too clear what a smart, beautiful woman like you saw in a dope like me. But I get it now. You like simple. Thank God."

She chuckled. "I know it's not big and fancy, but I don't need much more than this."

None of us really *needed* most of the things we had, but that didn't stop most people from wanting them. Though Bella wasn't most people. "If it makes you happy and it's safe, you should take it."

She squealed. "I'm going to!"

It made me happy to see her so excited. As far as I knew, this was the first splurge she'd made since coming into all that money, if you could even call it a splurge. She had to have made a good salary in her old job and could have afforded to live here. But she was conservative, and I liked that about her—probably could stand following her lead once in a while, too.

The real estate agent had stepped outside to give us a few minutes to talk. She knocked and let herself back in. "So what do you think?"

"It's nice," Bella said. "But do you think the landlord might come down a little on the rent?"

I had to cover my laugh with a cough. She could buy the damn building, if she wanted. Yet she was going to try to negotiate a better deal. I hadn't expected her to ask that question, and it actually made me fall a little harder. Luckily the agent hadn't recognized me, and I'm guessing she had no idea who Bella was either.

"Your annual salary is at least forty times greater than the monthly rent?" the agent asked.

Bella nodded. "Yes."

"And you have references from a current landlord?"

"I've lived in the same place for thirteen years and never made a late payment."

The agent smiled. "You'd be willing to sign the lease today?"

"Yes."

"Give me a minute and let me call the landlord to see what we can do."

The agent stepped outside into the hallway again, and Bella turned to me with a giant grin.

I chuckled. "You know you're going to have to fill out a tenant application and list your occupation and salary. The poor woman is going to shit her pants when she realizes who she was haggling with."

The agent came back with a smile. "I got you seventy-five dollars a month off the rent. Would that help?"

"Definitely," Bella said. She looked at me with a mischievous smile. "Should I do it?"

"I think you'll be able to swing it."

She turned back to the agent. "I'll take it."

The agent went into action, and while Bella worked on some paperwork, my phone began to buzz.

"It's Tyler." I showed Bella my phone. "I'm going to take it in the hall, so I'm not interrupting your reading."

"Oh, okay. Thanks."

I made sure to pull the door shut and walked to the other end of the hall as I answered. "Hey."

"I spoke to the detective who caught the case years back. He's still on the job. I'm going to meet him before my shift tomorrow to pick up a copy of what he's got in the file."

I ran a hand through my hair. "Damn, that was quick."

"You don't ever ask for shit, not even when you were a kid, so I figured it was important to you."

I blew out a deep breath. "It is. Thank you."

"No problem. I'm working until seven. Your game's at one o'clock, right?"

"Yeah."

"It's about a two-hour drive to the stadium from the precinct. You want to meet at eight? We'll each drive an hour."

"That sounds great. Thanks, Tyler."

"I'll figure out where there's a diner halfway and text you a place to meet."

"Perfect. I'll see you tomorrow night."

"Don't forget your wallet. Dinner's on you."

I smiled. "You bet."

The unexpected loss today didn't help my mood. My focus just hadn't been on the game. It was yet another reason I needed to get this shit with John's car sorted out.

Later in the evening, I made the hour drive to meet my brother after the game. He was already inside the Harvest Moon Diner when I walked in.

Tyler stood as I approached and gave me a hug. "Good to see you."

"You too, bro." I slid into the booth.

"Tough loss. Sorry, man. I listened on my phone while I was at work. A few guys driving eighty on the highway are going home without speeding tickets thanks to that last drive. I didn't want to be interrupted while I bit my nails."

I smiled halfheartedly. "This one hurt. I'm just glad it didn't knock us out of playoff contention since Dallas lost, too."

The waitress came over. She went to hand us menus, but Tyler waved her off. "You make Reubens?"

"We do. They're really good, too."

He looked over at me, and I nodded. "We'll take two and two Cokes."

"You got it. Coming right up."

Tyler waited until she was gone to lift a manila folder off the seat next to him. He slid it over to my side of the table. "I took a look at the file this afternoon. Not too much to go on. But you take a look. Maybe something will jump out at you."

I opened the envelope and scanned through all the paperwork. There were photocopies of notes, some typed forms, and a bunch of photos with labels on them. My brother pointed to one marked A12.

"I'd have to sign out the actual evidence. But the case file has photos of everything in the box. I figured if you found something that helped, we can decide where to go from there."

"Got it." I took my time, examining every page. When I got to a photo of what looked like pieces of a broken headlight on the street, I stopped. "Were they able to get a component number off the headlight?"

Tyler shook his head. "Nope. There were only a few small pieces, none of which had the ID number on it. That would've helped narrow things down a lot, seeing as the eyewitnesses couldn't even pinpoint the type of car. Their descriptions were pretty different. But the forensics report confirms that it was a classic car and places the type and make of the broken glass in an eight-year period of the fifties."

I nodded and kept going.

"I took out the graphic photos of the body—wasn't sure you'd want to see that. They weren't pretty. There weren't any skid marks on the street to indicate the driver attempted to stop before impact, so she got hit pretty hard—head was cracked open and stuff. But I have them, if you want. I just figured I'd ask rather than leave them in the file. You learn fast on the job that you can't unsee shit."

I nodded. "I'm not sure that would help any. Thanks."

I kept going through the file until I got to what looked like tire marks, only they were on a white surface and not the blacktop of the street that was in other pictures. "These are tire marks?"

"Yep. It's a blow-up to see the detail."

I pulled the photo closer to examine it. "Did the car jump the curb and these were taken on the sidewalk or something? Why is the background white?"

Tyler frowned. "That's skin. From the victim's leg. She had a skirt on."

I felt a little sick staring down at it.

My brother smiled sadly. "Think I made the right decision taking out the other victim photos, considering how pale you just turned."

I shook my head. "Someone ran the woman over and kept going like she was roadkill. What the fuck is wrong with people?"

"People leave the scene of a crime for two reasons. The most common is because they get scared. Often that's fueled by knowing they did something wrong—maybe they were on their cell phone or drinking."

"What's the other reason?"

"It was done intentionally."

"Jesus Christ." I raked a hand through my hair. "People are so fucked up."

"You don't have to tell me that. I see it every day. Just when you think you've seen it all and nothing could surprise you anymore, some perp goes and shows you you're wrong. The other day, I caught a case where a father had chopped off four of his three-year-old's fingers. She'd dropped a glass and broke it. That was her punishment."

"Don't tell me any more. I have no idea how you do your job."

I went through the rest of the file slowly. Nothing but the tire marks stuck out at me as something that could potentially help to rule out what I'd hoped to.

"Can tire marks be matched to a car years after an accident?"

"I'm no expert, but it probably depends on how much the tires have been driven. If you impound a vehicle soon after the accident, tire marks can be like fingerprints. The wear on them is unique, created from a combination of a car's alignment, the roads it's driven on, how it's driven, and a bunch of other factors. But if you keep driving that car for years, the fingerprint changes over time."

"This particular car is a collectible, so it sits in a garage most of the time. Though I have no idea if the tire has been changed."

"Welp, there's only one way to find out. Take an impression of the tire and do a comparison to the photo."

"How do you do that?"

"It's pretty simple. You dab some ink on the tire and roll it along a long piece of paper to catch the full tire rotation. Everyone and their mother wants to be a CSI these days, so you can get fingerprint kits, tire kits, and blood-detection spray all online."

I couldn't believe I was even considering doing this shit. Tyler stayed quiet as the wheels in my head spun.

"You want to fill me in on why this is so hush-hush?" he said. "You mentioned people could get hurt, but if it brings the truth out, maybe it'll be worth it in the end. Knowing the truth always helps victims and their families with closure."

"Bella's just started to move on. And if my hunch is right, finding out who is responsible is going to open a whole new can of worms."

"Who is it you think is responsible?"

I locked eyes with my brother. "This has gotta stay between me and you."

My brother pulled his head back. "You have doubt that I would put you over my job?"

I shook my head. "No, I'm sorry. I don't." I took a deep breath. "The car that might have been involved in the accident...belonged to John Barrett."

His forehead wrinkled as he tried to place the name. "The owner of the Bruins who died?"

I nodded. "And Bella's father."

Tyler leaned back. "Damn. You think her father killed her mother?"

⸻

Three days later, the impression kit arrived in the mail. I walked the damn package to the elevator at my apartment under my sweatshirt, like I was smuggling drugs. And the box wasn't even marked. Once I opened it in private, I stared at the contents and debated whether I was really doing this or not for the millionth time.

I should just let it go. Bella is in a good place now. Even if it turned out my hunch was right, how would that help her? It would be devastating all over again.

But she deserved to know the truth. It might even help explain why her father never made contact. Maybe he was too guilty to look her in the eyes.

Maybe neither of us knowing is the right way to go.

Would I be able to look at her in the eyes if I withheld that information forever? I struggled now, and she already sensed something was off. Not to mention, I couldn't play football for crap these days.

Fuck.

Fuck. Fuck. Fuck.

I picked up the test kit. The best thing that could come out of this would be that it proved me wrong. If that was the case, I wasn't going to tell her. Sure, there would always be a chance the tires had been changed, or the tread no longer matched because they were too worn. But if it was truly a dead end, I didn't want to dump all that on Bella. Not knowing an answer was harder than getting an answer you didn't like. Because you can never accept what happened and move on.

Maybe I should tell her either way.

I shook my head. Screw this. I could debate it all day and night, but why waste more time when I could go to the garage now? Coach wouldn't even have to know, since I already had the code to the combination lock.

I looked at the time on my phone. We had an afternoon practice today, but two-and-a-half hours might be long enough to get there and back. If it wasn't, I'd take the fine for being late. It would be worth getting this over with. So I grabbed my keys and headed out to the storage facility.

The test kit was simple enough to use. The ink was in a bottle that looked like shoe polish, with a felt applicator on the end to apply the fluid to the tire. Once that was done, I laid out the long, white paper and started the car, rolling it forward a few feet before shutting it off. Then I waited for the ink to dry, snapped a dozen photos, and rolled up the print before cleaning up the crap from the test kit. My heart pounded as I washed off the tire with the wipes that had been included and triple checked that I didn't leave anything behind.

I felt like a damn criminal and couldn't get out of there fast enough. So I waited until I was five blocks from the storage center to pull over and text the pictures to my brother. He'd said he would print them out and take them over to a buddy of his who worked in the crime lab for an official opinion. With that done, I took a few minutes to calm down before shifting my SUV into drive again. Though the calm didn't last long. Not when my phone buzzed from the cup holder.

Tyler: I'll let you know as soon as I hear. Shouldn't be more than a couple of days.

—

Friday morning, I'd just pulled my phone from my pocket to turn it off when Tyler's name flashed on the screen.

I swiped to answer and spoke low. "Hey, what's up? We're about to take off for our game in Vegas the day after tomorrow."

"Alright. I can be quick. I spoke to my guy who examined the tire prints."

"And..."

"They're a match, Christian. He can't swear to a hundred percent, but he said it's pretty much as good as it gets most times. There was a tiny pebble stuck in the tread on both pictures, and both alignments pulled to the right and have the same wear marks."

I dropped my head. "Fuck."

"I'm sorry. I know that wasn't what you wanted to hear."

"No, it definitely wasn't."

"My buddy said if he had the original impression you took, he could probably up his percentage of accuracy. But even with a photo of it, he feels comfortable telling you it's a match."

"Hey, Knox," the offense coach yelled. "You need a special invitation to shut your damn phone off?"

I whispered into the phone. "Gotta go, bro."

"I heard it. Let me know if there's anything I can do."

"I will. And thanks, Tyler."

I lowered my phone and was just about to swipe the call off when I heard, "Hey, wait!"

So I lifted my cell back to my ear. "What's up?"

"I almost forgot. In case I don't talk to you Monday, happy birthday."

He wasn't the only one who'd almost forgotten. "Thanks."

The five-hour flight gave me plenty of time to think about how I was going to break the news to Bella. Though when I landed, I was no better prepared than when we'd taken off from JFK. It definitely needed to be an in-person conversation, and since she was arriving at the game shortly before kickoff on Sunday and leaving right after it was over, I had a reprieve of a few days. But I'd have to tell her soon after we got back home because I was never going to be able to face her, knowing what I knew now.

Chapter 26

Bella

MY PHONE RANG as soon as I got into the waiting Town Car at the Las Vegas airport on Sunday.

"Hello?"

"Bella?"

The voice sounded familiar. "Yes?"

"It's Jake Knox, Christian's brother."

"Oh," I laughed. "No wonder your voice sounded familiar. You sound like Christian."

"Yeah, sometimes that works for me. Like yesterday when I talked your admin, Josh, into giving me your cell phone number. I told him I was Christian, and my phone broke, and I had your number saved and didn't know it by heart. Sorry about the little white lie, but I didn't know how else to get your number after he said you'd left the office for the day to go to a meeting and wouldn't be back until Monday."

"Couldn't you have just asked Christian for it?"

"Ah...no, that brings me to the reason I'm calling. It's Christian's birthday Monday. Well, and mine, too. Because that egomaniac couldn't even let me have all the attention one day a year. Anyway, I have a game in Philly tonight, and we're off on Monday, so I thought I'd drive up and surprise Christian. Lara is coming to the game with her sisters, so I figured maybe we could make it a little party. I'll see if Tyler can come, too. The last time we got to celebrate together was ten years ago, for our twenty-first."

"That sounds like fun. I'm sure he'd love that."

"Excellent. You think you can find out what time his practice is tomorrow, so I can make some plans?"

I smiled. "I think I might have an in with the coach to find that information."

"Perfect." He chuckled. "You have my number now, so text me, and I'll pull something together."

———

On Monday, I was dragging. The six PM flight I'd caught home last night really took off at nine Eastern Time. So by the time we landed, it was three in the morning. The team wasn't flying out until nine, so the birthday boy probably didn't walk in the door until the sun came up. Today's practice was just a team meeting at four, so I waited until one to text him, figuring he'd have to be awake by then.

Bella: Happy Birthday!

An incoming text notification buzzed from my desk a few minutes later.

Christian: Thank you. What time did you get home?

Bella: 4:30. You?

Christian: 8:00. But I slept on the plane.

Bella: Do you feel up to celebrating your birthday tonight? I made a reservation just in case, but wasn't sure how you'd feel.

Christian: Do you mind if we stay in and talk?

My brows knitted.

Bella: Do we have something we need to talk about?

I watched as the dots started to jump around, then stopped. A few minutes later, they finally started moving around again.

Christian: Sorry, I meant to write stay in instead. I just woke up, and my brain is still sleeping.

Bella: LOL. Okay. Staying in sounds good too. How about if I come to you? I'll bring dinner.

Christian: Sounds good. Should be done at practice by six. Eight?

Bella: See you then.

I switched over to my text chain with the other Knox football player.

Bella: Practice is an afternoon team meeting today. Should be over by six. I'm supposed to meet Christian at his place at eight. Maybe we could meet you at eight thirty?

Jake typed back right away.

Jake: How about we surprise him at his place first? Once word gets out where we are, we won't have ten minutes of privacy.

I wished I could offer to surprise him over at my place, but two people barely fit.

Bella: That would be great, but not sure we can get in.

Jake: Not a problem. Do you know the doorman's name?

Bella: I think Fred usually works weekday evenings.

Jake: What's he look like?

Bella: Maybe sixties, white hair, always smiling. Why?

Jake: Because when I stroll in like I own the place as Christian and tell the doorman I forgot my keycard, it's better to know his name.

Oh gosh. Alrighty then.

Bella: What should I bring?

Jake: I got everything covered. What's the earliest he'll be home?

Bella: I'd say seven since practice won't end until six.

Jake: OK. I'll be there by 6:30, just in case.

Bella: I'll do the same. But text me if anything goes wrong and you don't get in!

Jake: Will do. But won't be a problem. I've fooled our mother.

I laughed. I loved the relationship those two had, and I thought a little surprise party might be exactly what

Christian needed. He'd been so stressed this week about the game and making it into the playoffs. So a double celebration for the win and his birthday should be perfect.

—

"Hey, Miss Keating." Fred, the doorman, waved. He thumbed toward the elevator. "Christian got in a few minutes ago. He said you were coming by and to wave you up."

I hoped *Christian* meant *Jake*, since practice had ended even earlier than planned. I smiled. "Thank you."

When I stepped off the elevator inside Christian's apartment, I still wasn't sure until I saw Lara, Jake's fiancée. She was in the living room with two women I'd seen at Lara's party, but hadn't had a chance to meet. They were hanging a happy birthday sign at the top of the windows, and there was already a big spread of food set up on the dining room table.

"Hey." She came down and greeted me with a hug.

"I guess it worked?"

"It's a little scary how easy those two can pretend to be the other." She looped her arm through mine. "Come meet my sisters."

Lara introduced me to Kara and Sara.

"Your names are Lara, Kara, and Sara? Do you have any brothers?"

"Thankfully, no. Because if Kara was a boy, our mother was going to name him O'Hara."

Jake walked over and lifted me off my feet in a bear hug. "Hello, boss lady."

I laughed. "Did Christian tell you he calls me that?"

He set me down. "Nope. But we share the same DNA, so that doesn't surprise me."

It really was uncanny how much they looked alike. "I was thinking on my way up in the elevator—do you think Fred is going to spoil the surprise? He's going to see Christian walk in again when he never saw him walk out?"

"Thought of that earlier. So I called down a few minutes ago and said to let you and my twin brother come up when you arrive."

"Oh, good thinking." I looked around. "Was Tyler able to come?"

"Nah. He has to work until midnight."

I nodded. "Practice ended earlier than scheduled, so we probably won't have to wait long for Christian. Are we hiding when he walks in?"

"Absolutely. The two of us have been hiding behind doors and scaring the crap out of each other since we were kids. It would just be wrong if we didn't."

I smiled. "Alright. I'll put my bag and jacket in the bedroom then. I need to use the bathroom anyway."

Inside Christian's room, I found that his bed hadn't been made, and the throw pillows were strewn all over the floor. After I peed, I figured I'd make it for him so it would look nice if anyone wandered back here. When I pulled the sheet and cover up, there was something lumpy underneath. A manila envelope was buried halfway down, with a bunch of papers scattered haphazardly underneath. Neatening everything into a pile, I moved it all to the end table and finished making the bed. Then I walked around and picked up all the throw pillows. The last one was on the floor at the foot of the bed, and I tossed it toward the top.

It created a little breeze, and some of the papers I'd just set down blew onto the floor. I bent to collect them, not really paying attention until the bold heading at the top of one page caught my eye: *Bergen County Police Department.*

Had Christian gotten into an accident? I couldn't help but snoop. Though I only made it a few lines down before my heart stopped. *Victim's name: Rose Keating*

What the hell is this?

I scanned the rest of the page, confused. It looked like a copy of the police report from the accident that killed her. But why would Christian have this? I skimmed through the stack with a lump in my throat—they seemed to *all* be about my mother's accident. Some of them looked vaguely familiar from my weekly visits down to the police station after she was killed. The detective on the case had been so nice and treated me like an adult, even though I was only fifteen. He'd sometimes share updates and show me things from the file when he could. But after about a year, he'd told me the case was being moved to cold cases, and my weekly visits needed to stop. He'd promised to call if there was ever any new information. But my phone never rang.

After I went through the loose papers, I emptied the contents of the manila envelope onto the floor. *More stuff from the accident.* This had to be the entire police file. With each page I examined, my insides grew more and more shaky. One page in particular caught my attention— a picture of tire marks. Seeing them caused a fifteen-year-old memory to flash in my head.

I'd been sitting at the lead detective's desk at the police station a few weeks after the accident. It was the first time I'd gone down to speak to him. He'd opened the case file to show me some documents from his investigation, and a picture of tire marks had been on top. He'd quickly turned the page, and when I'd asked to see it, he'd said he didn't think it was a good idea. When I pressed, he'd frowned and quietly explained that the tire marks weren't on the street. They were on the body.

Looking down at the photo again, the tire marks faded away, and all I could see was what was underneath. *Skin.* The pale flesh of my mother's dead body. Nausea rushed up from my stomach. I took off running for the bathroom with the page still in my hand, stumbling to the toilet bowl just in time to empty everything inside me.

My head hung over the porcelain while a layer of sweat sheathed my forehead. I felt like I might vomit again, but the sudden urge to flee had me pushing to my feet to get the hell out of here first. The papers were still spread out all over the floor when I grabbed my purse.

Jake's fiancée was standing in the living room. She took one look at my face and put down the decoration in her hand. "Are you okay? You're so pale."

I shook my head. "Yeah, umm...actually, no. I'm not feeling too good. I think I ate something that is disagreeing with me. I just got sick."

"Oh no!"

I pointed to the door. "I'm going to go. I don't want to ruin the party and...just in case it's a bug and not something I ate, I wouldn't want to get anyone sick."

"You poor thing."

I forced a smile and waved a quick goodbye at everyone else before heading for the door.

The entire way home, I wracked my brain, trying to figure out why Christian would have my mom's old police file. I didn't come up with any answers, but my intuition told me when I eventually found them, I was going to feel a lot sicker than I did now.

Chapter 27

Christian

MY CALL WENT to voicemail for the third time.

"Still not answering?" Lara asked.

I shook my head.

I'd arrived home after practice and had the crap scared out of me by my brother, his fiancée, and her sisters. I hadn't even known he was in town today, but it was always good to see him, and it had been a long time since we'd celebrated our joint birthday together since we were born smack in the middle of football season. But my festive mood had taken a hit when Lara told me Bella had been here and then left, not feeling well.

"Maybe she's sleeping or her phone died?"

Either reason made perfect sense, but I still felt uneasy not knowing she was okay when she'd left to travel home while feeling sick. Knowing her, she probably took the subway and didn't even think about an Uber or a cab.

Jake walked over, eating a shrimp. He shoved it in his mouth and spoke with it full. "Go. We'll meet you at the restaurant."

His fiancée's nose wrinkled. "Go where?"

"He wants to go check on Bella, but he's trying to be polite since we're all here."

My brother knew me well. Plus, if it were Lara who had gotten sick and wasn't answering her phone, he'd feel the same way. So I nodded. "Thanks. I'm going to change my shirt, and I'll grab a cab and have him wait while I run up to check on her. Then I'll have him bring me to the restaurant."

My brother held a hand up. "No worries. Take your time."

I'd made it halfway to the closet in my bedroom when I froze mid-step.

The case file was all over the floor. My eyes flickered to the bed. The only time it was ever made was the day the cleaning people came or when Bella stayed over. *Oh fuck.*

Lara said Bella had gotten sick, so I walked to the bathroom.

Whatever small hope I'd had that maybe my brother or his fiancée had made my bed and accidentally knocked over the papers flew out the window when I saw the picture of the tire mark on Bella's mother's body sitting on the floor beside the toilet.

I shut my eyes.

This wasn't good.

I needed to get to her. *Now.*

———

I breathed a sigh of relief when Bella opened the door, and I wrapped her in my arms before saying a word. "I'm so glad you're okay."

She pulled back. "I'm not okay, Christian. What the hell is going on?"

"Can I come inside?"

She nodded.

I wasn't sure how or where to begin, and she wasn't going to give me any time to find a delicate way to explain things.

She shut the door and folded her arms across her chest. "Why do you have my mother's police file?"

I motioned to the couch. "Can we sit?"

"You're freaking me out, Christian. What's going on?"

"Please?" I walked over to the couch and extended a hand to her. "You're pale, and I'd feel better if you sat."

She huffed, but sat down. "I'm sitting. Talk."

I took the seat next to her and rubbed the back of my neck. "I asked my brother to get a copy of the file."

"Okay...but why? If you wanted to know more about it, I could've told you. It feels..." She shook her head. "I don't know. It feels like you invaded my privacy or something."

"I'm sorry. I didn't mean to do that."

"So why did you?"

I blew out two cheeks full of air. "It's a long story. But it started when you mentioned that the driver who left the scene was driving a collectible car. You said two witnesses gave different descriptions of the car, but one said it was an old blue Ford Thunderbird."

"So?"

"I knew someone who collected old cars and had a nineteen fifty-four blue Ford Thunderbird. He also worked at the arena."

Bella's eyes bulged. "Are you kidding? Why didn't you tell me?"

I held her gaze. "Because the person was John Barrett."

Bella's forehead wrinkled. "What?"

"I didn't want to tell you until I was sure."

"Sure about *what*?"

"That it was his car that killed your mother."

Bella clutched her heart. "You think John Barrett killed my mother?"

I took her other hand and squeezed. "I can't prove he was the driver, but it was his car that hit her, Bella. Coach inherited John's car collection when he died. He still has them, so I had someone compare the tire marks. It's a match."

Bella abruptly stood. "I'm gonna be sick again." She ran for the bathroom and knelt in front of the toilet bowl. I gathered her hair and held it from her face as she heaved.

Nothing came up, but her body tried anyway. After a few minutes, she lifted her head. "Are you sure?" Her face was pleading, and I wished with everything in me that I wasn't.

But I nodded. "I am."

"How could the police not have known? They went through all the local owners of both cars that the witnesses described. I remember the detective telling me that."

"Classic cars don't have titles, so they probably checked registrations. John owned a lot of collectible cars and bought and sold them under a corporate name. The corp was a dealership, so he had dealer plates he used to drive them—meaning he didn't have to register the individual cars."

She leaned an elbow on the toilet bowl and held her head. "The arena had cameras all around the exits, but the one that might've caught the accident was broken that night. At least according to the arena...which John owned." Bella shook her head. "How long were you going to keep this from me? Until your contract was renewed?"

"What?" I jolted back. "Of course not. My contract renewal has nothing to do with this. I didn't tell you because I hoped I was wrong and wanted to avoid having to dredge up a lot of stuff from your past. You said yourself you didn't want to look back anymore."

"How long have you known about it?"

"I don't know." I shrugged. "Maybe a month?"

"*A month?*"

"To be honest, I forgot about it for a few weeks. A while back you mentioned the type of cars involved in your mom's accident. John had once shown me his classic car collection, and I could've sworn he had a blue Thunderbird, but I figured I was crazy for even thinking he might be involved and no one knew. But then a few weeks later, the old cars came up again when I was talking to Coach, and I asked about them. One thing led to another after that."

"Does my grandfather know? Is that why he suddenly wants to get rid of the cars?"

"Definitely not. I've never shared my suspicion. When I asked him about the cars, it just reminded him that he'd wanted to donate them."

Bella stared off at nothing in particular. "Did he kill my mother intentionally?"

"I don't know, Bella."

She was quiet again, until her eyes grew wide. "Oh my God. Is John Barrett even my father? Or is the team a payoff for what he did to my mother?"

My brows puckered. "What do you mean? Didn't you have to prove he was your dad during the probate contest? I remember Tiffany and Rebecca holding a press conference when news first broke about the inheritance. They'd said they were going to court to ask for proof that you were John's daughter, because they didn't believe you were."

"My lawyer said it didn't matter because it wouldn't change the outcome of the inheritance. The will had been worded so that the team was left to Bella Keating, not to his daughter. All the stuff about him being my father was in a separate letter that wasn't part of the will. I actually didn't mind taking a test, but my lawyer was against it because it would have wasted more time and money. He also thought it was an unnecessary violation of my privacy and was against my DNA going in some database for no reason. The judge agreed. Plus, why would a stranger leave someone a billion-dollar inheritance? And my mom worked there, so it made sense since they'd have known each other."

"Jesus Christ." I raked a hand through my hair. "What do we do now?"

"I don't know. I need some time to process this."

"Yeah, of course."

Bella just kept shaking her head. "You should have told me, Christian."

"I was planning to. I'm sorry you found out this way instead."

"I am too." She frowned. "I'd like you to go."

"Go where?"

"I need to be alone, to think. I can't wrap my head around everything."

Leaving was the last thing I wanted, but I wasn't going to give her a hard time, not after the bomb I'd dropped. So I nodded. "Okay. I'll go to give you space, but promise you'll call me if you want to talk later or if you need anything?"

She sort of half nodded, not really committing.

I rose to my feet. "Can I at least help you up and walk you back to sit on the couch?"

"I'm fine."

I stopped at the bathroom door and looked back. On the tip of my tongue was to tell her I loved her before I left. Because I was head over heels in love with her. But this wasn't the time.

An uneasy feeling settled in the pit of my stomach as I walked out of the apartment. Pulling the door closed, I just hoped I *got* the chance to tell her.

Chapter 28

Bella

THE NEXT MORNING, I left the house to go to Miller's apartment. But that wasn't where I ended up.

"Kiddo?" My grandfather opened the door. "Well, this is a nice surprise. At least I think it is. Or did you tell me you were coming and I forgot?"

I leaned down to kiss his cheek, and tears unexpectedly stung my eyes. I'd come to get answers, but then it hit me that I might be about to hurt my grandfather, too. I hadn't cried before now, though tears had threatened a few times, and I'd stubbornly fought them back. Suddenly I couldn't do it anymore.

My grandfather took one look at my face and opened his arms. "Oh, sweetheart. Whatever it is, it's going to pass. Come here..."

I leaned down and let him console me. It had been a long time since I'd cried in the arms of someone and let it all out. When I finally stopped, my grandfather's shirt was all wet.

"I made a mess on your shirt." I laugh-cried as I pointed.

My grandfather's own eyes brimmed with unshed tears, yet he smiled warmly. "It's alright. As long as you don't blow your nose in it."

I snorted and wiped wetness from my cheeks. "I promise."

He tilted his head toward the living room. "Come on. I'll make us some tea, and you can tell me whose ass I'm going to kick for making you sad."

I followed him, but part of me regretted coming as I settled in. Maybe I should've gone to Miller's after all. But I needed answers, and I knew he'd only have more questions. When he returned, Coach balanced two steaming mugs on a tray on his lap, while his good arm moved his wheelchair. It wasn't easy to not get up and help, but he'd told me on more than one occasion that he liked to do things himself, that that wheelchair wasn't who he was, it was only his mode of transportation until PT could get him fully walking again.

"Here you go," he said. "Just like you like it, with a half teaspoon of sugar."

"Thank you."

He parked himself diagonal to where I was seated at the end of the couch. "Talk to me. It better not be Knox who's got you so upset. If it is, I'm going to need you to find me a big stick before you go, so I can whack him in the back of the knees and take him down to my level to get a solid punch in."

I smiled sadly. "It's not Christian, not really anyway." Tears threatened again as I looked into this kind man's eyes, but this time I managed to swallow them back. "I don't know where to start."

"The beginning is usually a good place. Take your time, sweetheart. There's no rush."

Over the next twenty minutes, I spilled my guts. If I'd had any doubt as to whether Marvin Barrett knew what his son had done, his face confirmed he was as shocked as I'd been.

But as I told the crazy story out loud for the first time, a lot of pieces clicked into place. It had never made sense why John Barrett would care enough to follow me—doing crazy things like donating a library next to the shelter where I'd lived—yet never come forward to admit he was my father. Now I understood it was because he had guilt, but his freedom meant more to him than clearing his conscience.

My grandfather shook his head. "I don't even know what to say. How could he have done such a thing and hidden it?"

That was the million-dollar question. If it had been an accident, he would have stopped. So it either wasn't an accident, or there was a reason he'd kept going.

"Did he drink in the owner's box during the games?" I asked.

My grandfather frowned. "He liked to have a few. There was a period of time right after Celeste died that he got carried away. I remember being worried he was taking things too far. He had the girls to consider and all. They'd just lost a mother, and the last thing they needed was a drunk for a father. But then something changed, and he seemed to go back to his old self. He didn't quit drinking, but he had more control over it, or at least I thought so."

"Do you remember when that was? Or maybe how long he seemed to have problems?"

Coach tapped his lip with his pointer. "Not exactly. But it was sometime right after Celeste passed, which was on St. Patrick's Day, I remember. And by the end of the season that year, he seemed to have things under control."

"His wife died seven months before my mom. I remember reading about it when I first found out he was my father. She died in March, and my mother's accident was in late October."

"Jesus..." He shook his head. "So you think he was drinking, and that's why he left the scene?"

"That's the only thing that makes sense. Either that or he intentionally hit her."

"I can't imagine that," Coach said. "But I also would never have imagined that he drove drunk, killed a woman, and ran away."

"Yeah..."

He was quiet for a long time. "Where do we go from here? Do we go to the police? Let them take a fresh look at the case with the new information? Maybe they can figure out the rest of the story? Interview people who might've been with John that night? I'll do whatever you want, whatever it takes to make this right. Not that it's possible to right this wrong, but you deserve to get the truth—the full truth."

"I think going to the police is probably the best way to handle it. But there's something else." I swallowed. "We never took a DNA test. What if John Barrett isn't my father, and he left me the team not out of guilt for never ac-

315

knowledging me, but because he felt guilty for killing my mother and running away?"

The look on my grandfather's face—*oh God, no!* Was this wonderful man even my grandfather? I had no idea why that didn't even dawn on me until now.

I clutched my stomach. "Marvin...you might not be my..."

He held up his hand. "Let's not even go there, sweetheart. We're family, no matter what."

I rubbed at my breastbone. "I think I need to know for sure. Would you...let a lab do a DNA test? We never had to prove John was my father during the court proceedings, but I really need to know..." Tears rushed to fill my eyes again. "...if you're my grandfather."

"Of course. I'll do anything you say." He took my hand and spoke into my eyes. "I'll take the test. But DNA doesn't make a family, love does. I'm your grandfather no matter what the results say."

I'd ignored all phone calls and texts today.

Christian had called a half dozen times and sent more messages than that, so when my phone rang again at almost nine PM, I answered.

"Hello?"

I heard the sigh of relief through the phone. "Thank God. I've been worried about you all day."

"I'm fine."

"Are you really?"

The truth was, I wasn't fine. And I was tired of lies.

"No, I'm not. But I will be. You don't have to worry about me, though."

"Of course I'm going to worry about you. You're all I could think about today. Hell, you're all I've been able to think about since I met you. I want to help you get through this, Bella. But I know you're upset with me for not telling you right away, and I'm afraid to push too hard and make things between us worse."

I'd spent half the night thinking about what Christian had done. "I'm not mad at you. In a way, I can understand why you didn't tell me. But that doesn't make it hurt any less. I trusted you, and it feels like that trust has been broken. The lie or the omission doesn't hurt half as much as losing something we had. It wasn't your secret to keep."

"I know. And I'm sorry. I handled it all wrong." He paused. "Can I come by and see you? I just need to know you're okay."

"I need some time, Christian."

"Time apart from me?"

"It's more just time for me. I spent the last two years learning to accept a family that might not even be my family now. I have a lot to figure out."

"Okay. I get it."

The line was quiet for a long time. "Take care, Christian."

"Wait!" His voice sounded panicked. "There's something else I've been keeping from you, and I don't want any more secrets between us. This isn't how I wanted to tell you, but I need you to hear it. I love you, Bella. And I don't mean I'm falling in love with you. Falling is when you haven't hit the ground yet, so there's a chance you can catch yourself. I've fallen, hit the ground, and I never want to get up. I love you so much that it scares the living shit out of me. So I'll give you the space you need, but you should know I'm not going anywhere. Not too long ago, I told you that if it ever got to be too much and you ran, I'd chase you. I still will, and I'll catch you eventually."

Tears streamed down my face.

"So I'm not saying goodbye," he added. "I'm saying I'll catch you later."

Chapter 29

Christian

I SAT IN my SUV across from her apartment, looking up.

It wasn't the first time I'd done it, and it wouldn't be the last at the rate things were going.

Two weeks had gone by since my birthday. The only times I'd seen Bella were when I parked a block away like a goddamn stalker just so I'd know she was physically okay. Emotionally was a different story. Neither one of us seemed to be handling that end of things too well. Bella had taken a leave of absence at work, and I'd lost my last two games. I'd broken down after a week and texted her, but I'd only received a sentence or two letting me know she was alive. Coach had been my only source of information. I'd avoided talking to him for a while, not knowing if Bella had told him anything or what I should or shouldn't say myself. But then he'd reached out and reamed me a new asshole for not telling him what was going on with the cars and his granddaughter. He'd told me he and Bella were taking a DNA test to find out once and for all if John Barrett was her father. Those results were due back this week.

Miller had been spending a lot of time at Bella's, so I wasn't surprised when he walked out tonight at nine o'clock—though I hadn't been expecting him to look straight at me as he exited. I sank down into my seat, hoping he hadn't seen me, but before I could sneak a peek to see if he was gone, he opened the passenger door to my SUV and climbed in.

"Drive a block or two away." He pointed up ahead. "I don't want her to look out the window and see me talking to you."

I started the car and pulled away from the curb. "Did you just see me on your way out, or you knew I was here the whole time?"

"I saw you down the block when we pulled up in the Uber. I've also seen you a few other times over the last couple of weeks."

My eyes flashed to Miller and back to the road. "Does Bella know?"

He shook his head. "No, but you could really do a better job of trying to be discreet. Didn't you ever follow a girlfriend you suspected might be stepping out on you?"

My brows pulled together. "No."

Miller rolled his eyes. "Figures." He pointed to an open space at the entrance to a small park. "Pull over up there."

I parked and shifted in my seat.

"You look like crap," he said.

I frowned. "Thanks."

"Matches how you've been playing lately, I suppose."

"Don't remind me."

Miller sighed. "She's fine. Well, that's not true. She's mentally exhausted from beating herself up. But she will be fine. My girl always is."

"Why is she beating herself up?"

"Oh, I don't know. Maybe because she has trust issues, and the first guy she trusted in forever was keeping a major secret from her. Or because she didn't insist on a DNA test to confirm John Barrett was actually her father two years ago before she uprooted her entire life. Or because she started to let her guard down and like that new life. Or because the only living relative she felt gave two shits about her might not be her grandfather. Should I continue?"

I raked a hand through my hair. "No, it was a dumb question."

"Got any better ones?" Miller put his hand on the door latch. "Or am I done here?"

"Will she ever be able to forgive me?"

"She won't even talk about you right now. But my guess is she'll come around. The one thing about Bella is, she looks at things from every angle. It's her personality, but also what she spent years doing for work. When you build algorithms for a living, you have to be able to think about how people respond to different scenarios. Deep down she knows you were only trying to protect her."

"Is she going to go back to work?"

Miller shrugged. "Don't know. I guess that depends on the results. She and her grandfather took a DNA test to find out if John was her father."

I nodded. "He told me. But even if he's not, she'll still own the team, legally. At least that's what she said—the way it was worded in John's will, she inherited the team even if they weren't related. That's why the judge denied the DNA request from her sisters, because it was a moot point."

"But if he's not her sperm donor, the only logical reason he left her the team is as a payoff for what he did. It'll be blood money to her."

I sighed. "Tell me what I should do. She wants me to give her space. But I want to be there for her. Do I push, or do I listen?"

"My personal opinion is that when a relationship is teetering on the edge, pushing usually forces it over to the wrong side. This is more about what she's going through and not about you two. So maybe find a way to support her with that stuff and not focus on fixing your relationship yet."

"How do I do that?"

Miller shook his head. "Fuck if I know." He opened the door. "But good luck."

—

The next day, every time my phone buzzed, I got my hopes up, even if I had no reason to since Miller had made it clear last night that Bella wasn't ready to talk yet. I still frowned, finding someone else's name on the screen. But I needed to answer because it wasn't the first time my agent had called.

"Hey, Phil."

"What the fuck? I've been calling you for a week. You don't answer texts or return my calls."

"Sorry. I've been dealing with some stuff."

"That's pretty obvious, since you've been playing like shit."

Does everyone need to tell me how crappy my game was? As if I wasn't aware. "What do you need, Phil?"

"Uh...how about the contract I messengered over ten days ago to be signed? Is there a problem with it?"

I looked down at the coffee table, at the stack of papers I'd opened but hadn't yet read.

"I haven't gone through it."

"Why the hell not? You know the terms. There's nothing in there that's gonna be a surprise to you. I would think you'd be anxious to seal the deal and become the second-highest-paid player in the league with the biggest guarantee at your age. Especially after throwing *four* interceptions last week. You waiting to *not* make playoffs to give them a chance to rethink the numbers?"

"Alright, alright. I hear ya. I'll read it and get it signed."

"I need to retire," Phil grumbled. "Call the office when it's signed, and I'll send someone to pick it up."

"Okay."

After I hung up, I grabbed the pile of papers and sat back on the couch. Phil had included a cover sheet with all the numbers. The total I'd be paid over the next five years was more than I knew what to do with. I'd be set for life. Hell, I was set for life already, so this was just an even cushier life.

Yet it didn't sit right. What if Bella walked away from the team because the reminder of the man who built it was too much for her to handle? It made my stomach turn to think about supporting the legacy of a person who cared more about his money and freedom than a young girl who was living on the street or in a shelter.

Then again, this was my career—everything I'd worked for from the time I was a kid. I'd been part of the team since straight out of college. It was my home.

I tossed the papers back on the coffee table and scrubbed my hands over my face. I needed to think about it more. Everyone would just have to wait a little longer.

Chapter 30

Bella

"SO I'VE RECEIVED both results," my lawyer said.

I already regretted telling Miller I needed to do this alone, but I took a deep breath and sat up taller. "Okay?"

"The independent lab confirmed the original, unofficial opinion on the tire marks you were given. With a margin of error of less than one tenth of a percent, John Barrett's Ford Thunderbird is a match to the tracks the police collected the night of the accident."

I nodded. I'd been expecting that. Though it was still tough to hear. John Barrett had killed my mother, either on accident or on purpose. The more important question was, who was John Barrett to me?

I wrung my hands together on my lap. "And the DNA testing? Is John Barrett my father?"

My lawyer lifted a piece of paper and looked down. "The conclusive range for single-grandparent testing is generally a finding of ninety percent or better. If both the grandparents are tested—meaning the mother and the father of the possible parent—the results can be ninety-nine-point-nine percent or higher." He turned the paper around and showed me. "Even with only one grandparent tested, your results came in at more than ninety-seven percent for exclusion." He shook his head. "John Barrett is not your father."

It felt like I couldn't breathe.

John Barrett was not my father.

John Barrett was not my father.

John Barrett mowed down my mother and gave me a football team to try to clean the blood off his hands.

"I'm sorry, Bella. I know this was not the news you wanted to hear. But as we discussed when you came in to ask me for these tests, the results do not change anything about your inheritance. In hindsight, it's clear that John Barrett chose his wording carefully in the will so your status as a beneficiary could not be disputed if these things were to come to light. Your name was specifically written without regard to any particular relationship."

I couldn't even think about the team or the money right now. All I could think was that my mother had been murdered, and I had no idea who I was. *Again.* My head spun as I realized it also meant Marvin Barrett was not my grandfather, and after that I couldn't hold back the tears. I'd grown to love that man. He *felt* like my family, and now I was back to having none that mattered.

My lawyer reached behind him and plucked a few tissues from a box, extending them to me. "I'm not sure how you'd like to proceed," he said, "being that there is no one to prosecute anymore. But I'm happy to take these findings into the police station so they can reopen the case."

When I said nothing, my lawyer shook his head. "I'm sorry. I realize you're not ready to make a decision like that right now. I only meant to tell you I can handle it, if that's the way you'd like to proceed."

I managed to nod and wiped my cheeks. "Thank you."

"Is there someone I can call for you?"

The only person I wanted to call was Christian. I wanted to curl up in a ball on his chest and let him tell me everything was going to be okay. But even that relationship was a mess.

I shook my head. "I'm just going to call an Uber."

He nodded. "I'm here if you need me to do anything at all."

"Thank you."

Two days later, I was still not out of my funk. I hadn't showered, my hair was a matted mess, and the only thing I'd eaten was some ice cream, which I didn't bother to scoop into a dish, and I now had a stain on my shirt where I'd dripped some of it.

Telling Coach had been even more devastating than I'd imagined. He'd cried. I'd cried. In the end, he'd promised it changed nothing between us. I wanted to believe him, but it felt impossible for that to be true.

My phone buzzed on the end table next to me, and I didn't even bother to look. I'd spoken to Miller a few times, and Christian had texted to ask if I needed anything, which I assumed meant he'd spoken to my grandfa—Marvin Barrett.

It stopped buzzing, but thirty seconds later it started up again. Still, I ignored it. When it happened a third time,

I rolled over and grabbed it, begrudgingly checking the screen. Miller's name flashed. I knew if he was worried he might call dozens of times, so I answered, even though I didn't feel like it.

"I'm fine," I groaned.

"You need to turn on the news in three minutes."

I sat up. "Why? What's going on? Is everything okay?"

"I don't know. But apparently Christian is holding a news conference at eight thirty."

"About what?"

"I have no idea. They didn't say."

"What channel?"

"Sports Network. I only found out because the *Hell's Kitchen* episode I'm watching is a rerun, so I was bored and read the dumb ticker at the bottom giving a news update."

"Alright, hang on." I grabbed my laptop from the nightstand and went in search of the Sports Network's livestream. "I'll call you back, okay?"

"Yeah, go. I'm going to watch, too."

I watched ads play on the screen until the news conference's stream went live. Christian walked in and sat down at a dais in front of a dozen microphones. The backdrop was a wall with the Sports Network logo all over it.

My heart fluttered. He was as handsome as ever, but his face looked thinner and his eyes were sunken, like he hadn't been sleeping well. I turned the volume all the way up as I waited for him to speak.

"Good evening." He smiled, but it wasn't a happy smile, more like a polite one. "Thank you for coming. I'll make this short and sweet because I'm sure you all have better news to cover than my sorry ass."

I couldn't see how many reporters were there, but a murmur of laughter went around the room.

"As you all know, my contract with the Bruins is up after this season. Today, I made the difficult decision not to continue with the team next year."

Holy shit.

People started shouting questions, but Christian motioned with his hands for everyone to settle down.

"The New York Bruins has been my home for ten years, and I very much appreciate the dedication they have shown me. But sometimes it's necessary to pick up your roots and plant them somewhere else. I'm sure you'll want to know if this is a contract dispute, and I'm here to assure you it's not. The Bruins made me what I consider a very generous offer to remain with the team. My decision is not about money."

Someone from the audience yelled, "Christian, are you injured?"

He shook his head. "I'm not injured. The tears in my knee that were repaired earlier this year continue to hold strong, and I've had no other changes in my health since I was cleared to return to play earlier this season." He leaned closer to the microphone. "This is not about my health or money. This is a personal decision I've made, and it was not made lightly."

Another person yelled, "Are you retiring?"

Christian shook his head. "No, I'm not retiring. You're all stuck with me for at least another five years, hopefully more."

The camera flashed to Mike Dietrich, a popular sports reporter. "This morning, New England announced some very unexpected trades to free up cash and stay under the salary cap. Can you tell us if that's where you're headed?"

"I'm not at liberty to discuss where I might be going yet. But I can tell you that once the deal is inked, you'll be the first to know." Christian flashed his signature cocky smile. "I'll also mention that I think New England is beautiful in the fall, and I recently purchased an old campground in Vermont that I hope to someday make into a football camp for kids when I retire."

My heart raced. *An old campground in Vermont?* That couldn't be a coincidence.

Christian knocked on the table. "Any other questions before I go?"

Mike Dietrich again spoke up. "Even with the trades New England made, they're not going to be able to pay you what it was rumored the Bruins offered—not by at least ten million. Does that mean you're willing to take a pay cut?"

Christian had been speaking to the room, but now he lifted his head and looked straight at the camera. "There are some things more important than money. I'm hoping this move will give me a fresh start, and I'm hoping I'll not be alone in making it."

I had no idea what anyone said after that. Christian answered a few more questions and then thanked everyone for coming and got up. Sports Network cut to its regularly scheduled programming—as if things could go back to normal after what Christian had just done. I sat in my bed stunned for a few minutes before my phone rang again. Of course it was Miller.

"Am I crazy, or did Christian just announce he's taking a ten-million-dollar pay cut because he can't work for the team of the guy who killed your mother? And instead he's moving to the city where you always wanted to live and bought the campground that holds your favorite child-hood memories?"

I swallowed. "I think that might be exactly what he did."

Chapter 31

Bella

I COULDN'T HAVE planned it better myself.

A few days later, Miller, his boyfriend, Trent, and I drove up to Vermont. The two of them were going to stay at some B&B for the night and check out the fall foliage, while I showed up unannounced at the hotel where Christian was staying. Coach had told me he was going up to sign his new contract with New England, but when we pulled in at the hotel, Christian's SUV was pulling out of the parking lot.

"Turn around quick!" I shrieked. "That's Christian's SUV we just passed coming in."

"Are you sure?" Miller said.

"I'm positive. I saw him driving."

Miller took a sharp turn and hit the gas to follow the SUV. But we were a half-dozen cars behind him.

"He's got a bike in the back," Trent said. "I can see the tire sticking up."

I leaned forward from the backseat to look.

"Is he going home?" Trent asked.

Miller shook his head and pointed. "Not if he's heading north. He just put his blinker on to get on 95, heading the opposite way of home."

"Oh my gosh." I gripped the seat. "I think he might be going to the campground. We took bikes there the last time we were here."

"You want me to follow him?"

I nodded. "The campground is only about ten minutes from here, if I'm right."

Since the road was a single lane each way, it was hard to stay close to Christian. We got stuck at a light, and by the time we moved again, Christian's SUV was no longer in sight. We didn't see it again until we pulled onto the road leading to the campground, and then it was already on the other side of the locked chain, blocking passage.

"Pull up to the chain," I told Miller. "I'll get out there."

"What are you going to do? Chase him down on foot?" Miller asked. "You're not exactly the fastest runner, and you got lost walking through the Museum of Modern Art."

"I'll be fine." We stopped, and I jumped out of the car.

Miller rolled down his window and yelled after me. "What if Wi-Fi doesn't work in there, and you can't find him, and you can't call me?"

"I'll take my chances! Go enjoy your day. I'll be fine here even if I don't find him. I'll call you later!"

It took a lot longer on foot than it did on bikes to get where I was going, even jogging. But when I arrived at the clearing with the picnic bench where Christian and I had stopped the last time and had our first kiss, I found him sitting on the table with his feet on the seat. He was facing the other way, and my heart beat wildly as I approached from behind.

When the leaves crunched beneath my feet, he turned. "Bella? What are you doing here?"

I smiled. "Looking for you."

"How did you know I was here?" He looked past me. "And how the hell did you get here?"

"Miller drove me up. He dropped me off at the entrance. We went to your hotel first, but you were pulling out, so we followed. My grandfa—" I paused and was about to say his name instead, but then I remembered the conversation he and I'd had two days ago. Test results didn't change anything. "My grandfather told me what hotel you'd be at."

"Your...grandfather?"

I nodded and pointed to the table. "Do you mind if I sit with you?"

Christian scooted over. He watched my every step like I was a puzzle he was trying to put together.

Sitting down on the picnic table, I sighed. "He still wants me to call him my grandfather. And I still feel like he is. I realize that's probably a little strange, considering I now know he's the father of the man who killed my mother. But he's my family."

Christian smiled sadly. "Not strange at all. We don't get to choose our genetics, so family is a gift from God. And that's what Coach is—to me, too."

"That's a really good way of looking at it."

I searched for the right words to say what I'd come to say. "I'm so sorry, Christian, for running away from you."

Christian swallowed. "I don't need an apology."

"You might not need one, but you deserve one. I'm sorry I pushed you out of my life. And I'm sorry I said hurtful things, like accusing you of not telling me so your contract negotiations would go better." I shook my head.

"I never really thought you would do something like that. I was just overwhelmed and confused, so I did what I do best and retreated, taking back the trust I'd given you."

"I should have told you sooner."

I sighed. "Yes, you should've, but I do understand that you were trying to protect me. The last time my world fell apart was when my mom died. My aunt said she'd take care of me, and then she died too. Then I went to live with my cousin, and she didn't want me around. So I learned to not rely on anyone. Since I was a teenager, I've thought my fear of getting close to people was because I was afraid of losing them. But I think maybe I was more afraid that there was no one out there afraid of losing me."

"Oh fuck." Christian shook his head. He scooped me from my seat onto his lap, then cupped my cheeks between his hands and spoke into my eyes. "I am terrified of losing you. Nothing else matters. For as long as I could remember, the only thing I was afraid of was not being able to play ball. But if I had to pick between you and playing, there would be no contest, sweetheart."

Tears slid down my cheeks as hope bloomed deep inside of me. "Did you buy this place?"

Christian smiled. "You said the time you spent here was the happiest you'd ever been. The real estate agent called me a week ago, to follow up after our visit again, and I realized that afternoon was one of the happiest days I'd had in my life, too. So I thought maybe there was some magic here, and I made an offer. I had no idea what I was going to do with it, but everything became easy to see after I made that decision. I knew the Bruins would be nothing but bad memories after everything sank in, and I didn't want my job to be heartache for you. So I had my agent put out some feelers to see who might be interested if I didn't sign my contract. The first team to respond was New England." He nodded. "It just felt right."

"I can't believe you've uprooted your entire life like this."

"You gotta uproot if you want to plant your roots somewhere new." He leaned closer. "I want to plant roots with you, Bella. It doesn't matter where, just needs to be a place you're happy."

"I finally know where that is." I sniffled. "The place I can be happy."

"Where?"

"Anywhere you are."

Chapter 32

Christian

"YOU'RE BEING CREEPY, Knox."

I smiled and brushed a lock of hair from her face. "How did you know I was watching you sleep when your eyes haven't opened yet?"

"I felt it."

I took her hand and slid it between my legs. "Why don't you feel this, instead?"

Bella giggled, and the sound warmed the inside of my chest. After a rough two weeks, the dark clouds hanging over us had finally started to lift. Once we'd returned from Vermont, Bella had some pretty big decisions to make. Not surprisingly, she'd handled them all with grace. She'd decided to take the information we'd found to the police so they could reopen the investigation into her mother's death. It took them less than one week to connect the dots and determine that the driver who'd killed Rose Keating had been John Barrett. We'd known the car had been involved, but the police had finished the job.

Since the stadium gave out all-access passes to guests in the owner's suite, everyone had to register with security.

Bella was able to get the list of guests from the night her mother died from security without the police even having to waste time on a warrant. They then interviewed everyone who had been in the owner's suite on the evening of Rose's death. Since it had been a game against the Bruins' main rival, and some of the guests had watched from the luxury box for their first time ever, many had a strong recollection of the night. Seven people confirmed that John Barrett had been drinking heavily, and he'd offered one of them a ride home in his antique car. The man had declined, knowing John was inebriated. After that, the police tracked down the guy who had maintained John's cars, and he confirmed that John had told him he hit a deer and needed some work done.

Bella had filled Tiffany and Rebecca in on what had happened, wanting to give them the courtesy of a heads-up in case the news got wind of the police poking around. Of course, they didn't believe her. But Tiffany told the new guy she was dating about what Bella had said, and he promptly sold the story to the tabloids. Everything blew up from there.

Bella tucked her hands under her cheek, and we laid on our sides, facing each other in bed. "I think I've made a decision about what I'm going to do with the team."

"Yeah?"

She nodded. "I'm going to create a charity in my mother's name and start donating all profits from the team to it. I don't want to keep anything that was John Barrett's, but others could really use the money."

I smiled. "I think that's a great idea. What about running it? Will you stay on as the team co-president?"

Bella shook her head. "I looked at the hierarchy of a few other teams, and many have the CEO holding both the CEO and president's positions. I think Tom Lauren can continue to handle both. And I'm going to ask my grandfather if he'll serve as an advisor to the president and also sit on the board of the charity I'll establish."

I loved that she was no longer hesitating to call Marvin Barrett her grandfather. If one good thing had come out of this mess, it was bringing the two of them together. Well, that and leading me to find the love of my life.

I nodded. "That all sounds like a solid plan. Though there are two other important decisions you should probably consider."

"Oh? What am I missing?"

I took her hand and brought it to my lips. "Move in with me? Stay here until it's time to relocate to Vermont, and then let's shop for a house together—somewhere with a big fireplace and a lot of land for our kids to run around on someday."

"You want me to live with you?"

I smiled. "I want you to be my wife, but I thought it might be a little soon for me to ask that. So I'm taking baby steps. Move in with me."

"But I just signed that lease for the other place."

"I'll buy it out, if they won't let you out. Waking up with you is the best part of my day, and I want you to be the last thing I taste when I go to bed at night."

She rested her hand over her heart. "Oh my. How can I say no when you ask like that?"

My heart sped up. "So that's a yes?"

She nodded. "It's a yes."

Leaning in, I cupped her face and kissed her with everything in me. When we finally came up for air, her cheeks were flushed. I went in for round two, but Bella stopped me. She nudged my chest.

"Wait. What's the other thing?"

"Huh?" All the blood in my brain had rushed south. I had no idea what she was referring to.

She laughed. "You said I had *two* important decisions to make."

"Oh, right." I grinned. "How do you want it this morning? All fours, spoon fuck, bent over the headboard, sixty-nine? Or maybe ride my face or my cock?"

Bella licked her lips. "I get to choose?"

"You do..."

She bit down on her bottom lip. "But they all sound so good."

We were still naked from last night, so I gave a little tug to the sheet and her luscious tits were on display—so full, with the sexiest natural lilt to them. While she decided, I leaned in and sucked a pert nipple into my mouth, fluttering my tongue and sucking before biting down to give it a strong tug between my teeth. Then I did the same to the other.

Bella's eyes were glazed over by the time I finished.

"What's it going to be, sweetheart?"

"It's hard to pick just one..."

"Oh, I wasn't asking you to pick just one. I was asking you how you want it *first* this morning. I don't have to be at the field for three hours. We have time for them all."

"Ride you," she breathed. "I want to ride you."

"My face or my cock?"

"Your cock."

God, those were the two best words to hear from her mouth. And the fact that she was shy about saying them, yet said them for me anyway, was sexy as shit.

I pulled myself up the bed to rest my back against the headboard, then held out my hand. Bella climbed on top of me, one thigh on either side of mine. I was about to check whether she was wet when I felt her dripping against my skin. "Lift..." I groaned.

Bella pushed up onto her knees, and I gripped my cock and positioned it near her opening. My crown glistened with anticipation.

"Look down while you take it. I want us both to watch your beautiful pussy swallow my cock."

Bella rested her hands on my shoulders for balance and never took her eyes from our connection as she lowered herself. She was so wet and smooth; it felt like I was gripped in a velvet vise.

"Christ..." My head fell back against the headboard. "You're so tight."

She lifted up and sank back down, each time taking more of me inside her. When her ass hit my balls, she looked up at me, and our eyes locked.

"Ride me." I reached around to the back of her head and fisted a handful of her hair, giving it a firm tug. "Ride me *hard*, sweetheart."

With her head back, I had access to her neck. So I sucked along her pulse line as she rode me hard, lifting almost all the way off and then slamming back down, only to gyrate her hips. She moaned when I pressed my thumb to her clit and massaged small circles.

I'd told her to ride me, but I couldn't help joining in. Grabbing her hips, I thrust up from underneath as she came down, sinking even deeper into her.

Bella's eyes rolled to the back of her head as her orgasm took hold. "Christian!"

"That's it. Say my name while you come, sweetheart."

Her pussy squeezed, and I took over, lifting her up and yanking her back down as I thrust. She chanted my name over and over until it became one long moan. Then I kissed her until every last quake had wracked through her body and buried myself to the hilt with a roar.

After, I was more out of breath than when I ran the full length of the field.

"I love you, Bella Keating. You're a gift."

She flashed a crooked smile and wiggled her brows. "I love you, too, Christian Knox. But don't get too comfy lying there just yet. If I'm your gift, I'm going to be one that keeps on giving."

Epilogue

Bella

7 years later

"I THINK YOU need glasses, ref!" I yelled. "How could you not see that offsides?"

"Oh crap." My husband climbed up the bleacher stairs two at a time. He looked at the person to the right of me, offering an apologetic smile. "Sorry. She gets hangry."

"I'm not hangry." I pointed to the field. "That ref has it in for us. He has since the start of the game."

Christian sat next to me and handed me a big pretzel.

I frowned. "Did you remove the salt again?"

"Doc said to reduce your intake since your BP is already a little high."

I rubbed my enormous belly and narrowed my eyes. "My blood pressure is a little high because *you* don't know how to do anything like an average person—like have *one* child at a time."

He leaned over and kissed my belly. "Who wants one little Bella when you can have two?"

"You won't be saying that in thirteen years when they're dating."

Christian's brows pulled tight. "Thirteen? Try thirty, sweetheart."

Sadly for the two little girls in my belly, their father was serious. At least I had some years to work on him before we had to deal with dating. Though our other twins—Drew and Ben, who were now in kindergarten—had gotten a sack full of valentines last year when they were only in preschool. I blamed that on them having inherited their father's dimples.

"There he is!" a teenage girl screeched behind us. "He is so freaking hot."

I turned to find them pointing toward the entrance to the field, where the assistant coach was currently jogging in. Wyatt was now twenty-four and the starting kicker for New England, the team my husband had retired from only last season. But he also helped out with Drew and Ben's pee-wee football team, assisting my grandfather, who was the head coach, whenever he could. Four years ago, Coach had moved up to New England to join us. He'd said he wanted to be closer to his family after the twins were born. And he was—because family has nothing to do with DNA. Tiffany and Rebecca had proven that when they'd stopped speaking to him after he called my boys his great grandchildren.

I leaned over to Christian and whispered, "I remember the days when the girls used to point to you and say that."

"It's a baton I will happily pass."

Wyatt joined Coach on the sideline. After years of physical therapy, my grandfather now walked pretty well with a cane. But he was currently using it to point to a ref and yell about the last call. The two of them talked for a minute before Wyatt went over to the players' bench and sat down next to Drew, who was currently sulking.

"I think you need to get one of them interested in a position besides quarterback," I told my husband. "I can't handle going home with one miserable child after every game."

Christian smiled. "The competition's good for them. Besides, Drew got the spot for the entire game last weekend. They'll figure it out on their own eventually, like Jake and I did."

My cell rang from my purse. Reading the name on the screen, I tilted the phone to show Christian.

He shook his head. "You're supposed to be on maternity leave."

"They're having a problem with the forecasting module. It keeps glitching and shutting down since they loaded it onto the new computer system. I think the problem is the new system, not the program." I tried to answer, but the phone disappeared from my hand before I could finish.

"Doc says no more work, or you're going to wind up in the hospital for the rest of this pregnancy. You know how miserable you were last time on bedrest for a month. You can't have stress."

"It's just a phone call. I'm not stressed..."

"It's never just a phone call, sweetheart. When you can't figure out what the issue is, you'll wind up working until four in the morning trying to fix things from your laptop."

Okay, so maybe I did do that the other night, but it wasn't easy to leave my coworkers hanging. Especially since I'd created the statistics and forecasting software they now used. After Christian and I had moved to New England to be with his new team, I was bored staying home all the time. I wanted to find a job with flexible hours so I could travel for his games and also go back to New York to see some of Wyatt's and visit my grandfather. That job fell into my lap when the director of team stats from the Bruins happened to take a job with New England. He'd always loved the forecasting module I'd been working on and invited me to consult with Christian's new team on how to improve their system. A year in, I was working full time and building a brand-new program from the ground up. I'd stayed on part time after the twins were born, but it wasn't easy because Christian was always on the road. Having another set of twins was going to make things more chaotic, but at least my husband was retired now and could help out more.

I frowned as the call went to voicemail and the phone remained in my husband's hand. "You know I'm going to call him back."

"I know you are. But how about when we get home? I'll do homework with frick and frack, and you can go up- stairs and get your geek on. At least if you do one thing at a time, you'll be a little less stressed. The game's almost over anyway."

A little while later, Christian and I walked down to the field. He carried the cooler he brought to every game. As we approached, the kids were down on one knee, listen- ing to Coach's post-game talk. But when they spotted my husband, every single player got up and ran toward him. Though these days, the kids were running to Christian Knox for a different reason.

"Do you have chocolate?" one of them asked.

Christian mussed his hair. "Did you complain because I only had vanilla last time?"

The kid smiled from ear to ear and nodded.

"Then I got chocolate this time too." He opened the cooler and had to step out of the way so he wouldn't be knocked over during the frenzied Chipwich grab. As soon as the kids got their ice cream, they ripped their cleats and socks off and ran around the field. I still found it amazing that Christian hadn't even prompted them to do that. He'd just brought the Chipwiches, and they did the rest—knocking each other over and laughing with their toes in the grass and ice cream in hand.

Christian hooked an arm around my waist, and we stood together quietly, watching the chaos on the field, both of us smiling.

"I just realized you have no grass at home right now," I said.

We'd recently dug up our backyard to put in an in-ground pool and some new landscaping. We planned on installing sod in the spring, but right now it was mostly mud. "Should I get some seed and make a little patch like you used to have on your balcony in your fancy New York apartment? I wouldn't want to rob you of your happy place to eat ice cream for six months."

Christian turned and pulled me close. Smiling down, he lifted a hand to my glasses and raised one side. I guessed they were crooked again. "I don't need my toes in the grass anymore," he said. "I've got my happy place right here, boss lady."

"Aww, that's so sweet."

He moved his mouth to my ear. "Plus, fuck the Chip-wich and your work. I'm going to eat you when we get home."

I laughed. That was Christian, the perfect combination of sweet and dirty. Sometimes I couldn't believe this was my life, that it was all real and I'd found true love. But I had. It had just taken me a while, because I'd found it where I least expected it—on the other side of fear.

Acknowledgements

To you—the *readers*. Ten years ago, I had an unfulfilling career and decided to write my first novel. I never expected my life to take the turn it did—selling millions of books in twenty-seven languages with hundreds of bestseller list appearances—and it's all because of YOU. Thank you for a decade of support and enthusiasm. I'm honored so many of you are still with me and hope we have many more decades together!

To Penelope – The best partner in crime a lady could ask for! Thank you for always helping me see the humor in any shitty situation.

To Cheri – Thank you for years of true friendship and support.

To Julie – Six more months until ten toes in the sand!

To Luna – It's the friends you can chat with at 5AM who matter most! Thank you for always being there, day or night. Your friendship brightens my day.

To my amazing Facebook reader group, Vi's Violets – nearly 25,000 smart ladies (and a few awesome men) who love books! You feed my soul and inspire me every day. Thank you for all of your support.

To Sommer –Thank you for figuring out what I want, often before I do.

To my agent and friend, Kimberly Brower – Thank you for being my partner in this adventure!

To Jessica, Elaine, and Julia – Thank you for smoothing out all the rough edges and making me shine!

To Kylie and Jo at Give Me Books – I don't even remember how I managed before you, and I hope I never have to figure it out! Thank you for everything you do.

To all of the bloggers – Thank you for all that you do! Without you, I wouldn't be in the same place. Thank you for always showing up.

Much love
Vi

Other Books by
Vi Keeland

The Summer Proposal

Inappropriate

The Boss Project

The Spark

The Invitation

The Rivals

All Grown Up

We Shouldn't

The Naked Truth

Sex, Not Love

Beautiful Mistake

Egomaniac

Bossman

The Baller

Left Behind

Beat

Throb

Worth the Fight

Worth the Chance

Worth Forgiving

Belong to You

Made for You

First Thing I See

The Rules of Dating (Co-written with Penelope Ward)
Well Played (Co-written with Penelope Ward)
Park Avenue Player (Co-written with Penelope Ward)
Stuck-Up Suit (Co-written with Penelope Ward)
Cocky Bastard (Co-written with Penelope Ward)
Not Pretending Anymore (Co-written with Penelope Ward)
Happily Letter After (Co-written with Penelope Ward)
My Favorite Souvenir (Co-written with Penelope Ward)
Dirty Letters (Co-written with Penelope Ward)
Hate Notes (Co-written with Penelope Ward)
Rebel Heir (Co-written with Penelope Ward)
Rebel Heart (Co-written with Penelope Ward)
Mister Moneybags (Co-written with Penelope Ward)
British Bedmate (Co-written with Penelope Ward)
Playboy Pilot (Co-written with Penelope Ward)

About the Author

VI KEELAND is a #1 New York Times, #1 Wall Street Journal, and USA Today Bestselling author. With millions of books sold, her titles are currently translated in twenty-six languages and have appeared on bestseller lists in the US, Germany, Brazil, Bulgaria, Israel and Hungary. Three of her short stories have been turned into films by Passionflix, and two of her books are currently optioned for movies. She resides in New York with her husband and their three children where she is living out her own happily ever after with the boy she met at age six.

Made in the USA
Middletown, DE
15 January 2023